The Warrior's Code
Peacekeepers X-Alpha #2

A Thriller

by Steve DeWinter

I0690634

Summary

Can a simple phone call change who you are?

On the same day that Alexander Chase is released from prison, he is approached by a secret organization with a simple request. Pose as an FBI agent and retrieve a cell phone from a small town police station.

He quickly finds himself alone and on the run while trying to destroy the technology that can convert anyone, anywhere, into a highly-skilled assassin.

THE WARRIOR'S CODE is the second book in the action-packed Peacekeepers X-Alpha thriller series, and marks Steve DeWinter's return to the genre two years after his underground bestseller, Inherit the Throne, thrilled readers worldwide.

This book is also available serialized under the following titles:
The Deep Cover Affair
The Deep Cover Connection
The Deep Cover Proxy
The Deep Cover Legacy

This book is a work of fiction. References to real people, events, establishments, organization, or locales are intended only to provide a sense of authenticity, and are used fictitiously. All other characters, and all incidents and dialogue, are drawn from the author's imagination and are not to be construed as real.

Ramblin' Prose Publishing
Copyright © 2015 Steve DeWinter
All rights reserved. Used under authorization.
www.stevedw.com

eBook Edition
ISBN-10: 1-61978-097-6
ISBN-13: 978-1-61978-097-2

Paperback Edition
ISBN-10: 1-61978-102-6
ISBN-13: 978-1-61978-102-3

Chapter 1

The peacefulness of the night was shattered by the intensifying wail of a dozen police sirens. Under the shallow reach of the street lamp, a battered car jumped the curb and cut the corner short, driving across the yard of a house and shearing away the mailbox that had stood for over two decades like a sentinel along the sidewalk's edge.

The driver clung to the steering wheel with white knuckles and pressed his foot on the accelerator as the right headlight exploded with a flash upon impact with the mailbox. Shards of tempered glass from the bullet-riddled rear window sprinkled the road as the car bounced back onto the asphalt. The tires squealed as the driver swerved back and forth until the car straightened out from its wild turn.

He had driven this road hundreds of times. But never this fast. And certainly never with half the Tampa police department hot on his heels.

The driver jumped the next curb and skidded to a stop in front of a house, leaving deep trenches in the front lawn. He flew from the car, leaving the door wide open. He ignored the car's warning signal indicating the engine was still running and ran to the front door. He hurriedly fumbled the keys and with jittering shaking hands unlocked the door just as the first of the police cars skidded to a halt in the street behind him.

He opened the open door, slipped through, and slammed it shut, leaning his back hard against the solid wood and looking worriedly over his shoulder. He glanced up at the security camera that watched the door at all times. "Hi, honey. I'm home," he called into the dark house.

The hallway light above flickered on and a woman appeared at the top of the stairs, cinching the belt of her silk robe. She looked down at him in confusion. "Alex?"

His heart skipped a beat. This was it. He took the stairs two at a time, ignoring the amplified voice shouting surrender commands at him from the street outside.

He stopped in front of her and gripped her hands in his. "I had to see you one last time."

She looked past him to the flashing red and blue lights visible through the etched windows above the front door, flicked her eyes to the security camera, then back at him with a mixture of suspicion and worry. "What happened?"

He glanced back and then looked deeply into her eyes. "I had a little more trouble than expected."

She looked up into his face, shaking her head slightly as the worry took over. She glanced again at the camera, took his hands up to her cheek and pretended to kiss them as she whispered, "Maybe we can still save it! You can hide! I'll tell them you ran out the back and went over the fence!" She turned her head to put her cheek on his hand to continue the loving scene.

Before she could act on the suggestion, he looked surreptitiously at the camera, then took her chin in his gentle hand, guiding her eyes back to his, then put her hands to his lips to hide his words. "It's no use. I'm going to be gone for a while."

He had second thoughts when she looked up at him wistfully, a tear forming along the rim of her lashes. "I understand. How long do you think?"

He was going to miss her, but it was too late now to change course. "I'm guessing a few years. If I'm good, I'm sure I can get that reduced to only a couple inside with some parole after."

Her eyes never left his as her hands turned to an iron grip around his wrists and her face took on a look of steel he knew all too well. "Tell me it was worth it!"

He couldn't answer, not yet. It was too soon. He gently removed her hands from his wrists, surprised she let him do it so easily, and then brushed her chin with his thumb as a silent thank you for going along with his plan after all they'd been through. He put all the confidence he could muster behind his eyes as he replied "We'll have to wait and see."

He was surprised when she raised her hand and stroked his cheek ever so tenderly. "I'll be waiting for you."

He smiled, trying to reflect a calm he didn't feel. Against all odds, they had grown close over the years, and he realized he was truly going to miss her while he was away. He put a reassuring hand on her arm, marveling again at her solid strength under the robe. He decided he'd leave her with the hope that they were doing the right thing. "It'll be okay. You'll see. The years will fly by. I promise I'll call you as soon as I can."

Both their heads whipped to the door as it was hammered repeatedly with a battering ram. She quickly turned back and pierced him in place with a look that almost made him flinch, knowing what normally came after for victims of that stare, than she flicked her eyes toward the camera and instead gave him a gaze that was a combination of an unmistakable threat as well as affection meant only for him. Her beautiful hazel eyes narrowed with the warning. "You better," she said just above a whisper.

At that moment the door gave way and Alex spun around with his hands in the air. Officers spilled up the stairs like a waterfall in reverse. They surrounded him on all sides and forced him to lie face down, handcuffing his hands behind his back. They wrenched a shoulder as they lifted him to his feet. The last thing he heard as they duck-walked him out the front door was an officer noticing the camera and demanding the footage from the woman still wiping the sleep from her eyes and looking as weak as she could beneath the robe that hid her true abilities.

Alex smiled. The footage would show the police why he had taken them on a wild goose chase after they were already in pursuit. He obviously had to see his lady one last time before going to the pokey; or whatever local vernacular the civilian police used when talking about the criminals they collared and the strange things they did right before being arrested.

He glanced back at the house as they loaded him into the car. She was standing just outside the front door, she inclined her head just so. He received the message. He nodded to her and she turned away, heading back into the house. He knew, no matter how long it took, she would wait for his call, and until he could see her again, he would miss her more than he would have ever thought possible.

Chapter 2

Angela cut herself on the razor sharp edge of a box and inspected the tip of her finger. The cardboard had torn a miniaturized version of the Grand Canyon through her fingerprint and it took a few seconds for the blood to well up.

She promptly stuck the finger in her mouth before a single drop splattered on any of the objects arranged in front of her.

Dressed in a herringbone-patterned short skirt, a sheer beige blouse over a black camisole, and black satin two-inch heels, she looked out of place in the basement. With her fiery red hair done up in a bun, she looked like she should be rubbing elbows with the elite at the cocktail party in the rooms above her rather than standing in the middle of the impromptu mail room, sucking on her finger.

Wes was only twenty years her senior, but the deep wrinkly crags on his face made him look eighty years old. He regarded her with a look like a long suffering parent whose wisdom was never heeded. He shook his head slowly, gesturing toward her injured finger. "I keep telling you Ang, you gotta wear gloves when handling these recycled boxes. Never had to worry what nasty critters was hiding in the boxes back in my day. Cardboard made from trees, as God intended, that's how it should be." He wrinkled his nose at her in disgust. "And I wouldn't be sticking no finger in my mouth after touching these things. Lord knows if they washed all that poop paper before recycling them into boxes."

He emphasized the word "recycling" with air quotes

before grabbing another package off the mail cart and slicing it open with a box cutter.

"They don't recycle toilet paper into cardboard boxes, Wes," she corrected him.

He glanced at her sideways. "They mix it all together, they do. Don't know what's in 'em or what they used to be."

His words trailed off as he continued to mutter to himself. This was not the life she envisioned for herself when she joined the campaign staff of the Honorable Judge Theodore Devon, Esq. during his bid to become the next mayor of the tight-knit community of Moscow, Idaho.

She certainly wasn't dressed appropriately for her current task in the basement of the house that served as campaign headquarters. She should be upstairs, mingling with the movers and shakers of Idaho's premier college town, instead of down in the basement ripping open envelopes and boxes filled with campaign contributions and other assorted gifts for the judge.

Wes peered in the box he had just opened. "Oh goody, more crap."

He held out a pink plush bear with a bright yellow bow tied around its neck. "Who in their right mind even thinks a mayoral candidate needs a teddy?"

She took it and inspected the bright pink bear before handing it back to him. "It's probably a gag gift."

Wes regarded her with a confused expression right before the wrinkles in his face smooth as he laughed. "Oh I get it. Theodore. Teddy."

He wiggled the teddy back and forth in synchronized motion with his own head. "Hi. I'm Mayor Teddy."

She couldn't help but laugh. The menial tasks of a political staffer, far too many to count on a daily basis, would've been unbearable without Wes. They had been paired up early on in the campaign and it worked out much better than she originally thought it would.

She would've quit months ago if it weren't for him.

Her cell phone rang in her purse.

Finally!

The judge must've remembered she was still down here and was calling her back up to the party. When she dug it out, it rang again with that same muted sound as if it were still deep inside her purse.

Only, it wasn't her phone ringing.

Wes shrugged his shoulders. "Don't look at me, I don't have one of those things. Somebody wants to call me, they can damn well wait till I get home."

The muffled ringtone sounded again, coming from one of the packages on the mail cart.

Wes leaned over the small pile of boxes and envelopes and cocked his head to the side. After it rang again, he plucked a box off the cart and cut it open.

He unfurled the tightly wound bubble wrap and held the cell phone up as it rang much louder this time. Had somebody accidentally boxed their cell phone up instead of the gift? What other reason would they be trying to call it, except to find out where it had ended up?

"Aren't you going to answer it?" she said as it chirped again melodically.

He held it out to her with nicotine stained fingers. "No way. These things give you brain cancer."

She took it from him with an exasperated sigh and answered it. "Hello?"

There was silence on the other side followed by a rapid clicking sound.

"Hello?" she said again.

The clicking promptly stopped and was replaced by the sound of a fax machine. She hadn't heard that sound in nearly a decade. Emails and PDF attachments had replaced the fax machine as the primary document transfer pipeline. They still had a fax machine in the main campaign office, but it sat in the corner, unplugged, and slowly gathering dust. Somebody, some high level staffer, insisted it was relevant technology, so it had never been thrown out.

She listened to the screeching tones coming from the cell phone, and understood everything. When the computerized tones completed their transmission, she set the phone down on the table in front of her and meticulously planned out the order of her next few important tasks.

She had a lot to do, and very little time to do it.

Chapter 3

Angela scanned the room around her with a fresh pair of eyes. She was in the basement while her target was located in one of the rooms above. The basement had been turned into a makeshift mail room; exactly where she needed to be.

The only other person in the room was staring at her with a puzzled expression on his face. "Are you okay Ang? Who was on the phone?"

She probed the recesses of her original memories and matched his face to a name. The transition happened faster each time. She was quickly merging her original memories with her new ones.

The man standing before her was named... Wes.

She smiled reassuringly at him. "I'm fine."

The worry lines in his deeply wrinkled forehead smoothed. "You zoned out for a moment there. You sure you're okay?"

She glanced at her watch.

"The judge's party will be winding down soon. We should finish opening these boxes."

As soon as Wes turned his attention back to the cart, she snatched up the box cutter and sliced his throat with the skilled hand of a professional assassin. As she coldly watched him fall, gurgle, and ineffectively try to use his hands to stop the life blood flowing out of his open artery, it occurred to a part of her mind that she had never so much as harmed a fly the whole time she was growing up in this quiet college town.

She stepped aside quickly to avoid being splattered by the spraying blood from her first victim. Somewhere in the back of her mind she quietly asked herself how she had known to do that.

She picked up the pink plush teddy bear with the yellow ribbon and cut into it. She pulled out the stuffing and let it fall around her feet until she found what she was looking for.

She slid the automatic pistol out of the teddy bear and gripped it with the practiced hand of someone who had fired thousands of rounds, even though this was the first time she had ever held a gun.

Her thumb flicked off the safety and she yanked on the slide to chamber the first round.

Her mission was to make her target's death personal. It could not look like a political assassination. It was up to her to make sure nobody probed too deeply into why the judge was killed.

Fortunately for her, she would have a room full of witnesses eager to spread her carefully calculated misdirection. Every one of them would scramble to be the first to say why the judge was killed when the news trucks showed up.

She couldn't remember who she was doing this for, but that didn't matter. She would use her newfound skills to the best of her ability and accomplish her mission. It was imperative. It was why she lived.

She stepped over the body of her former colleague, internally thanking him for handing the phone over to her. It would've been a much harder sell to the witnesses if he had been the one to pull the trigger.

Chapter 4

Angela stepped into the crowded great room of the Victorian mansion where the Honorable Judge Theodore Devon, Esq. was holding his latest fundraising event. She chuckled silently to herself as she thought of her target's name.

The Honorable Judge Devon.

Tonight was going to be as much a character assassination of the judge as it was a literal assassination.

Her clothes no longer looked out of place and she blended perfectly in with the crowds milling about the rooms of the mansion.

She held the gun tightly against her leg with her left hand. She would need her right to shake hands with anyone who stopped her to force an introduction with another of Idaho's elite.

Fortunately, she made her way through the crowd with minimal interruption. She was just a staffer on the judge's campaign, and not someone the elite felt compelled to meet.

She circled the room a second time, not finding the judge anywhere.

She stopped next to Billy, another staffer who had the luck of being related to the judge through some distant cousin and was never relegated to menial tasks. He had been at the party the entire time. She accidentally stood a little too close and realized her perfume mesmerized him like it usually did boys her previous personality wanted to attract. She marveled that boys raised on the privileged side of the tracks always thought they were God's gift to women, which made them easy prey. But she didn't have time to be bait.

She purposely avoided looking into his eyes, which would've derailed the mission further by forcing her to focus on redirecting his unwanted attention, and carefully scanned the crowd. Then, her new personality found a way to use his undesired interest. She engaged his eyes with hers and looked at him with a very sly half smile as she said, "I can't find the judge."

He nodded to the open French doors on the other side of the room. "He's out in the garden trying to convince one of his biggest contributors not to withdraw his support, but I don't think you can help with that right now."

She put on her best pouty disappointed puppy dog look and asked, "Maybe, maybe not. Anybody else out there with them?"

"Don't think so. My guess is that's a very private conversation."

So much for a quick and speedy end to her mission. There had to be plenty of witnesses around for what she had planned. She would have to wait until he came back inside.

She tucked the pistol up under her blouse and into the front of her skirt. She couldn't risk someone spotting it before she was ready for them to see it.

She watched, waiting for him to return, when a familiar high-pitched voice pulled her attention away from the open French doors. The judge's wife, Marguerite, was pulling a distinguished looking gentleman by the arm toward her.

"Ah, here she is. Senator Jules, I'd like you to meet Angela, a very bright young lady who has been with us since the very beginning."

The senator graciously extended his hand and Angela shook it with an easy smile on her face. "It's very nice to meet you, Senator."

The senator's face brightened when he caught a whiff of her essence. She found that it had paid, more often than not, to spend the extra bit on perfumes that advertised to be infused with pheromones. He took advantage of the handshake to move in closer. "The pleasure is all mine."

Marguerite motioned to the room in general. "None of this would be possible without Angela's help. She is a godsend."

The senator breathed in her scent. "I could use someone like you when the next election comes around. I just barely beat out my opponent the last time."

He clung to her hand, even though the shake had officially ended. She did her best to not make it feel like his prolonged handholding was unwanted. She glanced sideways at Marguerite.

"Actually, I was hoping for a more permanent position once the judge becomes mayor."

The senator gripped her hand tighter and winked. "Now why would you limit yourself to working in a small town mayor's office? I'm sure I could think of several positions for you in my office."

She pulled her hand out of his slowly and suppressed the emotions bubbling up from deep inside that urged her to react to his obvious meaning. She had more important things to do tonight.

"I appreciate the offer, senator, but I belong here. I grew up here."

And then inspiration hit her and she knew what to say to lay the groundwork to accomplish the mission.

"And I plan to start a family here."

Marguerite smiled. "I didn't know you were married."

"I'm not, but I've been spending a lot of time with someone lately. And we've become very close."

Marguerite stiffened at her comment. That confirmed to her that it was Marguerite's decision to banish her to the basement for the duration of the party. All those late nights working alone with the judge, despite nothing ever happening, had made the wife suspicious and jealous. Luckily for Marguerite, her paranoid suspicions were about to be realized in front of dozens of witnesses.

During the short conversation with the senator, Angela had positioned herself so she could keep an eye on the doors leading out to the garden. She spotted a man walking in, glancing around, and then heading for the front door. That must be the contributor the judge was trying to persuade to maintain his support. It didn't look like he had been successful.

It didn't matter. The judge was alone in the garden, and that was best for her new plan.

She nodded politely at the senator. "It was very nice to meet you. If you'll excuse me there is someone I need to talk to."

She didn't wait for his response as she quickly made her way out to the garden.

Thankfully, he was alone. Her heels clicked on the paving stones as she approached him from behind while he turned. "Did you have a change of heart, Walter?"

His face registered surprise. "I'm sorry, Angela. I thought you were my contributor coming back to apologize for his behavior."

The next thing she did was out of character for her, and this man had done nothing to deserve it. It made it hard for her to do, but it had to be done to accomplish her mission.

She swung hard and slapped the smile off his face.

She spun around on the balls of her feet and stomped back through the garden toward the French doors that would lead her back into the middle of the party.

She was making a big scene, pushing people out of the way as she forced herself through the middle of the great room.

The judge called out to her as soon as he reached the French doors.

"Angela!"

She spun around and screamed at him. "You promised! You promised!"

The judge looked even more confused now than in the moment after she slapped him. "What did I promise? What are you talking about?"

By now, everyone at the party looked like they were watching a tennis match, their heads pivoting from the judge, to her, and back again to the judge.

"I'm tired of the lies. We can't hide this forever."

"Hide what forever? What's gotten into you?"

Every guest's head pivoted to her, waiting for a response. She had to make it good.

She laughed hysterically to show the witnesses she'd been pushed, not to the edge, but over it.

"Excellent choice of words, darling. What's gotten into me? What's gotten into me? I'll tell you what got into me."

She reached under her blouse and yanked out the pistol.

She ignored the cries of terror as everyone shrank away from her. She shouted, clearly and loudly for everyone to hear. "You got into me. I'm pregnant you son of a bitch!"

There were nine rounds in the magazine of the automatic pistol.

The first eight she pumped into Honorable Judge Theodore Devon, Esq. Even though she had never fired a weapon in the twenty-eight years she had been alive, her groupings were tight and the judge was dead before he hit the floor.

The last one, she saved for herself.

Chapter 5

The prison guard stopped in front of the bars to Alexander Chase's cell. He peered in and grinned. "Today's your lucky day, Chase. Did you remember to pack?"

Alex stood up and stretched his tall, muscular frame before holding up a frayed toothbrush. "Didn't really come here with much."

The guard circled a finger in the air and the doors popped open with the prerequisite buzzer sound. Alex followed the guard away from the six foot by eight foot box that had been home for the last two years. Inmates hooted and hollered all manner of obscenities as he walked past their locked cells.

The guard laughed. "Seems you have quite the fan club."

Alex ignored them and kept walking. "Nah. They say that to all the guys."

Processing was handled quickly and Alex found himself standing at the front gates to the prison waiting to be released.

He stepped over the threshold, marveling that the difference between imprisonment and freedom was but a single step. As the gate slowly rolled closed, the guard nodded at him. "See you soon Chase."

Alex squinted against the harsh sunlight that reflected off the whitewashed prison walls. "Don't think so Tony."

Tony smirked. "They all say that. And they all come back."

Alex scanned the circular driveway and saw only one car parked along the curb. It was a brand new Aston Martin sports car. Not the kind of car you would expect to be waiting in front of a nondescript prison in the southeastern United States. He thought back to everyone he came in contact with on the inside. None of them seemed the type to have friends who could afford to spend $300,000 on a single car.

He certainly didn't know anybody with that kind of money to throw around. "When's my taxi get here?"

Tony pointed to the shiny green sports car with the butt of his shotgun. "That's your ride."

"Who is it?"

Tony shrugged his shoulders. "Maybe it's your parole officer."

Tony walked away laughing, pleased with how clever he was.

Alex walked up to the sports car and tapped a knuckle on the tinted window of the passenger side. The whine of the window's internal motor brought him face-to-face with a beautiful blonde sitting in the right-side driver's seat of a car produced for British roads.

She smiled sweetly. "Get in Mr. Chase."

Her refined British accent made her that much more attractive.

She started to roll the window up when he put his hand in to stop it. "Who are you?"

She lowered her tinted sunglasses with a dainty leather gloved hand so he could see into her sparkling blue eyes. "My name is Samantha Fox. I'm your new parole officer."

Chapter 6

Alex shoveled the last forkful of gravy slathered biscuit into his mouth and looked out the smudged windows of the diner. Samantha's car easily cost ten times more than all the other cars in the parking lot combined, but she hadn't parked on the far edge of the lot to leave a protective bubble around her expensive sports car. Instead, she wedged it between two beat-up trucks right in front of the diner.

Looking back, he noted she hadn't touched a single bite of the biscuits and gravy she'd ordered. He was surprised when she told the waitress that she'll have what he's having, because she didn't look like she usually ate that way.

"Aren't you going to eat?"

"No. I ordered it for you."

She pushed her plate over to him. How did she know he would still be hungry after finishing his meal?

Who cares how she knew. He hadn't eaten anything this good in over ten years. And that included his eight years serving in every climate imaginable before spending the last two in prison.

She waited patiently with her hands folded in her lap while he used the final piece of biscuit to mop up the last of the gravy and popped it into his mouth. He would hit the gym and work off any extra pounds he had just gained by next week. But for now, it felt good to stuff himself. Who knew when he would get the chance to eat like that again?

He sat back, rested his hands on his stretched belly, and regarded the thin blonde sitting across the table from him. She was not what he would've expected a parole officer to look like, or behave. He glanced out the window at the expensive sports car. What kind of civil servant could afford a car like that?

It was time to find out what was going on.

"Why don't you tell me who you really are?"

She sat back, her eyebrows raised in surprise. "I'm here to get you integrated back into society and working again. In fact, I already have a job lined up that would be perfect for you."

"Really? What kind of job?"

"It's a courier job. You go somewhere, pick something up, and bring it back."

"Would I get to use your car?"

"Nobody would believe a courier drives an Aston Martin."

"Nobody would believe a parole officer drives an Aston Martin."

The faintest of a smile picked up the corners of her mouth. "Touché, Mr. Chase."

"Collection and retrieval, huh? Why me?"

"Because you hold a special set of skills. The retrieval may require some improvisation on your part. But I believe you're up to the task."

"You don't know anything about me."

"On the contrary. I know everything about you. Most importantly, I know why you went to prison after having a flawless record in the army."

"Anybody can find out why I went to prison. It's public record."

She leaned forward in a conspiratorial manner. "You and I both know the public record's been tampered with. One month after you were recommended for promotion to the

Green Berets, you were dishonorably discharged from the army and sent to prison. And we both know it had nothing to do with a bar fight in Tampa. I know the real reason your friends, your fellow soldiers, even your government, turned on you in an instant. I know the reason not found in any public record."

Chapter 7

The gravy settled like lead in Alex's stomach as he studied Samantha's face for any indication she was lying. One of the things not found in any public record, with the private records sealed to all but the most privileged eyes, was his extensive training in counter-espionage and interrogation tactics. He was able to tell when someone was lying to him. She was either telling the truth, or she was very good at lying.

It was time to call her bluff.

"You don't have anything."

"Isn't that the same thing the tribunal told you when they released Saqr and sent you to prison?"

She had done her homework, he mused. She knew which button to push to set him off, and he didn't want to disappoint her by letting the comment slide.

He reached across the table in the blink of an eye, grabbing at her throat to choke out the rest of her unspoken sentence.

She was faster.

Before he realized what was happening, she had him face down on the floor with his arm twisted back to the breaking point.

She convinced the waitress not to call the police, but it seemed everyone had a cell phone these days. In the time it took her to calm down the restaurant staff, three other patrons had already dialed 911.

She pressed her knee deep into his spine and whispered into his ear. "We should leave before the police get here, don't you agree?"

He wiggled his head an attempt to nod. It was the best he could do with his face pinned to the ground by someone nearly half his size.

She lifted him back on his feet and hustled him to the door while throwing twenties on the front counter to pay for breakfast. "It's okay everyone, my brother has seizures like this all the time. I'm taking him to the hospital now."

The waitress scooped the bills off the counter. "The police can give you an escort," she said instead of offering to make change.

Samantha guided him to the car as she hollered over her shoulder at the waitress who stood in the open door of the restaurant, "His medication's in the car. We really don't need to make a big deal out of this. Sorry for any trouble."

She shoved him into the passenger seat and hopped behind the wheel.

Five minutes later, they were on the highway, the diner but a distant memory in the rearview mirror. She made the V12 engine in the Aston Martin work for it and there was not a police cruiser manufactured in any country that could catch up with them.

He massaged his tender shoulder and watched her expertly slalom the Aston Martin around the other cars on the highway as if they were standing still. She seemed to be in complete control despite eliciting angered honking from the other drivers as she darted around them with millimeters to spare.

Without taking her eyes off the road, she said, "It's not polite to stare."

He hadn't realized he had been watching her for so long and shifted his view to the road ahead.

He had been wrong about everything. He had made

assumptions about her. The expensive car. The skin tight business suit. Even the loosely combed long blonde hair that fell softly down her back. Together, these individual elements drew a picture about how she would behave in any given situation.

He had scored very well during training on being able to read people. He scored well on every test they threw at him. It was why he'd been recommended to the Green Berets, the elite of the elite in the United States Army.

He had already observed all the signs for Samantha Fox. He knew exactly who she was. A spoiled girl from privilege used to getting her way.

But she had become an entirely different person the moment he reached for her neck. She moved with the speed of an elite soldier who had perfected the art of hand-to-hand combat.

Anyone able to get him to the ground after he made the first move, was someone he needed to keep an eye on.

After an hour of silence, she pulled off the highway and rolled to a stop behind a gas station. She shut off the engine and twisted in her seat to face him.

"It appears we've gotten off on the wrong foot. What can I do to set things right?"

"How about the truth."

"What do you want to know?"

"What do you want to tell me?"

She let out an audible sigh. "How about you ask me questions and I answer them?"

"Are you going to tell me the truth?"

"When you ask something I feel compelled to lie about, I will tell you that I cannot say; which will be the truth."

He studied her mannerisms. She certainly gave every

indication she was telling the truth. Time to put that to the test.

"What is your name?"

"Samantha Fox."

"What is your real name?"

"I cannot say."

"Are you a parole officer?"

"Not exactly."

"Then who, exactly, are you?"

"I cannot say."

"Let me put this a different way. Who do you work for?"

"I cannot say."

They were getting nowhere, but at least they were getting there quickly.

"You seem compelled to lie an awful lot."

She shrugged. "Hazards of the job."

"And what job is that?"

She smiled. "I cannot say."

It was his turn to sigh audibly. "Okay then, what can you tell me?"

"I can tell you that the skills you possess are something I need to get a specific task done. And I will pay you $50,000 to do it."

"$50,000?"

"Yes."

"How long would it take me to do this task?"

"Three days."

"$50,000 for three day's work?"

"That's right."

"Sounds illegal."

"It is."

Chapter 8

Alex pulled himself out of the Aston Martin and twisted his torso back and forth, stretching the knots out of his back from sitting in the same position for too long. What Samantha "not her real name" Fox had failed to mention, when he first agreed to take the job, was that the first day would be spent driving halfway across the continental United States.

They would have been here sooner if she'd let him take a turn at the wheel. Instead, they spent a couple of hours of fitful sleep in a cheap roadside motel with a lumpy mattress and broken springs. He almost wished he was back in the comfort of his prison cell. Even the thin roll-up mattress from his boot camp days would've been better.

The sun was setting for the second time since his release and he wondered if he was making the right choices. Should he have taken this job, or should he have waited? She had been waiting for him upon his release, so it seemed like going with her was the right thing to do.

Samantha smoothly glided out of the car as if this was something she did every day. Who knows, maybe this was something she did every day. He massaged his stiff shoulders. Before he could answer that question, he had to know more about her.

He looked around and saw they were in the parking lot of yet another seedy motel.

"Please don't tell me we're staying here tonight."

"We are an hour away from the target. If we stay any closer, you run the risk of bumping into someone beforehand and blowing your cover."

He shook his head. "No one's going to believe I'm an FBI agent."

"Of course they are. You will have all the credentials you need to prove you are who you say you are. Besides, we've already tapped the switch coming out of town. If they call any of the listed, or unlisted, numbers for the FBI, they will be talking to my people. We'll vouch for you."

Statements like that made him wonder why she needed his help in the first place.

"Why do you need me to play this FBI agent? Why can't you do it?"

"I already visited a few days ago under the credentials of a newspaper reporter. I can't go back as somebody else. It's a small town. They might remember me."

Might remember her? They would definitely remember her. That knockout body, combined with the singsong lilt of her British accent, made her unforgettable to the entire male population. It had nothing to do with the size of the city or the frequency of out-of-town visitors.

"Can't we stay someplace... nice?"

She placed her hands on top of the Aston Martin and looked at him across the roof. "You can either spend the night somewhere that costs $25 or somewhere that costs $300,000."

She pointed to a vending machine that hummed noisily next to the motel office. "Either choice puts you within walking distance to what you Americans believe is the pinnacle of twenty-four hour access to haute cuisine."

He'd already spent long enough in the bucket seats of the Aston Martin. He would never pull off being an FBI agent if he tried to sleep in the car.

"Fine. But if this bed is as bad as the last one, I'm gonna

make you regret not checking us in to a Four Seasons."

She gave him a wry smile. "I'd like to see you try."

Chapter 9

The next morning, Alex woke up feeling much better. The mattress on his bed was made out of memory foam, and it had cradled him perfectly while he slept.

Just like the night before, Samantha had checked them in to separate rooms. She either trusted him enough to not escape during the night, or she didn't trust him enough to be in the same room with her and a bed. Since he had spent the last two years in prison, and the eight years before that in the army, it was more likely the latter. While he wasn't a Greek god, he wasn't ugly by any stretch of imagination.

And it had been a very long time for him.

Sadness washed over him as he fought against the tidal wave of depression. Images flashed in his mind of... her.

He took three deep breaths to steady his nerves and pushed those memories back into the dusty corner. He would never let it go, but he wasn't ready to deal with it yet. There was still something he had to do before he could resolve that memory from a lifetime ago.

A knock on the door snapped him out of it.

He peeked through a corner of the drapes. Samantha was holding a cup of steaming coffee in one hand and a dark blue suit on a hanger in the other. She knocked on the door again.

As he opened the door, she quickly swept into the room and handed him the cup of coffee.

"Drink all of that first. I don't want you spilling on the suit."

The heat from the sweet elixir of life seeped through the cup and the cardboard ring around it. How did she know he liked his coffee scalding hot? And what more did she know about him?

He decided to put her through a little test.

"The coffee's a little hot," he said.

She hung the suit on the hook that dangled from loose screws on the bathroom door and ripped open the thin plastic cover, exposing the dark blue suit.

"Nice try. I also know you like two and a half packets of sugar. Not two. Not three. Two and a half." She looked at him sideways while peeling the rest of the plastic away and shook her head disapprovingly. "You've got some pretty odd habits, but you were in the right place at the right time. Tonight, you'll be $50,000 richer and headed anywhere you want."

"Technically, I wasn't supposed to leave the state, four states ago."

"Don't worry Alex. As an added bonus, we've handled all the paperwork for your parole. By tomorrow morning, you'll be a free man."

This was something new.

"A free man?"

"We can put information into the system just as easily as we can take it out. As a thank you for accepting this job on such short notice, we've expunged your record. Anybody doing a background check will find nothing but your exemplary military record, your release from service with accommodations, and a steady job with a private security firm oversees for the last two years."

His mouth gaped open in surprise.

She winked. "You're welcome."

His earlier doubt eroded away in an instant. He definitely made the right decision going with her rather than waiting for something else to come along.

And then just like that, she was back to business. "Here's a shaving kit and some shampoo from the front desk. You have half an hour to make yourself look like a respectable FBI agent."

He inspected the tiny bottle and disposable razor. They looked even smaller in his powerful hands. "What? No conditioner?"

She put her hands on her hips. "Where do you think you are, the Four Seasons?"

Chapter 10

Samantha had given him only thirty minutes to get ready. He was ready in twenty. He could've done it in ten if he hadn't spent half the time fighting with the skinny tie.

Ties were not needed during combat situations and would prove even more dangerous as part of a prison uniform. Of all the skills he maintained during his two-year incarceration, tying a knot that was designed for fashion was not one of them.

Thank God this wasn't one of the tests back in the army.

He struggled with it for another minute before tucking it under his collar and buttoning his jacket over the uneven bottom sections.

He inspected himself in the mirror.

It had been a good idea to keep his hair trimmed short rather than let it grow long and unruly like most of the other inmates in his cellblock. That seemingly insignificant decision kept him as an outsider during his full two-year stint. The fact he refused to get any tattoos ostracized him from everybody else in the prison, which is how he preferred it.

He'd always fancied himself an outsider.

A lone wolf.

A rogue.

Even when he was part of a well-trained unit, his favorite missions were the ones where he could strike out on his own.

Whatever task Samantha had in store for him, it looked like he would be on his own for most of it. And that was exactly the way he liked it.

Speaking of Samantha, there was another knock on the door. She was a few minutes early. Probably another one of her little tests.

"Come in."

She looked at him for only a second before all her attention focused on his neck. "That will not do."

She tugged roughly at the knot, trying to loosen it as she dug her fingers in between the tie and his Adam's apple. He tried to push her hands away from his neck, but she slapped them away.

"You're choking me."

"We are on a tight schedule. If you were having trouble, you should've called me in."

"If I knew what I was going to be doing, I could stay on schedule."

She forced the tie loose and slipped it out through his collar with a single pulling motion.

"You will be told what you need to know, when you need to know it."

"Maybe that's not how I operate, stumbling around in the dark."

She unbuttoned his jacket and flipped up the collar of his shirt.

"That's exactly how you operate. Why do you think I picked you?"

"You said so yourself. I was in the right place at the right time."

She looped the tie around his neck and, with practiced fingers, tied a perfect Windsor knot in no seconds flat.

"Amongst other things."

"What's that supposed to mean?"

"You are good at what you do, Mr. Chase. That is why I

picked you. It was a bonus that I didn't need to break you out of prison first."

Chapter 11

Alex parked the rented Lincoln Town Car, painted in the prerequisite FBI black, in the lot of the Moscow, Idaho police station between two police cruisers.

He shut off the engine and sat there for a moment, collecting his thoughts, while the engine ticked as it cooled down.

The task Samantha had given him seemed simple enough. He would present himself as an FBI agent to the desk officer and ask to review the evidence from a local murder-suicide that took place a few days before. Because the victim had been running for mayor, the FBI preferred to independently investigate the evidence. At least that was the story he would give.

What he was really supposed to do, was swap out the cell phone in the evidence locker with the cell phone in his pocket.

For that, he would be paid $50,000.

He twisted the rear view mirror and inspected his face. It was still shocking to look in the mirror and not recognize himself.

The sandy red-haired toupee, along with the bushy same-color mustache would have been enough. But then a team of makeup artists aged his skin, adding deep crow's feet around his eyes, and dotting on plenty of freckles.

It still seemed odd, with the resources she had at her disposal, that she needed him for this task. Her makeup crew, which had magically appeared as soon as he was dressed, could've made anyone look different. Why did she need him, specifically?

Why indeed.

It was his good fortune that she did seek him out. If he did well on this task, she would call on him again. Maybe even offer him more jobs for the people she worked for.

All in good time, he reminded himself.

Before he could plan out his future, he had to take the next step. Right now, that next step was to steal a cell phone from a police station.

He slipped out of the rental car and headed up the steps, not even bothering to lock his car. Crime was typically low in a small town, and it was parked right in front of the police station. It would be safe.

He reached the door and it opened quickly. A thin man in an ill-fitted suit and horn-rimmed glasses rushed past him.

Alex jumped back to keep from being knocked back. "Hey, watch where you're going buddy!"

The Thin Man mumbled an apology of sorts and hurried down the stairs.

Once inside the door, the desk officer raised his head from the dog-eared paperback novel in his hands. "Can I help you?"

Alex flipped open his FBI badge and draped it over the open book. He waited silently while the officer scanned his phony FBI credentials.

The officer looked up and pasted on the same "let's get you out of my hair as fast as humanly possible" smile every local law enforcer gave when somebody came in waving a federal badge to intrude on their jurisdiction.

"What can I do for you, Special Agent Sanderson?"

He snapped the document wallet shut and tucked it back into the inside pocket of his jacket.

"I would like to see the reports and all related evidence for the murder-suicide case."

The desk officer looked bored. "Which murder-suicide case?"

Alex cocked an eyebrow. "You have more than one?"

The officer stuck the bookmark into his book and closed it.

"No. But another agent from the FBI was just in here asking for the exact same thing. You probably bumped into each other in the parking lot. You guys need to learn to communicate better."

His mind reeled. The FBI was here? Samantha hadn't said anything about the real FBI coming here. The only person he saw leave was the Thin Man, and he certainly hadn't behaved like a real FBI agent. It seemed that Samantha wasn't the only one interested in the cell phone.

He nodded to the log book. "What was the name of the agent?"

The officer leaned over his logbook. "Umm, Agent Smith."

It was time to improvise.

He looked the desk officer squarely in the eyes. "Don't you think a name like Agent Smith is a little too convenient? Did you even look at his ID?"

He whipped out the cell phone from his pocket and pretended to dial before sticking the phone to his ear.

"Sanderson here, get me Hal on the line immediately."

While he pretended to wait, he looked at the desk officer. "I need to see that bag of evidence."

When the desk officer seemed to hesitate, Alex bellowed, "Now!"

The desk officer ran behind a door and came back out

moments later, evidence bag in hand. Alex held his hand out for the officer to give him the bag while he shouted into his phone.

"I don't care where he is! Get him on the phone now!"

The officer handed him the bag.

While cradling the cell phone in the crook of his neck, Alex ripped open the evidence bag and spilled its contents on the counter.

There were not a lot of items in the bag.

But most importantly, there was no cell phone.

The Thin Man had taken it.

Chapter 12

Alex bursts through the doors of the police station and scanned the streets around him. The Thin Man was nowhere to be seen.

This time he dialed the cell phone for real as he ran for the rental car. It was answered on the first ring. He didn't bother waiting for Samantha to speak.

"The cell phone's gone."

"What?!"

"A thin guy, five-six, hundred and twenty pounds, dark hair, horn-rimmed glasses, gray suit. He took it."

"Are you sure?"

"There are four roads at compass points leading out of here. How soon can you have them covered?"

"Already in place."

"Good. Pass on the description and let me know immediately when they spot him."

He hung up his phone, not waiting for her response. He was the one on point. That meant he was in charge, whether she liked it or not.

She wanted a lone wolf?

She wanted a rogue?

Well, she got one.

He reversed out of the parking space with a squeal of tires, shifted into drive, and shot forward down the street.

If he were the Thin Man, where would he be headed right now?

He had scanned a map of the city and outlying areas last night when Samantha said they were at the place for his task. He had done it to make sure that, if Samantha turned on him, he would know possible escape routes.

Now, that same knowledge would help him decide where to go next.

If he were the Thin Man, he would want to put as much distance between him and the city in as short a time as possible. That meant he would want to get to an airport. And he'd want to do it soon.

Moscow, Idaho was far enough from any major city, with a commercial airport, to be considered smack dab in the middle of nowhere. His mind's eye swooped over the city like a homing pigeon, circling higher and higher as he pictured the city map he had studied.

The city of Pullman, to the west, had a regional airport for private planes.

If the Thin Man had similar resources to Samantha, he would have access to a plane. And possibly a pilot.

The other three directions out of Moscow went to God knows where. If he was the Thin Man, he'd be headed for the airport to the west. If he turned west on 3rd Street, it would take him out of the city and in the direction of Pullman. And hopefully, in the direction of his prey.

His cell phone rang.

"Did you find him?"

Samantha did not sound pleased. "When you get the cell phone, we are going to have to discuss who's in charge."

"Where is he?"

"He just passed one of my checkpoints on Pullman Road, west of Moscow."

"I know where he's going."

He disconnected the phone and stomped down on the accelerator of his rented Lincoln Town Car. Now would have been a good time to have had the Aston Martin.

Chapter 13

Samantha stared at her silent phone. Maybe she had chosen poorly. Maybe she was wrong about Alexander Chase. She had seen the file on Chase. Even the un-redacted and recovered records that somebody, very high up the food chain, had tried to erase.

For the first time, in over twenty years, her organization was building a new alpha team from scratch. The previous team had been disbanded and scattered to the wind. They had been infiltrated and compromised at nearly every level and her boss decided the only way to clean house was to demolish it completely and start anew.

And he wanted her to build his new team.

As she dialed Alex again, she worried that her first choice might be too unstable. But then again, in her line of work, a loose cannon would hit the target more often than not.

Before she finished dialing, her radio crackled to life.

"Come in Fox. This is Sky reporting in."

She lifted the radio to her lips.

"This is Fox, go ahead Sky."

"Suspect pulled off the highway onto Airport Road. He is headed for the Pullman-Moscow Regional Airport. Over."

"Any visual on the operative?"

"He is a mile behind the target and making excellent time."

"How long until he reaches the target?"

"If both cars maintain their present speeds, he will catch up with the target in five minutes."

She felt relieved. They had not lost the cell phone yet. If the target was exactly as described, Chase would have no problem getting the phone once he caught up with him.

A chill ran down her spine as the radio crackled with Sky's next comment. "Only…"

She gripped the radio tightly. "Only what, Sky?"

"The target will be at the airport in less than a minute."

Chapter 14

Alex skidded off the highway onto Airport Road, ignoring his own red light and the honking of other drivers.

His phone rang and he scooped it up off the passenger seat to answer it. "Little busy right now."

"The target boarded a private charter, tail number November Whiskey 17592. It's taxiing to the runway."

Why was she just watching the Thin Man do all this?

Why weren't her other agents doing something? Anything?

"Why didn't you stop him?"

"You're the only operative on the ground."

"You said you had people all over the city."

"I have one, watching via satellite."

He disconnected and tossed the phone into the back seat. He didn't need any more distractions if he was expected to stop that plane by himself.

He sped around a slow moving truck, kicking up loose gravel from the shoulder of the road as he fishtailed back onto the pavement.

Keeping one eye on the road ahead of him, and the other on the GPS screen built into the dash, he screamed around the last curve of Airport Road, seeing the edge of the airport spread out before him.

He pressed hard on the accelerator, smashing it down into the floorboard, trying to get one more horse to push the car just a little bit faster.

He watched his green arrow refresh its position in leaps and bounds on the GPS map as he sped down the pavement, weaving around the sparse traffic.

Up ahead, he saw an unmarked access road that led straight into the airport from the road he was on. The official entrance was still three quarters of a mile ahead of him. If he tried to go in the correct way, he would be too late.

He twisted the steering wheel and skidded off the pavement at a thirty-five degree angle. The Lincoln Town Car was not a nimble car, and he fought against inertia to keep it headed in the direction he wanted; straight for the locked gate that was supposed to keep cars, like his, off the runway.

He clung to the steering wheel and let the mass of the rental car rip through the chain-link gate like it was made out of paper.

If he had done something like this fifty years earlier, he would've gone through that gate with nothing more than a few scratches. Nothing a little touch up paint couldn't fix. But it seemed that today's cars were more fragile than Faberge eggs.

The chrome grill on the town car crumpled inward on impact and, as he bounced up and over the collapsed fence, the bent metal pipes that formed the frame of the gate ripped the front bumper off in a last-ditch effort to do its job to stop the speeding car.

Thankfully, he hadn't popped the tires and was able to barrel full speed down the gravel lined access road.

The gravel ended and his tires gripped old pavement, pressing him into his seat as he shot forward even faster.

At the same end of the runway he was fast approaching, a small private plane was readying for takeoff.

From this angle, he could make out the "N" and the "W" that started the tail number sequence. He hadn't been paying attention when she rattled off the rest of the numbers to him.

Close enough.

The plane started rolling down the runway.

He didn't have time to slow down to make the curve coming up and enter the runway properly.

He twisted the steering wheel and bounced off the paved road, kicking up dirt and grass behind him as he cut a path through the field that butted up against the end of the runway.

His front tires hit the edge of the runway, nearly blowing them both out as he bounded up on to the smooth tarmac. Finally, he found himself in the environment the massive town car thrived on.

Smooth and straight.

He kept the accelerator pinned to the floorboard as he raced up behind the single prop plane and swerved around to come alongside it.

He made direct eye contact with the Thin Man in the copilot's seat, the large headphones making his tiny head look even smaller. Fear reflected behind his horn-rimmed glasses right before he turned to yell at the pilot.

Alex kept his foot down hard on the accelerator, the town car just barely matching the speed of the plane, but starting to lose ground.

If he didn't act fast, the plane would lift off and he would end up in the field at the other end of the runway, empty-handed.

If he were trying to stop another car, he would use the infamous pit maneuver the police used to end a car chase. He would steer the front end of his car into the back end of the other and spin them out. Maybe something like that would work on the plane.

The front of the town car was parallel to the back end of the plane, and he was already going as fast as he could, with the plane inching away from him every second he wasted.

It was now or never.

He turned the steering wheel just enough to nose his front end in to the side of the plane.

And right under it.

He shot out on the other side of the plane, without even touching it.

The town car fishtailed wildly and spun off the edge of the runway. The massive car did two three-hundred-and-sixty-degree turns before stopping in the middle of the grassy field, a cloud of dust enveloping him.

He leapt from the car as the dust cleared, just in time to watch the private plane lift off into the sky with the Thin Man and the cell phone. He'd lost them both.

He kicked at the side of the town car as the wail of sirens, carried on the wind, headed in his direction.

Chapter 15

For the second time this morning, Alex found himself walking through the front doors of the Moscow, Idaho police station. Only this time, he was in handcuffs and being escorted by two of Moscow's finest.

The desk officer gave him a sideways glance before returning to his book. If only the desk officer knew how much more interesting his life was than any book, he would have paid him a little more attention.

He was led into the interview room, with the two-way mirror stretching across the back wall and a microphone in the center of the table that was connected by a long cable with the video camera mounted in the corner of the ceiling.

As soon as he sat down, they secured him to the metal chair with a second pair of handcuffs.

He wasn't going anywhere.

Alone in the room with his thoughts, he wondered how long before he would find himself back in prison with no hope of parole. It hadn't even been twenty-four hours since he got out, and he'd already tried to ram a plane off the runway with, he was surprised to learn, a vehicle reported stolen from the local car rental place.

Maybe he was hanging out with the wrong crowd. He'd already wasted his one phone call with the only phone number he had been given since getting out of prison. And, for one reason or another, Samantha refused to answer. If he thought real hard, he probably knew the answer.

So that was it. Just like that, he was on his own.

Maybe she was testing him. Looking to see if he could figure a way out of the situation he had put himself in.

The door opened behind him and he heard the soft click of woman's heels circle around the table into his field of view.

Samantha had come after all.

He was about to react when she shook her head slightly and gave him a stern look, keeping him silent.

She set her briefcase on the table and snapped it open.

"I am your court-appointed attorney until such time, if and when, you decide to hire your own." She spoke without a hint of her British accent and perfectly mimicked the Midwestern twang. He wondered if the British accent was also an act. That was a question for another time and another place.

"I'm going to ask you a couple of questions, and I want you to keep in mind that everything you say and do is viewable through that camera over there."

He'd just spent the last two years of his life living under the scrutiny of wall-to-wall cameras watching even the most intimate and private moments of his daily life. Surely, she didn't think he'd missed the giant camera, with the red blinking light, in the corner? Or maybe she was trying to tell him that she was also tapped into that camera, and could see everything that happened in this room.

Out of view of both the two-way mirror behind her and the camera in the corner, she briefly showed him a handcuff key before setting it under the picture she placed on the table in plain view of everything.

She slid the picture over to him while asking her question loudly enough to mask the sound of the key scraping across the table top.

"Have you ever seen this person before?"

He cleared his throat as he slid the picture off the edge of the table, letting the key fall into his lap, and lifted the picture to inspect it closely.

It was a picture of him on the day he enlisted in the army, the day after he graduated from high school.

There was little resemblance to the man with sandy red hair, a bushy mustache, pale skin and freckles sitting at the table now. If all the makeup and fake hair were removed, there would be no doubt in anyone's mind that this was a picture of him ten years younger.

He set the picture down on the table.

"Good-looking kid. Friend of yours?"

She took the picture and snapped it shut in her briefcase.

"Actually, it is a friend of my Uncle Martin's. If I were talking to that boy today, I would tell him that Uncle Martin will always be there for him."

He sat back as far as the handcuffs would let him. "So are you going to take care of me?"

She smiled. "As your court-appointed attorney, I will do the best that I can."

She stood up and exited the room.

When he was certain that all eyes behind the two-way mirror were on her legs, he coughed into his hands and secreted the handcuff key under his tongue.

She wasn't gone five minutes before two detectives walked into the room. They stood with their backs to the two-way mirror and stared down at him. He did a double-take as he realized these cops weren't only related, they were twins. He found himself staring at the local good ol' boys equivalent of Tweedle Dee and Tweedle Dum.

He did his best not to mumble or spit the key out when he spoke. "Let me guess, you guys are gonna play a little game of bad cop, bad cop?"

The cop on his right, Tweedle Dee, tossed the FBI credentials on to the table.

"After you left this morning, we called the local FBI field office and verified you."

Alex smiled and lifted his hands.

"I guess we can take these off."

Tweedle Dum was the next to speak. "After your little stunt at the airport, we decided to dig a little deeper and called our cousin who is an analyst at the main FBI offices in Washington D.C."

It was Tweedle Dee's turn again. "He said there's no record in the FBI employee database for an agent named Gerard Sanderson."

He lowered his hands back into his lap. This wasn't sounding too promising. "He should look harder."

Tweedle Dum leaned in close. "Nor has there ever been."

Alex barked out a surprised laugh, almost slurring his next sentence as he nearly lost the key. "I find that hard to believe."

Tweedle Dum cocked his head. "What's in your mouth?"

Uh-oh. "Nothing."

"Say 'she sells seashells down by the seashore' for me."

"That's ridiculous. I'm not gonna say that."

Tweedle Dee got in on the act. "Yeah. Say it."

He looked from one twin to the other. Saying that many S's would make him lose the key for sure.

"I'm pretty sure the Fifth Amendment protects me from having to say that."

Tweedle Dee vaulted over the table and gripped his jaw. He held his other hand tightly against Alex's throat so he couldn't swallow the key.

"Spit it out. Spit it out!"

Tweedle Dee's vice-like grip tightened around his throat. His other hand squeezed just under the jaw line, forcing his mouth open.

Tweedle Dum moved behind him, grabbed his head with both hands, and tilted it sideways. Alex tried to resist, but the twins must've worked out together on a daily routine. It was like wrestling with twin Incredible Hulks. They wrestled with him until the key clattered to the ground.

Once the key was out, they both released him.

Tweedle Dum picked the key up from the floor and held it in front of him. "Where did you get this?"

And then his eyes grew wide.

He took a step backward as Tweedle Dee said what they both must've been thinking. "What the hell?"

Alex looked past them at the two-way mirror and saw his reflection. His bushy mustache had peeled halfway off his face and hung limply over his lip. His sandy red hair was tilted all the way to one side of his head, exposing his natural short-cropped hair underneath. And part of the pale and freckled skin on the side of his face had peeled off like a snake shedding its skin.

He wasn't getting out of here anytime soon.

But if there was one thing his training taught him, it was, when everything collapsed around you, cling to the cover.

He glanced up at the camera and silently prayed that Samantha had a backup plan. If not, he might be spending the rest of his life rotting in a federal prison.

Chapter 16

Samantha watched the two burly detectives wrestle Alex out of his disguise.

Skyler, her technician on loan until she could confirm an official member for the new alpha team, had tapped into the interview room camera and transmitted the feed to the display embedded in the dashboard of her Aston Martin.

She watched them strip off the rest of the disguise and listened in on their conversation as one of the detectives waved the toupee in Alex's face as he spoke.

"We were pretty sure the FBI badge was fake. But we had no idea you were fake."

She switched off the audio, leaving just the video feed, and punched the number on her cell phone that she hadn't wanted to call this early into her first active operation.

No matter what time of day it was, anywhere in the world, this number was always answered on the first ring.

An elderly man's voice spoke as soon as it stopped ringing. "What can I do for you Sam?"

She was glad to be talking to him on the phone, rather than in person, so he couldn't see how sweaty and clammy her hands had become as soon as he answered.

"I need some help Robert."

"I've been following the exploits of your latest candidate, on the Internet, no less. I just watched a YouTube video, uploaded by somebody with a cell phone, of him chasing a plane down the runway of an airport in an automobile. Our organization prides itself on secrecy, Sam. On our ability to remain in the shadows. He may not be the best fit for clandestine operations."

"I won't say you're wrong..."

She heard his faint chuckle through the phone's speaker. "But you're thinking it. I picked you to rebuild the team because I saw a little bit of me, the me that I used to be, in you. When I was younger, I was much more willing to take chances."

"Then take a chance on Alex."

"In one day he's gone from Mr. Chase to Alex?"

She was glad he couldn't see her blush.

"It's not like that."

He chuckled again. "I know it's not. It's just fun to make someone like you blush."

Her heart stopped and she looked around outside the car until she spotted the traffic camera.

Robert's voice came through her phone. "Whoops. Looks like you found me. As you can see, I've been keeping a very close eye on you. When you agreed to help me rebuild X-Alpha, you became family. I'm afraid I can be a bit overprotective sometimes. There. I've turned off the feed."

"Did you also see what happened to Alex in the interrogation room?"

"I did. And I must say, despite how public his actions were today, I've been impressed with him so far. Even though he lost his disguise, he never broken cover. He's still claiming to be with the FBI, and arguing with the twins that their cousin doesn't have the clearance to see his personnel records. Someone, even with his level of training, might have broken when his rope unraveled so quickly. But he's still clinging to it. I think I'm beginning to see what you see in him."

"Then you'll help?"

After a moment of silence, he finally responded. "I'll make a call."

She let out the breath she had been holding.

"Thank you Robert."

Chapter 17

The only reason the muscle twins hadn't started taking turns punching Alex in the face, when his disguise had, literally, fallen apart was because he was in a police station in the heart of the United States and not in an interrogation camp in any other part of the world.

His year and a half of intensive training, preparing him to venture into the world's most volatile hotspots, easily prepared him to deal with Tweedle Dee and Tweedle Dum.

The longer he held to his cover, the easier it was to maintain it.

It also helped, when they ran his fingerprints, the results came up empty. It didn't come up as classified. It didn't show as restricted. It was as if he didn't exist. He wasn't in the system.

That little tidbit seemed to set off the twins more than anything.

It made them even more determined to break him.

They were beginning their ninth round of them taking turns asking the same questions in the same order when there was a knock at the door and a uniformed officer poked his head in.

"The Chief would like to speak to the two of you right away."

Tweedle Dee stuck a thick finger in Alex's face. "Don't you go nowhere."

They both laughed as they exited the interview room.

The officer closed the door and walked swiftly over to him, dropping his phony FBI wallet on the table.

"The Chief would like to extend his sincerest apologies

for the behavior of his men, Special Agent Sanderson."

He unlocked the handcuffs and took a step back.

"Please understand, under the circumstances… We had no idea that… The director of the FBI himself called and straightened everything out. He promised to have a talk with their cousin about breaking protocol."

Alex massaged his lightly bruised wrists. "I wouldn't take it that far. I'm sure I would've done the same if I were in their position." He looked squarely at the camera in the corner. "It's tough to do your job when you don't have all the information."

The officer seemed relieved. "Thank you. Rest assured, Detective Johnsons will be reprimanded."

"Wait a minute. Are those guys' last name Johnson?"

"Yes sir."

"Detectives, Johnson and Johnson?"

"Yes sir. But because of their size, nobody really teases them about it."

"I can see that."

"I've been instructed to take you out the back. Your partner is waiting for you."

"Thank you, Officer…" He trailed out the last syllable, like a singer holding a note, to draw a name from him.

"Wallace, sir. Officer Wallace."

"Well, Officer Wallace. I will be sure to include how helpful you were in my debrief report."

Always maintain your cover.

Wallace grinned like a schoolboy handed a lollypop bigger than his head. "Just doing my job, sir."

He patted Wallace on the shoulder. "Keep up the good work, Officer Wallace. Now if you will kindly get me out of here, I still have a job to do."

Chapter 18

In the alley beside the Moscow Police Department, Alex stood next to the hunter green Aston Martin on the passenger side, the British passenger side, and waved to Officer Wallace.

As soon as his butt hit the seat, Samantha accelerated, forcing the car door to close rather quickly.

"Whoa. What's the hurry?"

"You put me in an awkward position, Alex. I had to call in a favor to get you out of there."

"So I gathered. The director of the FBI. Sounds like some important people owe you some pretty big favors."

She took the next corner tightly, ignoring the angry honks from oncoming traffic.

"I can't guarantee I can save your sorry ass every time you get yourself in a jam. You're going to have to operate with a little more... discretion."

"Discretion? I'm the epitome of discretion."

"You chased a plane down a runway. Somebody caught it all with a cell phone. You're a YouTube sensation."

"I thought it was the right thing to do at the time. You told me to get the phone, and since you wouldn't tell me why it was so important, I could only assume it was extremely important. So I did what I had to, to get the job done."

"You let him get away."

"He was in a fucking plane!"

They hit a straightaway and she punched it, glancing at him sideways. "We've wasted enough time to start after the target."

He gripped the door handle tightly as she skidded around another corner. If he hadn't been holding on for dear life, he would've ended up in her lap. "I've seen your driving skills, and I have no doubt that you are willing to try, but there's no way you're going to catch up with a plane in this."

"You're right. That's why I ordered you something... faster."

She whipped around another corner and slammed on the brakes right before she collided with a Harrier jet sitting in the middle of the road.

"According to the registered flight plan the target will be landing at the Boise Airport in an hour. That," she pointed at the jet, "is going get you there in twenty minutes."

"What about you?"

"You're on your own for a few hours, so don't do anything stupid."

"I never do anything stupid."

"Okay, don't do anything public."

"Don't worry. I'll get that phone."

He reached for the door handle and was about to get out when she placed a hand on his arm.

"I got your message, back there in the interrogation room."

"What? About keeping me in the dark all the time?"

"You will find out what you need to know…"

He interrupted her. "When I need to know it. So you told me."

"If I could tell you more, I would."

"Maybe, when this is all over, you can tell me everything."

She smiled and let go of his arm. "Maybe."

Alex didn't know much about fighter jets, since most of

the aircraft he rode in during his army days, were C-130 transports. The one thing he did remember, from the few times he spent aboard aircraft carriers, was that the Harrier jet had a single seat in the cockpit for the pilot, and little room for anything, or anyone, else.

He climbed up the side of the Harrier and came face-to-face with the pilot.

"I don't have to sit in your lap, do I?"

The pilot grinned. "Nope. This is a trainer. Your seat's in the back. Put this on and hook up the oxygen once you're settled."

He clambered into the back and buckled himself in. Once he placed the helmet on his head, he could hear the pilot through the integrated headphones.

"Name's Hastings. You ever been in a fighter before?"

"First time."

"I'd like to say I'll be gentle, but it is my understanding you are in a bit of a hurry."

"Got any advice for a virgin?"

"Just keep your hands off my stick."

"Excuse me?"

"The flight stick in front of you. Since this is a trainer, they're connected. Don't touch it."

"Got it. Hands off the stick. Check."

"You ready for the ride of your life?"

Hastings powered the engines up and the plane lifted straight up, sending Alex's stomach into one somersault after another.

As they rocketed through the sky, he alternated between closing his eyes and keeping them open. He wasn't sure which one lessened the feeling of dizziness from the increased gravitational forces inflicted on his head.

Even more disconcerting was watching the flight stick move around between his knees, as if operated by some ghost, even though it was only the pilot in front of him controlling each delicate movement.

Hasting's voice echoed through the helmet intercom.

"You doing okay back there?"

Alex swallowed another bit of bile that threaten to come up again. "Just get me there in one piece."

The pilot's only response was laughter.

Chapter 19

Hastings checked the readouts in the dash in front of him. As usual, Bessie was purring like a kitten. They'd only been in the air for ten minutes, and already they were nearing the halfway point.

Usually, the first time he took someone up, he would give them the grand tour of this unique fighter jet's capabilities. The maintenance crew had complained, on more than one occasion, about the mess left in the rear of the cockpit by his petrified passengers.

Unfortunately, this was a special mission, and he was under direct orders to get his live cargo to the destination as quickly as possible. Still, they would easily be arriving well ahead of the other plane tracked on his visual display. So why not have a little fun?

"You ever pilot an aircraft?"

His passenger responded quickly. At least he hadn't passed out yet.

"Nah, I was a ground pounder myself."

"An army man, eh?"

"Eight years."

"Tell you what? How about I give you a little turn at the stick?"

"Really?"

"Sure. Grip that bad boy in front of you, but try not to move it too much just yet."

He felt the control stick vibrate in his hands as the Army Man grabbed hold of the paired flight controller behind him.

"I'm going to take us through a few easy maneuvers first.

Just hold the stick loosely and let me do all the work."

"Okay."

He took them through a few barrel rolls, providing instruction the whole time.

"Do you feel how I just do slight adjustments?"

"Uh-huh."

"You think you could do that, without sending us into an unscheduled landing?"

"I think so."

He slowly released his grip on the stick, and watched its movements with intensity, ready to grab it within a moment's notice and save both their lives if he had to.

"It's all yours."

The plane wobbled a little, but the Army Man recovered quickly and was doing a better job than most of his first-year pilots.

"Take us through a barrel roll."

By the third maneuver, his new copilot had settled into an easy rhythm and controlled the fighter with ease.

"You should ask for a transfer into the Navy."

"Oh, I'm not with the Army anymore. Strictly freelance."

Whoever he was freelancing for, had some pretty heavy connections to commandeer a fully armed Harrier jet for a half-hour jaunt across Idaho.

A red square blinked in the corner of his display, signaling an incoming priority communication.

"Hey Army Man, I need to switch off the intercom for a moment to take a call. You can let go of the stick now."

"Okay. And, thanks."

"Don't mention it."

He switched off the intercom and pushed the button to route the secure channel to his helmet comm.

"This is bravo echo sierra. I am receiving."

Instead of the radio operator's voice he was expecting, his headphones filled with electronic noise, similar to the sounds his modem made when he was a young kid connecting to the local bulletin board systems.

His confusion was immediately replaced by clarity of purpose.

He scanned the displays in front of him and smiled.

His target was still several miles ahead.

He flipped several switches, arming the air-to-air missiles mounted to the underside of the Harrier's wings, and adjusted his flight path to put him directly behind his target.

Chapter 20

Alex couldn't contain his excitement. He just wished he had somebody to tell. Maybe Samantha would be just as excited as he was about actually piloting a fighter jet.

The plane changed direction slightly and started losing altitude. They must be getting ready to land at the air national guard base attached to the Boise Airport. As soon as they landed, he would be driven over to the regional aviation hangar, where he would wait to surprise the Thin Man. And finally get that super important cell phone for Samantha.

Lights blinked rapidly on the panel in front of him.

The multifunction display shifted to show the forward view, while another display showed the missiles on the fighter being armed, one by one.

"Hastings?"

There was no reply from the pilot up front.

"Hastings. Can you hear me?"

The internal intercom was still shut off.

The digital dial on the altimeter continued to spiral down as they dropped through the sky.

"Hastings!"

The speakers in his helmet crackled to life.

"...traffic control. Military aircraft designation bravo epsilon sierra, you are entering controlled airspace in an unauthorized descent. Please resume your registered flight plan. Respond, over."

Hastings made no attempt to respond.

Alex banged on the canopy, the noise he made barely perceptible over the roar of the jet engine.

"Hastings! What are you doing?!"

The same voice crackled through his earphones, sounding a little more frantic this time.

"This is Boise air traffic control. You are in an unauthorized descent through controlled airspace. Respond, over."

Alarms sounded from the dashboard in front of him.

Maybe Hastings had passed out and they were about to crash.

He grabbed the flight control stick and pulled back, trying to put the jet back into a climb. The control stick fought him and pushed itself forward.

Hastings voice came through the speakers in his helmet.

"Stop that."

"What are you doing, Hastings?"

"I am following orders."

"Your orders are to take me to the airbase."

"I have new orders."

"What new orders?"

Hastings didn't reply, but the weapons lock alarm told him everything he needed to know.

Hastings was going to shoot down the Thin Man's plane.

Chapter 21

Alex watched in shock as Hastings made tiny adjustments to put the Thin Man's plane in the crosshairs of his targeting computer.

Private planes were not outfitted with military defense systems. They would have no warning before they were shot out of the sky.

He watched the display, unsure of what he could do to stop this, when the lock broke as the target plane shifted too far from the center of the targeting reticle.

Hastings quickly adjusted for the slipstream that buffeted the Thin Man's plane and the beeping from the targeting computer increased in intensity as it reacquired its lock.

The missiles mounted on the Harrier had a narrow field of view where they could successfully lock on to a target.

He watched as Hastings struggled to match the motions of the single prop plane ahead of them, trying to keep them in the center of the display so the missile could lock on.

His eyes were riveted on the display as the plane moved in and out of the center, the missile acquiring its lock, and then losing it again.

He prayed for another gust of wind to knock the plane out of the missile's field of view.

And then his prayers were answered.

An air pocket sent the small plane dropping several dozen feet.

The flight stick banged against his leg as Hastings struggled to keep the target in his sights.

He watched the control stick undulate wildly between his knees and realized he didn't need to wait for an act of God to stop Hastings.

He could stop Hastings himself.

He grabbed the control stick in both hands and yanked hard to the left.

Chapter 22

Hastings was finalizing the minute corrections to put the target plane back in the center of his display when the flight stick jumped from his hand and the fighter did a barrel roll to the left before cutting off into a wild arc in the opposite direction from his target.

He reactivated the intercom.

"I told you not to touch that."

"Who ordered you to shoot down that plane?"

"That's classified."

"By whose authority?"

"My authority. I'm the pilot and this is my plane."

"Patch me through to your commanding officer."

"Negative."

He grabbed the flight stick and tried to wrestle control back from his stowaway, but the Army Man wasn't going to give it up so easily.

The plane rocked back and forth as it streaked through the sky, leaving a contrail of white vapor in its wake.

He pulled back on the thruster controls, slowing the Harrier down until it hovered in place, thousands of feet above the surface of the earth. He wasn't going to be able to complete his mission with this freelancing mercenary interfering.

He unhooked his restraints and slid the automatic pistol out of the holster on the side of the seat. As soon as he disposed of the Army Man, he could finish what he really had to do.

Chapter 23

Alex frantically searched the dashboard in front of him for inspiration. There were so many switches and buttons, and he had no idea what any of them did.

Everything was labeled, but the labels were incomprehensible abbreviations. They might as well have been written in Klingon.

Hastings had slowed the plane down to keep him from crashing the jet. At least he wasn't actively targeting the other plane anymore.

Hastings grunted as he struggled to turn around in his seat.

Everything had been normal until he'd received that special communication. Who was giving him his new orders? It couldn't be Samantha. If she wanted to destroy the cell phone, she could've ordered the plane shot down without involving Alex.

No. This had nothing to do with Samantha.

This was somebody else. But not somebody who wanted the cell phone. Somebody who wanted to destroy the evidence that could... link them to the murder-suicide.

Alex leaned against the side of the canopy and looked around the back of the pilot's seat to see what Hastings was up to.

In a flash, he saw the gun in Hastings' hand.

Hastings pointed the gun at him and he ducked away just as Hastings fired.

The bullet ricocheted inside the cockpit and shattered the glass canopy.

"Hold still Army Man."

He had to appeal to the pilot's logical side. Convince him he was making a mistake. A big mistake.

"You don't want to do this."

"I have to do this."

"You don't have to do this. You said so yourself. You're the pilot. You have the authority on your jet. Nobody can force you to do anything."

"I'm not being forced to do anything."

Alex ducked instinctively as another bullet ricocheted inside the cockpit. This time, the bullet punched a fist sized hole through the top of the glass canopy.

This maniac was going to destroy the jet, with them inside, if he didn't do something quick.

He started turning dials, punching buttons, and flipping switches on the dashboard.

A pulsating klaxon sounded and, outside the window, the missiles dislodged from the wings one at a time and fell to earth.

The klaxon pulsed at just the right frequency that, even with his helmet on, it throbbed deep inside his brain.

When the last missile fell away, the alarm stopped.

In the deafening silence, Hastings had stopped firing.

Alex slowly peeked around the edge of the pilot's seat.

Hastings had collapsed against the side of the cockpit, his face pressed against the shattered canopy. A stream of drool ran down from the corner of his mouth.

Just past Hastings, outside the shattered glass, two A-10 Thunderbolts screamed by unnervingly close to the hovering jet.

The loud thump-thump of rotors rose above the whine of the Harrier's jet engine and, through the hole in the canopy, a helicopter gunship rose into view. As the helicopter pilot's head moved, the twin guns mounted along the bottom pointed wherever he looked.

The speaker in Alex's helmet crackled to life again.

"Occupants of the renegade Harrier. Stand down or we will open fire."

Chapter 24

There was no way Alex was going to be able to fly, let alone land, the Harrier jet himself. After careful negotiations, and remanding Hastings into custody once they pulled him unconscious from the hovering Harrier, they lowered another pilot from the helicopter into the Harrier.

The new pilot landed them swiftly at Gowen Field Air National Guard Base, where they ushered Alex into a room and left him alone to await Samantha's arrival.

Technically, he wasn't under arrest. But the one time he opened the door, two armed guards sternly requested he go back inside and wait.

There was nothing to read. There was nothing to do. The only furnishings in the room were a brown leather couch, two brown leather upholstered seats, and a coffee table at the center. The last person to decorate this room must have died of old age back in the nineteen-seventies.

He stretched across the couch and closed his eyes. With how this day had been going so far, who knew how long it would be before he got another chance to rest.

The squeaky hinges of the door alerted him to someone entering the room. He lifted his head and watched Samantha enter and toss a black duffel bag onto the coffee table. "Here's your $50,000. Thank you very much for your help."

He stared at the duffel bag as she turned and started out of the room. He jumped up and stood in her way.

"That's it?"

"That's it. Thank you very much for your help."

She tried to go around him, but he moved in front of her again.

"That's not it. You hired me to do something, and if you're going to pay me, I'm going to do it."

"There's nothing left for you to do. We're done."

"Did you get the phone?"

She shook her head. "We followed him with the satellite as he got off the plane and took a shuttle to the main terminal. Once he went inside, we lost him."

"Then we're not done. Use whatever contacts you have. Check the boarding logs. Check the rental car logs. We can pick up his trail again."

"I don't think we need to do that."

"Why not?"

"Tell me exactly what happened to your pilot."

Why was she asking about him?

"I don't know. One minute he was giving me flying lessons and we were joking around, the next minute he was targeting the other plane with missiles and turning the world's most cramped environment into the gunfight at the O.K. Corral. Only, I didn't have a gun."

"When did the change happen?"

"We really need to talk about getting me a gun."

"Focus, Alex. Focus. When did the change occur?"

"Right after the call."

"What call?"

"He said he was getting a priority transmission and shut off our internal intercom. After that, he changed direction and all Hell broke loose."

"Are you sure the pilot's behavior changed only after getting the transmission?"

"Yeah. Why?"

"Thank you very much for your time, Mr. Chase. Enjoy your $50,000."

She started to leave again, but he blocked her at the door.

"Whatever it is you're planning to do, I want in."

"I don't have any more money to offer you."

"I don't think this is about money. What was so important about that phone that now, after the pilot flipped out, isn't so important anymore?"

"I cannot tell you that."

"Is this about those computer sounds?"

She looked at him and squinted one eye. "What computer sounds?"

"Right before the pilot shut off my intercom, I heard this noise. Sort of like when a fax machine is making its initial connection."

Worry spread over her face as she took a step backward. "How much of that did you hear?"

"Only like half a second. Why? Is it important?"

She regarded him for a full minute before speaking again.

"I can't offer you money."

"I'm not motivated by money."

"So, what does motivate you, Mr. Chase?"

"Doing the right thing."

"Would you be willing to help me a little while longer, if it meant you'd be doing the right thing?"

"Only if you tell me this time what it is I'm doing."

She started for the door and he blocked her yet again.

"How about partial disclosure?"

She hesitated. "How about I tell you what you need to know, right before you need to know it?"

If that was the best she could offer, he had very little choice in the matter. He stuck out his hand to seal the deal with a handshake.

"I'll take what I can get."

She took his hand in a firm grip.

"Welcome to the team."

"So, how many others are on this team?"

"Just you."

Chapter 25

Alex sat across from Samantha at the cherrywood stained table in the tiny room they had checked into at the Boise Airport Motel 6. It wasn't a Four Seasons, but it was a lot better than her previous two choices. If he was going to be spending more time working with her, he would have to get used to her less than stellar choices for accommodations.

She placed an automatic pistol on the table, within easier reach to her than him, and adopted a serious look.

"Let me preface, before I begin, that everything I tell you from this point forward is the most important thing you will ever hear in your life. And should you repeat it to anyone, at any time, I will be forced to kill you."

He started to laugh, but then her look stopped him.

She continued. "The same thing that happened to the jet pilot today, happened a few days ago in Moscow, Idaho."

"The town where you wanted me to collect the cell phone?"

"Correct."

"And what exactly happened?"

"People were, to put it bluntly, programmed to kill."

"Programmed to kill?"

"A similar transmission to the one you overheard with the pilot was sent through the cell phone to make a young woman kill a respected judge, who was running for mayor."

"Made her kill? You mean like hypnosis?"

"These were not simple hypnotic suggestions. The brain was reprogrammed, as if it were a computer. The woman killed two people with the precision of a highly trained assassin, even though she had never handled a gun before in her life. She also, according to witnesses, claimed to have been pregnant. We obtained a copy of the autopsy record. She was not pregnant."

"Who's we?"

"Right now, we, is you and I. Stay focused on what's important here. The ramifications of killing a judge in a small town in the middle of America are very small, politically speaking. He was not targeted personally, or politically, to achieve anyone's long term agenda."

"Then why was he killed?"

"Moscow was a preview."

"A preview for what?"

"To prospective buyers of what this technology can do."

"What exactly are you telling me?"

"There is somebody out there with the capability to use random individuals to carry out a suicide mission without prior contact or training."

"Suicide mission. Are they able to convince a person to kill themselves?"

"The woman in Moscow turned the gun on herself immediately after killing the judge."

"What about the pilot?"

"He woke up, claiming to not remember anything about what happened. I don't know whether that was part of the original plan or whether something happened up there to interrupt the program."

He tried to think about what had happened in the jet. He was fighting for his life and everything happened so fast. Maybe when he released the missiles the pilot knew he would be unable to complete his deadly mission, and the program had erased itself.

A chilling thought dawned on him.

"So anyone hearing this transmission could be told to do anything, including kill themselves?"

"Yes."

"So the President of the United States could answer his phone during breakfast and suddenly stab himself in the heart with a butter knife?"

"That's why we have to find out who developed this, and stop them before they use it again."

An even more chilling thought occurred to him.

"Or sell it."

Her cell phone buzzed and she answered it. "Yes. Uh-huh. Yes. We're on our way."

She disconnected and slipped the phone into her pocket. "Skyler tracked the signal sent to the plane. It originated from an address here in Boise, so he adjusted the satellite to watch the area. The man you chased on the runway entered the house about ten minutes ago. Other than that, no external activity. The house, and both houses on either side, is shielded against infrared viewing. We have no idea who's inside with him, or how many there are in any of the houses. We will be going in blind. Are you sure you want to do this?"

"Do I get a gun?"

She finally cracked a smile and slid the automatic across the cherrywood table. "This one's yours."

Chapter 26

Samantha negotiated the Aston Martin around the garbage bins scattered haphazardly in the back alley behind the row of houses. She nestled the sports car between two garbage bins, painted roughly the same hunter green color as her car, and shut off the engine.

She handed Alex a tiny flesh colored in-ear hearing aid.

"Stick this in your ear."

He took it and stuffed it into his ear. "This is so we can communicate back and forth?"

"No. It's the decoy." She held up a small ceramic tooth in her fingers. "This is so we can stay in contact with each other. Press this over one of your upper back molars. You'll be able to hear me, since it resonates the audio through the bones in your skull, and I'll be able to hear you because… well, it's in your mouth."

He rolled it around in his palm.

"How long does the battery last?"

"Your body acts as both the battery and the antenna. It has the added bonus of being undetectable when scanning for communication devices since it uses your body's natural conductivity to do its job. Its range, however, is extremely limited and the Aston Martin acts as the base station. As long as we stay within a quarter-mile of the car, we shouldn't have too much trouble communicating."

He stuffed it over his molar and bit down on it to wedge it firmly in place.

Samantha pointed to the GPS screen in the dashboard.

"We are here. The three houses are two blocks over. Our target is the center house."

"How sure are you that this is the house where the signal came from?"

"My source is rarely wrong."

"You said rarely."

"Okay. Never wrong."

"So what's the plan if we bust in there and scare the hell out of an innocent family?"

"We'll cross that bridge if we get to it."

"How do you propose we sneak up to that house unnoticed?"

She gave him a curious look. "Who said anything about sneak?"

"You can't just walk right up to the front door?"

"You can if you're holding one of these."

She reached into the back seat and produced a Bible.

Chapter 27

Two hours later, Alex and Samantha walked out of the house two doors down from their target. Samantha thanked the elderly woman for listening to them while Alex helped himself to a few more snickerdoodles from the plate she held.

When they got to the front sidewalk, Samantha looked back and waved one last time at the woman. "The people here are so friendly, but they ask too many questions. I wasn't expecting it to take this long to work our way down the street."

Alex popped another cookie into his mouth. "And excellent cooks. I swear, I'd weigh three hundred pounds if I lived anywhere near that last lady. You sure you don't want one?"

A small dog's incessant yapping echoed through the neighborhood. Samantha spun around, putting her back to the three target houses, and held a hand up against his chest to stop him. "There's activity at the house."

Alex looked up and saw somebody stepping out into the bright sunlight with a tiny dog on a leash. His eyes grew wide with recognition. He had never seen the dog before in his life, but at the other end of the leash was somebody he had bumped in to very recently.

It was the Thin Man.

He let the snickerdoodles drop to the ground as he reached for his automatic.

Samantha placed a hand on his arm.

"I don't want a repeat of the airport."

He gave her a wink. "Relax. I got thith, thith, thh…"

For some reason, he couldn't finish his sentence and slurred the last of his words.

Samantha looked at him strangely. "What are you doing?"

His mouth felt numb, like he had just been to the dentist.

Suddenly, the world tilted at a sharp angle and he groped at Samantha for support.

He weighed nearly twice as much as she did and she struggled to hold him up. "Alex? Are you okay?"

He tried to say… something. But he couldn't remember what. His brain was becoming as numb as his tongue as he fell face first into the exquisitely manicured lawn of the nice old lady.

Chapter 28

Samantha couldn't hold on to Alex any longer, he was just too heavy, so she let him fall into the yard.

He lay next to the small pile of cookies he had dropped moments earlier so he could reach for his gun.

Something was very wrong.

She already had her pistol out of its holster when she felt two sharp needles pierce her back and 50,000 volts coursed through her body.

Her convulsing muscles threw her own gun from her hand as she collapsed into the yard next to Alex.

Even though the Taser had stopped sending an electrical current down the wires, every nerve in her body still felt like it was on fire.

Her eyes focused on Alex across the low cut grass. His eyes were glazed over and drool ran out the side of his mouth.

Chapter 29

"Shit! Shit! Shit!"

Skyler stood up in his chair as he watched the live satellite camera feed. Both Samantha and Alex were down, and armed men were approaching them from all sides.

He hit a key on his computer to speed dial Uncle Robert and listened as it rang once.

Uncle Robert was not his real uncle, but had sort of adopted him while he was still in college. It was on Uncle Robert's personal recommendation that he got into the SIS, Britain's Secret Intelligence Service or, as it was more commonly known thanks to a certain infamous fictional spy, MI6. And it was upon Uncle Robert's personal request that he help Samantha rebuild the X-Alpha unit.

Uncle Robert's phone rang a second time.

He did a double-take.

That never happened.

Not, usually never happened.

It never happened.

He switched the audio feed on his monitor to the same frequency as Samantha's tooth transmitter.

Dead silence. The Taser must've shorted out its fragile electronics.

He switched the frequency to Alex's transmitter.

Sound crackled through the speakers in his headphones.

He listened intently, trying to focus on what the men around him were saying.

He couldn't hear anything beyond Alex's constant moaning.

Uncle Robert's phone rang a third time.

Why wasn't he answering?

He momentarily refocused his attention on the droning sound coming through Alex's transmitter and verified his system was recording everything.

He pulled down on his flexible mic and spoke into it. If he could hear Alex, Alex could hear him. "Stop moaning. I can't hear what they're saying."

Uncle Robert's phone rang again, and then a female voice answered with a hint of uncertainty in her voice. "Hello?"

He was so focused on the garbled voices coming through the tooth transmitter, he hadn't realized the clear female voice was coming from Uncle Robert's phone.

"Hello?" The female voice said again.

He pushed a key on his keyboard and spoke into his mic. "Who is this?"

"My name is Nurse Hathaway. Who is this?"

Why had a nurse answered his phone? All of the attendants Uncle Robert had hired to assist him in his old age had been given explicit instructions to never answer his phone.

"Where's Robert?"

"Who is this?"

"I'm his nephew. Where is he?"

"I'm sorry to be the one to tell you. Your uncle has suffered a transient ischemic attack and is in surgery now."

"A transient what?"

"It's a mini stroke."

"Shit."

She was obviously used to getting various types of reactions when delivering bad news and made no comment about his foul language.

"Would you like me to give you the address of the hospital? He should have family around him when he wakes up. We've found that usually leads to a faster recovery for the patient."

"Yeah, go ahead."

He let the computer record and transcribe the hospital address as he switched the audio of his headphones back over to Alex.

He watched, his eyes transfixed on the screen, as Samantha and Alex were carried into the middle house, out of view of his satellite camera. They had no idea that the only person who could get them the resources they needed at a moment's notice was in the middle of surgery.

Whatever happened next, they were on their own.

Chapter 30

It was dark and the worst smell ever to invade Alex's nostrils kept returning. He gagged as he turned his head away from the smell. Someone gripped his cheeks tightly and held his head in place as the putrid smell assaulted his nose again.

It was then he realized that it wasn't dark, his eyes were closed. He opened them and focused on a rough, unshaven face, in front of him.

The rough face grinned and released the vice grip on his cheeks, also thankfully taking away the smelling salts he had used to wake him up. The man spoke to him in English, but with a thick Eastern European, possibly even Russian, accent.

"How are you doing brother?"

Alex stretched his mouth. The numbness had faded, but it still felt like his tongue was made out of cotton.

He tried to shift his weight and discovered he was tightly bound to a dining room chair. He looked around the room, but it was just him and the burly man with the beard in the small kitchen of a house. The sun shone brightly through the window over the sink. Either he had been unconscious for more than a day, or not long at all.

"Are you looking for your lady friend?"

He tried to speak, but it came out hoarse and raspy.

The bearded man held a glass of water to his lips.

"Drink. You will need to speak when Umarov asks you a question."

Umarov? That was a Russian name. Was he in Russia? How long had he been knocked out?

He gulped the water down and his tongue started to feel normal again.

"Where am I?"

The bearded man laughed. "Umarov asks the questions. You only answer."

"Where is the woman I was with?"

The bearded man shook his head, frowning. "You don't listen very well. You only speak when spoken to."

"Where have you taken us?"

The bearded man responded by back-handing him across the face.

A new voice intruded on the room. "Vakha!"

The Thin Man walked into the room and stood next to his thug. "I need to ask him a few questions before you kill him."

Vakha smiled down at Alex. "I was just teaching him some manners."

Alex sucked on the blood oozing from his split lip without saying another word. He knew when it was time to keep his big mouth shut.

Vakha pointed out Alex's silence. "See, he learns much faster than his friend."

Alex strained against the ropes holding him to the chair. "If you hurt her…"

Vakha raised his hand for another powerful strike, but Umarov stopped him. "Go get Madina. I want to make sure our guest tells me the truth."

Disappointment spread across Vakha's face, most likely at not being able to hit him again. He left the kitchen to do as he was told.

Umarov crouched down to meet Alex at eye level. He squinted at him through his horn-rimmed glasses. "What kind of door-to-door false religion peddler walks around with a gun?"

Alex glared back at him. "What kind of FBI agent speaks with a Russian accent and steals evidence from police stations?"

Umarov's upper lip curled. "How dare you call me Russian?" He spit on the tile floor in disgust after saying the name. "I am pure Chechen and neither you, nor your pretty girlfriend, can stop me from forcing those oppressive invaders from my home."

Chechen? What were Chechen rebels doing in the middle of Boise, Idaho? If he was still in Idaho. Or even the United States, for that matter. And what did somebody, from halfway around the world, want with the cell phone? Unless...

"You're the buyer," he said abruptly.

Umarov raised his eyebrows. "What?"

"Moscow was the trial run for... Moscow. You're going to kill the Russian president."

The scenario formed in his head as he kept talking.

"You're going to make it look like somebody within his own inner circle killed him. Somebody without ties to any terrorist group."

That got a rise out of Umarov. "We fight for our independence. We are not terrorists."

"You're going to throw the government of Russia into disarray. That would destabilize the entire Eastern European bloc. But why?"

Umarov looked impressed. "Isn't it obvious? If they are too busy fighting amongst themselves..."

He finished Umarov's sentence. "They are too busy to fight with you."

A woman in a tight black leather cat suit and stiletto heels walked into the room carrying a doctor's bag in one hand and a car battery with booster cables in the other.

Umarov stood up. "I have some questions for you. Madina here, will ensure you answer them truthfully. And then I will kill you."

Chapter 31

Skyler pressed the headphones tightly against his ears and listened intently as the Chechen terrorist began his interrogation.

He was recording everything coming in through Alex's transmitter, but there was nothing else for him to do but listen in and look for a clue, any clue, on how to save them.

Which was not going to be easy to do, since he was nearly five thousand miles away, deep underground, in London.

He'd already punched in the three names he overheard into the SIS database.

Umarov, Vakha, and Madina.

He added additional parameters to cross-reference them against Chechnya, Russia, and Islamic Terrorism to narrow down exactly who had his team.

While he waited for his search to produce results, he whispered into his flexible mic. "Just stay cool, Alex. I'm working on trying to get you and Samantha out of there."

Alex's voice echoed loudly from his headphones. "Don't take too long."

Because he'd said that out loud, the first voice to respond was Umarov's.

"I'm afraid death will not come quickly for you, no matter how much you beg."

Sklyer wasn't sure if Alex's next question was for him or his interrogator. "What are you doing?"

Umarov's response answered his question. "Don't worry. These patches are harmless, really. Any doctor will prescribe these to anybody who asks. In small doses, they help with motion sickness. Adding additional patches simultaneously, like this, will make you a little more cooperative. I wouldn't worry too much about the side effects of overdosing. You won't be alive long enough to experience them."

Suddenly, Umarov's voice dropped in volume and Skyler strained to hear him. "Keep this rag in your mouth. It would be most unfortunate if you bit your tongue off when Madina caresses you with the wires from the battery. It makes it very difficult to understand your answers without a tongue. Now, I see from the expression on your face you are afraid. Before we begin, Madina's going to touch you with the wires, just a little bit, so you know what to expect should you refuse to give me an answer right away."

The extreme pain in Alex's voice was evident as he let out a primal scream.

The scream ended suddenly, replaced with the steady hiss of electronic silence. The electrical shock had blown out the transmitter in his tooth.

With the infrared shielding keeping him from seeing inside the house, and both audio transmitters shorted out, Skyler was blind, deaf, and of no use to the agents in the field.

His computer beeped and drew his attention to a monitor off to one side. His query had netted some results.

He clicked his mouse and switched the database results to the main screen in front of him, now that he had nothing else to look at.

Vakha and Madina, both born in Chechnya, fought on the side of the Chechen resistance during both Chechen wars with Russia in the mid and late 1990s. After Chechnya was reintegrated into Russia, Vakha and Madina joined with Chechen extremists and participated in many bloody acts of terrorism.

But Umarov did not match the profile. He was born in Russia to wealthy and connected parents.

Umarov was born into a life of privilege, and even during the collapse of the Soviet Union and the formation of the Russian Federation, his family remained strongly connected to those in power.

His personal history did not fit with his proclamation for wanting a free and independent Chechnya. His wealth was tied directly into the well-being of the Russian government. Umarov would suffer along with the rest of Russia's elite if everything collapsed.

Skyler read the rest of the intelligence report on Umarov. There was nothing in it to show why he had taken up with two known terrorists.

There was plenty of information about the documented and alleged exploits of Vakha and Madina. Skyler took note of their psychological profiles. They had killed often, and without remorse. One of the biggest reasons they were not currently in prison was that they killed anyone who found out who they were. Umarov had been so free with calling them by name in front of Alex, there was no way they were going to let him live to tell anyone.

Uncle Robert was in the hospital with a stroke, and the only two agents in the newly formed X-Alpha unit would be dead within the hour.

He set down the headphones and started switching off the many displays around him. With the head of the unit in the middle of surgery, and every field agent captured and compromised, there was nothing left for him to do but follow pre-established protocols.

Unfortunately, he couldn't pass on any of the

information he'd learned about the threat to Russia, or it would reveal to the world that this organization existed. This organization was not supposed to exist. Maintaining secrecy of X-Alpha was more important than the current stability of Eastern Europe, especially since there were no more agents left in the field to stop any threat.

If Uncle Robert died on the operating table, Skyler would be the only one in the world who knew what was going to happen to the fledgling Russian government. That was an awesome responsibility to place on the shoulders of a young technical analyst who, at age nineteen, was still considered a teenager.

That was a responsibility he couldn't bring himself to bear alone. He broke from protocol and replicated the entire system on a high capacity jump drive that was still small enough to fit into his pocket. He would let Robert decide whether to plug the jump drive into a new computer, and pick up where they left off, or smash it with a hammer. Once the operating system and database were copied over, he shut down all the computers and armed the self-destruct mechanisms.

Five minutes after he sealed the doors on the old World War II bunker, the magnesium burn units reduced everything inside the steel room to ash.

Chapter 32

Alex sat up quickly and sucked in a deep breath of air.

He was disoriented for a moment until he recognized his surroundings.

He was in the passenger seat of Samantha's Aston Martin. And he was not alone. He looked at Samantha slumped over in the driver's seat, her head resting against the side window.

He felt for a pulse and found it was strong. Thank God. She was only asleep.

The last thing he remembered was ringing the doorbell at the first house on the target street, Bibles in hand for their cover.

How did they get in the car?

Where were they?

He glanced out the window. They were parked on some dirt road in the middle of a forest and the sun was just setting.

Had they lost the entire day? Or had it been longer than that?

He scratched at an annoying itch on his bicep, and felt the outline of something through his shirt. He rolled up his sleeve and exposed the square flesh colored transdermal patch stuck to his arm.

He peeled it off, crumpled it up, and shoved it in the ashtray.

He rolled up both of Samantha's sleeves, found the same type of patch on one of her arms, and peeled it off.

He patted her cheeks lightly to wake her up.

She jerked up and lashed out. He ducked away before

her fist connected with his jaw.

"Easy Samantha. It's me, Alex."

She looked around, disoriented. "Where are we?"

"I was hoping you could tell me."

She looked out the front windshield. "I don't know."

Was she suffering from the same memory loss he was?

"What's the last thing you remember?"

"I… We… We were just leaving the third house."

He pointed to the wadded up patches. "I think there was some kind of drug in those patches." He closed his eyes against a sudden wave of dizziness. There definitely had to be some kind of drug in those patches.

Samantha sat up and started touching menus on the GPS display in the dashboard. "I'm not getting Skyler on any of the standard comm lines."

"He's not answering?"

"There's not even a signal. It's like he switched them all off."

"Why would he do that?"

"Maybe whatever happened us, happened to him too."

"What did happen to us?"

Samantha fiddled with the GPS display. "We're only about ten miles away from the target house. I think they drugged us and moved us?"

"How?"

She looked at him with alarm. "The cookies!"

"What cookies?"

"The old lady drugged the cookies. I wasn't drugged, because I didn't eat any of the cookies."

She looked down at her disheveled and torn clothes. "I didn't eat any of the cookies. So what happened to me?"

"The only way to find out, is to go back."

She nodded and reached for the push-button start when he grabbed her hand. "Wait! What if they placed an explosive in the engine?"

She looked at the button on the dash. "Triggered when I started the car."

She pulled her hand away and placed a finger lightly on the automatic door lock button, and paused. "Or they set the trigger up for when I unlocked the car."

"Roll down the windows instead. We'll climb out that way."

"Can't. Not without turning on the car first."

He took a deep breath and let it out slowly. They were stuck in the car with only one option.

"Go ahead and unlock the doors. If something happens, it's been a pleasure working with you to save the world."

"We haven't save the world yet."

"If it ends here, at least we will have died trying."

"Here goes nothing."

She grimaced as she pushed down on the automatic door lock button.

Chapter 33

The door locks popped up with a hollow thunk. Alex and Samantha wasted no time bailing out and running from the car. They went in opposite directions deep into the forest.

Alex ran until he felt there were enough trees to create a buffer between him and the exploding car.

He leaned against a tree and sucked in large gulps of air, trying to catch his breath. He'd done his best to maintain himself while in prison, but aerobic exercise was not something looked upon favorably by the other inmates. They were all about lifting weights and bulking up. They weren't as interested in staying in shape as much as they were in looking like somebody you didn't want to mess with.

There had been no explosion. Either, it wasn't going to explode, or there was some other trigger that would set it off.

When he finally recovered, and stopped wheezing heavily, he started to walk back slowly.

The forest thinned as he neared the road. The car sat quietly in the road with both passenger doors open and the hood raised up. Samantha poked around in the engine.

She slid back from the car as he approached, dusting the grease off her hands as she smiled.

"No explosives. And it doesn't look like anything's been tampered with."

She slammed down the hood and settled back into the driver's seat of the Aston Martin. She pushed the start button and the engine purred to life without exploding and shredding them to bits.

She leaned over and looked at him through the open door.

"Are you coming?"

Something just didn't feel right about any of this. If they had been discovered and captured, by the very same people they were investigating, why were they alive with no memory of what happened? Ignoring how their memories were erased, why would they be taken only a few miles away? Surely, their target was smart enough to realize they would come right back after discovering they were still so close.

Maybe they had expected to erase more of their memories. Maybe they hadn't expected them to remember going there in the first place.

Memory was still a mystery, even to scientists who devoted their life to unlocking the secrets of how the human mind worked.

No. It was too risky to expect them to forget everything. They had to have known they would remember something. And once they remembered, they would be back.

That was it.

They knew they would remember.

Perhaps even counted on it.

"Pop the trunk."

Samantha give him a quizzical expression. "What?"

"Pop the trunk. I want to see what's in there."

"There's nothing in there but the spare tire."

"Just pop it."

She sighed and pulled the lever just under the dash. The trunk sprang up and he walked to the back. As the contents of the trunk came into view, his jaw almost hit the ground.

Chapter 34

The trunk of Samantha's Aston Martin was filled with jewelry, cash, and various audio and video electronic components, with the cables still attached as if they had been yanked hastily from a home entertainment system.

Samantha joined him at the back of the car. "Oh my God. What is all this?"

"My guess? This is all evidence to support a robbery around the same time we were in the neighborhood. Can you get television signals on the video screen in your car?"

"No, but I can access the Internet."

He shut the trunk and they were both back in their seats when she started poking at the touchscreen.

"See if you can find anything about a robbery that happened earlier today in Boise."

One of the first results in her search was a link to the local Boise major news network affiliate.

He pointed to the link. "Check that one."

She touched the link and the local news station's web page loaded.

At the center of the page, a video buffered and started playing, the news anchor's voice filtering out to them through the car's stereo speakers.

"Residents of a peaceful neighborhood are in shock today. A bold, daylight robbery turned into a violent assault, sending a beloved elderly woman to the hospital, where she fights for her very life. Our field reporter, Parker, has more details."

The video shifted to show a reporter holding a microphone in front of a quaint house with a neatly manicured lawn. Samantha pointed to the screen. "That's the house with the cookies."

The field reporter paused a couple of seconds before speaking.

"The tragedy took place earlier today in this normally peaceful neighborhood, where neighbors still wave hello to each other and children play together in the street. A man and a woman, carrying Bibles and pretending to be discussing their faith, forced their way in to the house behind me, assaulted the homeowner, and stole everything of value.

"Unfortunately, these vicious criminals took more than just worldly possessions. Tonight, there are no children playing outside. Every door is locked and every window shuttered along both sides of the street. It may be a long time before this neighborhood can return to a sense of normalcy. Back to you, Dave."

The screen shifted back to the desk anchor with two hand drawn sketches, superimposed behind him, of Alex and Samantha.

"Thank you, Parker. One of the neighbors of the elderly woman has offered a $250,000 reward for any information leading to the capture of these two suspects. They are believed to be driving a green late-model Aston Martin sports car and are considered armed and extremely dangerous. Should you see them, or their car, call the police immediately. Do not attempt to approach or apprehend them yourself."

Samantha shut off the display. "That keeps us from going back."

"That also keeps us from using your car."

She frantically jabbed at the screen again with her index

finger, cycling through menus faster than he could keep up. "What are you doing?"

"Trying to reach Skyler. There's nothing on any of the channels."

"What about calling him on your cell phone?"

"I don't know where my cell phone is. Whoever brought us here, kept it."

"Okay. So we'll find another phone, and you can call him from there."

"The security measures built into the phone prevented the telephone numbers from being stored as readable digits. I can't call anybody without that phone!"

Her frustration mounted and she punched the dash with her fist, cracking the touchscreen display.

She sat back roughly and placed her head against the headrest, staring at the ceiling with her eyes closed. "This is not how this is supposed to be going."

"Correct me when I get something wrong, Samantha. We're cut off from all support and we are wanted fugitives with our pictures splashed across the television screens of millions of Americans who not only think we are heartless bastards but see us as a quick pay day to bolster their kid's college fund."

She tilted her head sideways to look at him. "That sounds about right. Why are you smiling?"

"Because we finally have the upper hand."

Chapter 35

The creases on Samantha's forehead deepened.

"The upper hand? Did you not hear yourself just now? We're cut off and on the run where, potentially, everybody with a television is on the lookout for us. And here in America, that's a sodding number of people."

"Exactly. And as long as the Thin Man thinks that, he won't be expecting us to come after him. We thought we had the element of surprise when we were trying to get close to his house, but we were wrong. Now, we actually do have the element of surprise. He won't see us coming, because he won't be looking."

She was shaking her head. "We have no idea where he is. I doubt he's still anywhere near that house, what with all the news trucks and police around."

"Skyler was watching that house. He's probably tracking the Thin Man right now."

"I can't get in touch with Skyler."

"Where's your failsafe? The number you call or the address you go when the mission self-destructs around you?"

"It really has self-destructed around us, hasn't it?"

"I can't see how it could get any worse."

She reached into her mouth and extracted a capped tooth. She crumbled the tooth between her fingers and pulled out a tiny rolled piece of paper with a string of numbers on it.

"Entering these numbers into a phone will send the police to that location within minutes. It's a failsafe, of sorts. Should I be captured and the tooth located, after letting myself be tortured for a little while, I admit it's a phone number to my agency. They call it, and I wait for rescue."

He ran through that scenario in his head. It didn't look good.

"By the time we were able to convince somebody we never assaulted that lady, or robbed her house, that brain programming technology would've been sold to the highest bidder. That doesn't exactly work in our favor."

She continued. "However, entering these same numbers into a GPS unit provides the coordinates of a safe house. From there, I can get what we need."

They both looked at the darkened, and cracked, display of the GPS. This in-dash GPS unit was not going to be helping them find anything. He couldn't help but smile at the irony of it all.

"Let's figure out how to hide the Aston Martin. Then we'll steal a car with a built-in GPS unit."

Chapter 36

It was the middle of the night by the time they had driven the Aston Martin deeper into the forest, covered it with leaves and branches, and then hiked back the ten miles to civilization.

The leather dress shoes Alex wore may have been the final touch he needed to make him look like an FBI agent earlier in the day, but they were not the best footwear for long hikes down a dirt road under the shadowy light of a pale moon. Samantha's heels were even less so, yet she had kept up with him every step of the way. He remembered someone telling him once that, when it came to dancing, women were better than men. They matched every step of their male partner, but did it backward and in heels. Hiking ten miles through rough terrain may not have been dancing, but she kept up with him despite the hindrance of her shoes.

But he doubted she would categorize it as fun. In the stillness of the night, he heard her mumble something quietly to herself. "Note to self: change dress code of field agents to include hiking boots, or at least tennis shoes."

Whoever she worked for, she felt she had the latitude to define mission parameters. She never said what agency she worked for and he had started to formulate a guess of who it wasn't. She had a British accent that hadn't faltered once, even under pressure. So it wasn't a cover. That was her natural accent. She couldn't be with the FBI, or the CIA, or the NSA. She wasn't American and would be precluded from joining anything in the United States.

It made more sense that she worked for British

Intelligence and, whoever she reported to, had a lot of strong contacts in the U.S.

But if she was a British agent working here, she would have an American handler working with her. What he gathered from the limited information she had given him, or inadvertently let slip, contact with an agent of the United States government was not something she had to maintain. And it was not like the United States to let a foreign agent operate within its borders without oversight; even a British agent.

So, she wasn't working with any of the American agencies. She couldn't be with the Chinese, or the North Koreans, or any other government that was against the United States. Why would she be trying to stop some new technology from falling into the wrong hands, if she was already the wrong hands?

No. She operated independently from any of the agencies most of the world knew about. It had to be independent, and not British Intelligence either, because she had been too easily cut off from any kind of support when things went south. There was no infrastructure that kept her in contact with the people giving the orders. It didn't appear that she worked for an agency that was yet established to operate around the globe without interruption.

She worked for someone hidden.

Someone new.

Chapter 37

Hunkered down in the bushes that lined the edge of a shopping mall, Alex and Samantha debated which vehicle, in the sparsely populated parking lot, would give them access to a GPS and, potentially, a few hours reprieve before the police zeroed in on the stolen vehicle.

Samantha whispered in the darkness afforded by the thick bushes and pointed to a car sitting under a lamp post.

"Our best bet is to get one that is very commonplace. I think there are enough Toyota hybrids on the road, we can easily blend in. Looking at our other options, I think it's the only one with a GPS in the dash."

She held up the key fob from her Aston Martin. "It's also the only one that will allow keyless entry for my universal remote. I can be in the hybrid and start it up in less than two seconds."

The world had changed much in the two years he was in prison.

"I didn't think they made universal remotes that worked on any car."

She gave him a mischievous smile. "They don't. How long do you think it will take you to get the plates?"

Alex gripped the screwdriver he'd retrieved from the trunk of the Aston Martin before they abandoned it in the middle of the woods. Switching license plates with another one of the cars would give them a little extra time in case they were spotted. The police would be looking for a vehicle and license plate match before stopping them.

"Shouldn't take but a minute."

They watched the silent parking lot for a short while

before she finally stood up.

"Won't get any quieter than this."

She headed for the hybrid while he went to the other side of the parking lot and started unscrewing the back license plate from a thirty-year-old rusted Dodge. It would've been faster to grab a license plate from the nearest car, but then they ran the risk that, once the police were called for the stolen car, the license plate swap might be noticed. People had a tendency to become more involved, the closer they were to any given situation. Someone parked right next to the crime scene might hang around and talk to the police long enough to observe the license plate number on their car was different than they remembered. A person parked on the far side of the parking lot might give a cursory glance toward the police activity on the other side, but then they would just drive off.

With the back license plate in hand, he walked around to the front and bent down to work on removing the second plate.

As soon as he bent down, a loud and angry voice cut through the silence like a knife. "What the hell?!"

Thirty-year-old hinges squeaked as the driver opened his door and stepped out, baseball bat in hand, to confront the man stealing his license plates.

Alex wasn't a small man, by any stretch of the imagination, but when he stood up, he still had to crane his neck to look into the alcohol infused bloodshot eyes of the bruiser who had just climbed out of the Dodge. The red and white checkered flannel shirt, unbuttoned and draped over a dingy white T-shirt, was a dead giveaway that this guy was a doer rather than a thinker.

His mind went into overdrive, trying to come up with the

one possible response that would keep that baseball bat from cracking against his skull.

Best to feign ignorance.

"Wait a minute. I may have the wrong car."

"You're damn right you got the wrong car."

He set the license plate from the back of the car on the hood and raised his hands. "I don't want any trouble."

Bruiser took a step forward and swung the bat around like a policeman swinging a baton. "Should've thought of that before you tried to steal my plates."

He pointed with one hand. "Your plate is right there. In fact, here's a screwdriver so you can put it back on."

As he placed the screwdriver on the hood next to the license plate, Bruiser lunged at him, swinging the bat high. Alex ducked under it easily and came up with a clenched fist just under Bruiser's chin.

Bruiser's teeth rattled and he stumbled backward a couple of steps. That hit usually sent someone to the ground.

Instead, Bruiser shook it off and smiled, showing he didn't have many teeth left to lose in this fight. "I'm glad you did that. My parole allows for me to defend myself."

Alex's hand was already throbbing. The likely result of hitting Bruiser again would be broken fingers. He needed a weapon.

He grabbed the only one available to him.

Bruiser stalked forward and laughed. "If I was looking for somebody to screw me to death, I woulda stayed with that blonde up north."

Bruiser's bat extended his reach beyond what Alex could do with a screwdriver. If this was a fair fight, the man with the three-foot bat would have the advantage. But Bruiser was a whole head taller than he was and must've outweighed him by over a hundred pounds. He'd already delivered his fight ending knockout punch, only to have it shaken off.

This was not a fair fight.

If Alex wanted to win, he could not fight fair.

So he did what anybody needed to do to survive until the next fight.

He ran.

This only angered Bruiser more.

He ran in a straight line, diagonally across the parking lot, toward where Samantha was waiting for him in the hybrid.

Bruiser roared and took off after him, his large work boots pounding on the pavement behind him, and getting closer. Apparently, Bruiser's height was all in his legs and it gave him a longer stride once they were at a full run.

Alex pumped his arms, willing his legs to move faster. If his black leather shoes weren't designed for hiking, they certainly weren't up to the task to take him through any kind of evasive maneuvers while running at his top speed through a parking lot. It was times like this he was glad he ignored the catcalls of his fellow inmates when he maintained his rigorous aerobic training.

If he had succumbed to peer pressure and only worked on his strength training, focusing on bulking up like the rest of the prisoners around him, he would've been at the mercy of the Louisville slugger long before it clipped his shoulder and spun him off balance.

His smooth dress shoes refused to regain purchase on the oil-slicked pavement and he fell. His training kicked in and he shoulder-rolled across the ground to pop back up to a standing position, his screwdriver ready to inflict some damage.

Bruiser skidded to a halt and swung the bat around like a baton again. "Go ahead, pretty boy. Make your move."

A strange, high-pitched whine, accompanied by an increasing brightness, drew their attention away from each other.

And directly at the car speeding toward them through the parking lot.

Bruiser stood transfixed, like a deer in the headlights. He snapped out of it and dove away moments before the car hit him.

The car skidded to a stop in front of Alex and Samantha hollered out the window. "Get in!"

She didn't need to tell him twice.

He flung open the back door and catapulted himself headfirst into the backseat. She punched it, and the sudden acceleration automatically shut Alex's door as the hybrid shot forward.

Bruiser was on his feet, and shattered one of the side windows with his bat, as Samantha did her best to peel out of the parking lot in a severely underpowered hybrid.

Samantha jerked the wheel and they careened around another corner. "We need to get rid of this car as soon as possible. That bloke's probably calling the police right now."

Alex climbed between the seats and dropped into the front passenger seat. "I don't think he'll be calling anyone."

"How can you be so sure?"

"He's on parole. People like that, generally don't call the police. However, we didn't get to switch the license plates, and that will give us less time."

"Then let's not waste any." She held the tiny roll of paper out to him. "Type in the coordinates to the GPS. Let's see where we should be going."

Chapter 38

Alex stared at the tiny rundown motel, with attached restaurant, in the light of the early rising sun.

"Can't you ever take me any place nice?"

Samantha checked the GPS.

"These are the exact coordinates. All I have to do is mention Robert's name and we'll get whatever we need."

"Who's Robert?"

She give him a steely stare.

He put his hands up. "Okay. Sorry. Sorry. No more questions."

The hybrid had a near full tank of gas when they stole it. They were able to make their six-hour journey to Government Camp, Oregon a nonstop trip, and Alex's bladder was sending him strong signals.

"If this is the place, then let's go in. I have to see a man about a horse."

"Horse?! What horse?"

"It means I need to take a piss."

She nodded. "Good idea. We should both avail ourselves of the facilities before continuing."

"If you have to use the crapper too, just say so."

"I'm not as crass as you."

He grinned sheepishly. "Sorry. Two years of prison will pretty much beat the crass right into you."

He stepped out of the hybrid and stretched his back. It was a crisp, bright morning. He breathed in the fresh mountain air deeply and let it out slowly, savoring every molecule of the sweet aroma.

A faded banner hung over the restaurant, advertising

karaoke every Friday and Saturday night.

The neon open sign blazed in all its glory. At least they wouldn't have to wait.

The bell above the front door dinged as they entered. The dining room was empty and someone called out to them from the back.

"Just sit anywhere. I'll be right out to take your order."

Alex and Samantha looked at each other and picked the booth nearest the front door. They weren't planning to be here for very long.

Alex's bladder goaded him again and he looked around for the restroom sign, thankfully spotting it in the far corner.

"I'll be right back."

The door with the restroom sign opened into a back hallway that was lined with shelves, making the small area additional storage space for the kitchen. At the far end, the open door to the bathroom beckoned.

He had only gone two steps when the waitress entered the hallway from the kitchen, a purse slung over her shoulder and car keys in her hand. She looked up at him with a shocked expression.

She recovered quickly. Almost too quickly. "I thought I told you to have a seat."

He looked at the purse and car keys. "You also said you'd be right out."

She looked ready to say something, and then bolted for the back door.

His bladder would have to wait.

He called out as he took off in pursuit. "Samantha! Outside!"

Chapter 39

Samantha had just plucked a sticky menu out of the holder on the table when Alex cried out.

She didn't bother to determine if she was running from something, or to something. She just reacted by drawing her gun from its holster, another of the inexplicable items the Thin Man had let her keep, and bolted out of the restaurant.

There was a scuffle around the back of the restaurant followed by a cry of pain. As she ran for the corner, she heard the rumble of a car engine start.

She dashed around the corner, just in time to jump back out of the way of a gold colored muscle car speeding away from the restaurant. Her arms shot up to protect her face from the gravel the car tires spit at her as it slid sideways onto the road.

Alex limped quickly up to her. "Let's get after her!"

She ran back to the hybrid, Alex hobbling as fast as he could behind her. "What happened?"

He greeted his teeth with each step. "I'm not sure. When I went back there, she was already ready to leave, purse in hand. She bolted. I went after her and she attacked me as soon as I came out the door. She's good. She's had training."

Samantha hopped into the hybrid and pushed the start button.

Alex fell into the seat next to her. "I think we found your contact."

As she gunned the hybrid and steered it onto the road in pursuit, she glanced over at him. "But why did she run?"

Chapter 40

The waitress pushed the accelerator down hard on the gold colored 1974 Firebird that was a present from an ex-boyfriend. The name tag on her polyester waitress outfit claimed her name was Janet. That was a lie, along with just about everything else in her life.

She should never have returned.

But she had returned for him, only to have them not work out. The only reminder of a life she could never have obeyed her every command as she took it through the twists and turns of the two-lane mountain road.

Everyone thought she was dead. Even if they suspected she was still alive, they would never think to look for her in Government Camp, Oregon. It would've been stupid for her to return. To her, that made it the smartest decision she could make.

When she saw the hybrid pull in with a shattered back window, she suspected the people in the car might be trouble.

When they both climbed out, their special forces training was evident in how they moved, talked with each other, and even stood.

She knew they were trouble.

And if they came, others would follow.

So she ran.

She cussed herself out for leaving her gun at home. She had let her guard down because nothing had happened for so long. She would not make that mistake again.

She was so busy running through what she should do, where she should go, what she should take, that she almost missed her turn. She hit the brakes and skidded the car onto the dirt road. She gunned it, kicking dirt and rocks up behind her, and was out of sight of the main road in less than twenty seconds.

Chapter 41

Alex massaged his aching knee. The waitress had kicked him the moment he came out the back door. If he hadn't trained himself to the point of instinct, he would be nursing a shattered kneecap right now.

Samantha's question still echoed in his head.

Why had the waitress run?

It didn't make any sense.

They hadn't had the chance to say anything to her. They had not even met her yet when she decided to run.

The waitress had seen something in them that frightened her.

But what?

Samantha had been quiet the whole time they had been speeding down the road after the Firebird. Maybe she knew what happened? It was, after all, the coordinates on the paper inside her tooth that brought them here. She had to know more than she was saying, because she wasn't saying anything.

Before he came in contact with the waitress again, he needed to know more to prepare himself.

"Who is the waitress?"

Samantha never took her eyes off the road, focusing on keeping the hybrid from flying off the edge of the road. "I don't know."

"Bullshit. The message in your tooth took us there. Surely you knew what to expect once we got there."

She stayed focused on the road, and even more annoyingly, remained silent. She had to learn to start trusting him if she expected him to help.

"You promised to start giving me information, before I needed it. What happened back there?"

"I didn't know she would run."

"Did you know she would attack me?"

"No."

"Why don't you start by telling me what you do know?"

She gave him a sideways glance, just as the road curved. She whipped the steering wheel around and fishtailed back to the center of the road.

"It won't help."

"You let me be the judge of that. I need full disclosure. Without it, she just might break my leg the next time."

"I barely know anything."

"Just tell me!"

Her shoulders drooped slightly as she gave in. "Okay. Robert used her on a contract basis in the past."

"There's this Robert again. Who is he?"

"Are you going to let me talk?"

He put his hands up, and then promptly gripped the door handle again as she careened around another corner.

"Go ahead."

"He told me she was no longer active, but should the need ever arise, she had a way to get in touch with him that was known by nobody else. A way outside normal channels."

"Why did he tell you?"

"He didn't tell me how she would contact him, or even who she was. He just said, if I ever go to the GPS coordinates in my tooth, to use his name and ask for her help."

He scanned the road ahead. They were never going to catch up with a 1970s muscle car. "I don't think she wants to help."

He spotted something in the road. "Stop the car!"

Samantha slammed on the brakes and they skidded to a stop in the center the road at a thirty degree angle.

"What is it?"

He pointed to a fresh set of skid marks that arced off the road and onto a dirt path. "She went that way."

Chapter 42

The waitress hastily packed and threw the duffel bag into the backseat of the Firebird. She had just stuck the key in the ignition when she heard a high-pitched whine coming from the twisty dirt road that led to her house.

It was the sound of a hybrid laboring up the deeply rutted road. The Firebird barely made the trek each day, she didn't think a hybrid would fare much better.

The whine increased in pitch and intensity, but never got closer.

The hybrid electric motor revved briefly before falling silent.

She slid her SIG Sauer pistol out from the duffel bag and crept silently from the Firebird. She left the door open, not wanting to let the sound of closing it echo in the forest around her.

She walked a few feet into the dense woods, and then paralleled the road. As she approach the hybrid, voices echoed from the road.

First a woman's voice, and then a man in response.

"Bloody hell! The car's buggered in a rut. Are you sure she came this way?"

"Pretty sure."

"Well if she didn't, we've lost her."

"And if she did, she's not going back this way. Nobody's getting around this Toyota without towing it away first."

"Brilliant! Isn't it just like an American to state the obvious?"

"Don't get mad at me. I didn't say anything to make her run."

"Well, it certainly wasn't me. I never even saw her until she tried to run me over with her car."

"Let's not fight about this Samantha. There has to be another way to contact your boss."

"She was my last link to Robert. I've got nothing else."

Her gripped tightened involuntarily on the handle of her pistol. Did she say Robert?

Chapter 43

Alex clamped his mouth shut before he said anything else. Now was not the time for them to be fighting.

They had barely eaten in the last twenty-four hours, they had lost their target, after possibly being captured and inexplicably released by the very same target, and they were cut off from all levels of support. In this situation, tempers could easily run hot.

Samantha seemed like she was typically a cool character, but she was giving back just as much as she was getting, and from what little he actually knew about her, that seemed very much unlike her. He needed to learn to hold his tongue if he didn't want to make the situation worse than it already was.

Fortunately, Samantha had already quieted down on her own. He scanned the dirt road they came up and was surprised the hybrid had made it this far. Maybe if they walked farther up the road, they could find out where the waitress had gone.

He was just about to make this suggestion when he looked over at Samantha, who was standing perfectly still, her eyes locked on something in the forest.

He looked in the direction she faced and froze.

The waitress was standing just off the edge of the road, holding a gun aimed at Samantha's head.

The waitress was the first to speak.

"Who are you?"

Samantha replied. "We're friends of Robert. He said you could help us."

"I don't know what you're talking about."

It was Alex's turn to reply to that one.

"Then why did you kick me in the knee and run?"

She looked over at him. "What would you have done in my situation?"

He shrugged his shoulders. "I don't know. Maybe come out and take our breakfast order?"

"You weren't there for the food."

"Actually, I was kinda looking forward to it. It's been a while since I've eaten, and I did need to use the restroom. So, you running, was quite inconvenient. In fact, if you'll excuse me for just a moment."

All this talk about needing to use the restroom moved his bladder's urgent prompting right to the front of the line. He turned away from the waitress with the gun and cringed at her next statement.

"If you don't think I'll shoot you in the back…"

"I really have to go. I swear, I'm not trying anything funny," he said over his shoulder as he took another step toward the woods.

"Stay where I can see you," she demanded.

He pointed to his left. "How about I use this tree right here?"

Thankfully, she did not shoot him in the back while he relieved himself. Even when his toilet had been in clear view of everybody who walked by his prison cell for two years, it was still awkward to stand near a tree with his back to two women and urinate down the side of it. He had hoped for a little more privacy once he was out of prison. So far, he wasn't getting his wish.

He finished and made himself appropriate again before turning around to face the waitress.

"Are you going to help us, or not?"

She held the gun study. "You never answered my question."

Full disclosure seemed like the best way to deal with the waitress. Especially, if she could help them.

"My name is Alex, and this is Samantha. She hired me and now we're completely cut off from the people who hired her. She had GPS coordinates embedded in her tooth that brought us directly to you in the hope that you could get us in touch with someone named, Robert. Did I forget anything, Sam?"

Samantha, wisely, had not moved from her spot. "No. I think you just told a complete stranger everything."

The waitress took a step closer to Samantha, but kept the gun steady. "Do you work with Robert?"

"He hired me directly."

"Did he hire you to kill me?"

"No. We are only here because I can't get in touch with him. He told me you were the only one, outside his inner circle, who had his private phone number."

"Prove it."

"Prove what? I don't have anything that can link me back to him."

"No. Prove that Robert told you about me."

"If you're the person he told me about, your name tag is wrong."

"Is it? Then what's my name?"

"Stone. Your name is Melissa Stone."

She let her arm drop to the side and held the pistol loosely in her hand. Samantha started for her and Melissa's arm snapped up immediately as she took a step back.

Samantha froze again.

Melissa thumbed the magazine eject on the SIG Sauer

and pulled on the slide to eject the chambered round before tossing the empty pistol on the ground in front of her.

Samantha watched her disarm herself, but did not attempt to charge at her this time.

Melissa held her arms out to her side, so that neither of them would think she was going for another weapon. "It's been a long time since I called Robert. There's no guarantee I still have his number."

Chapter 44

In the tiny one room cabin that Melissa called home, she handed Alex a cup of tea. "Sorry I don't have anything more substantial."

"That's okay," he said as he sipped it slowly. His stomach rumbled with the knowledge that, finally, something was headed its way. He didn't have the heart to tell his stomach it was only tea.

Samantha set her tea aside, untouched. "So can we call Robert now?"

Melissa sat down on the chair across from them with her own steaming cup of tea. "I don't have a phone."

Samantha bristled at that comment. "I'm not calling him to chat. Something is going to happen and I need to contact him. It is extremely urgent."

Melissa seemed unfazed by Samantha's outburst. "It is always urgent, with him. Something is always happening in the world, and Robert has a knack for getting right in the middle of it. I made the mistake of getting involved once, and it cost me my life."

That seemed like a strange comment. Alex placed his tea on the coffee table in front of him. "Your life? You seem very much alive to me."

"As far as everyone I care about is concerned, I'm dead. When I look in the mirror, I am constantly reminded that the person I used to be, is gone."

She looked over at Samantha. "You are the first person to use my real name in two years."

Samantha leaned forward. "I need to get in touch with Robert right away. Can you take us to a phone?"

Melissa regarded her for a while, silently sipping at her tea, before she responded.

"No."

Alex could tell it took every ounce of her strength not to vault over the coffee table, strangle Melissa, and force her to take them to a phone.

"Excuse me?"

"I'd rather not get involved this time, if it's all the same to you."

"It's not all the same to me. If you know how to get in touch with Robert, you have a responsibility to…"

Melissa slammed her mug onto the coffee table, spilling some of the tea.

"I don't have a responsibility to you, or to Robert, or to anyone. My responsibility ended when my life ended."

Samantha sat back on the couch, gritting her teeth as Melissa continued.

"When he helped me save my family, he instilled in me an undying loyalty to always be there for him. When my family was in danger again, he offered no help. I sought him out and found nothing but a shell of his former self. He was a broken and beaten man, wallowing in self-pity."

Samantha leaned forward. "He's not like that anymore. He has a renewed sense of purpose and asked me to help him set things right. He's once again the man you knew."

"Even if that were true, I'm not the Melissa he knew. She disappeared when he walked away and left her vulnerable on a park bench in the middle of the night."

"Please, Melissa, I beg of you. Help us reach Robert."

"I will not call him for you…"

Samantha started to explode again, but Melissa held up her hand.

"Let me finish. I will not call Robert myself. But I will give you the phone number, and then, kindly ask you to leave."

Samantha visibly calmed down. "Thank you."

Alex, staying quiet this entire time, had a thought.

"If we could intrude on you for one more favor?"

Melissa raised her eyebrows, prompting him to continue.

"Could we get a ride back into town?"

After Melissa wrote down the lengthy phone number for Robert, they piled into the Firebird. Melissa was driving, Samantha was in the front passenger seat, and Alex was in the back, leaning forward between the two front bucket sheets, his arms perched on the head rests.

"You sure it's no problem to get rid of the hybrid for us?"

Melissa backed out of the nook that served as her driveway and pointed the Firebird away from the house. "Won't be the first time."

The car bounced down the uneven dirt road and Melissa slammed on the brakes as she rounded the first bend, nearly hitting a police officer holding his hand up for her to stop.

Alex leaned back quickly in his seat. "Are the police normally on this road?"

Melissa shook her head.

"Let me handle this." She rolled down her window and leaned out. "Morning Fred. What are you doing here?"

The officer squinted against the morning sun as it rose above the tree line. "I was just coming to see you, Janet. There's a stolen vehicle blocking your road. Tow truck will be here in twenty minutes."

"My shift started a half hour ago. Do you think I could get around it?"

He approached and leaned down to peer inside the Firebird. "Got stuck in a narrow part. Don't think you'll fit. Who's your friends?"

"This is Sally and Jack. Friends from Portland visiting for the week. You sure we can't get around?"

"Your friends got any ID?"

"Hank will kill me if I'm an hour late for another shift. Can't I just try to squeeze past the other car?"

Fred squinted into the car and recognition flashed across his face. He took a couple steps back and drew his service revolver while shouting commands. "Everyone out of the car and keep your hands where I can see them."

Before any of them could react, his head vaporized into a fine red mist and his headless body crumpled to the ground.

Chapter 45

Madina squinted through the scope of her high-powered sniper rifle. She swiveled it away from the headless police officer and focused on the gold colored Pontiac Firebird that held her two targets; and a third person who might prove to be of interest to Umarov.

She unclipped the walkie-talkie from her breast pocket and whispered into it even though she didn't think there was anyone close enough in the surrounding forest to hear her. It paid to never be too careful.

"If you can hear me, signal by flashing your headlights."

She watched the driver of the gold Firebird stare in shock at the headless body of the officer. Even from this distance, she could see the driver react to her voice coming through the officer's shoulder mounted radio.

They could hear her.

Now to verify they would listen.

"I know you can hear me. Flash the headlights on your vehicle."

She squinted through the scope and watched the Firebird's headlights flicker on and off.

"Excellent. I suggest you get moving before any more police arrive."

The car started up immediately and continued down the road, unfortunately the car entered a thicker part of the forest and she lost sight of them.

Right before they disappeared from view, she could see the heated debate going on inside the car. Oh, how she wished she could hear what they were saying, but Umarov was the only one listening to the bugs sewn into the lining of their target's clothing.

All she had was a GPS unit with two dots representing each target. It was her job to make sure the path was clear so they could get to wherever it was they were going.

She would have preferred to be by Umarov's side when he completed his big, world changing, mission, but then he was a man who ran a varied and complex game.

When this new opportunity fell into his lap, he entrusted her to lead this new mission to success.

And she would not fail him.

She lifted the rifle and swung it in a shallow arc before settling it back on its tripod. There was only one way down to the main road, and they would never make it past the stolen Toyota hybrid.

The GPS unit clipped to her belt would tell her when they reached the area where the Toyota was, but nothing beat tracking a target with her own eyes.

She squinted through the scope.

And waited.

The driver became expendable once the car could go no farther.

Her orders were very clear.

Eliminate everyone they came in contact with.

Chapter 46

As they drove away from the slain officer and continued down the dirt road, Melissa and Samantha screamed at each other. Melissa claiming to have been lied to, and Samantha claiming to not know who killed the police officer.

Alex sat in the backseat, running through the events over the past two days in his head. There was no indication that Samantha had anyone working for her beyond those he already knew about, or suspected.

In the past several hours, she had been out of contact with her organization and had never left his side. Even if she did have an opportunity to call in reinforcements, or overwatch, she'd had no access to a phone.

Plus, she had been just as shocked as he was when the police officer's head exploded. Whoever was out there helping them, Samantha did not know about it. And if she didn't know about it, she didn't have control over it.

That last thought was the most sobering of all.

He raised his voice to be heard over their arguing. "Ladies. Ladies! Please! Calm down, both of you."

Samantha quieted, but Melissa was not so compliant. "You killed a police officer, on my property! That is exactly the kind of trouble I knew you would be. You asked me why ran when I first saw you? That's why I ran."

He tried to persuade her that she was making the right choice in helping them.

"We had nothing to do with that. We are in the dark as much as you are as to who killed him, and why."

Melissa laughed. "Why? He was about to arrest you two for God knows what. Whoever killed him, is helping you.

And now, I'm an accessory. And it was on my property! Thanks to you, I have to leave and never look back. I'm gonna have to change my name, again!"

Samantha also pleaded their case. "Believe me, Melissa. We don't know what happened back there."

Melissa skidded to a stop. "I'll tell you what happened back there..."

Alex cut her off. "It doesn't matter what happened. All that matters is that we get out of this alive."

Melissa became deathly calm as she gripped the steering wheel. "How do I know you will let me live?"

Alex couldn't help raising his voice. "We had nothing to do with that!"

He quickly took a deep breath to calm himself down and lowered his voice. "Right now, we must work together. We need to focus on getting out of here. Why did you stop?"

Melissa pointed to the hybrid stuck in the road in front of them. "Fred was right. There's no way I'm getting around your car. We'll have to walk down to the main road and hitchhike from there. Alex, hand me my bag."

Alex grabbed the duffel bag with one hand, kicking up dust. It had obviously been in storage for quite some time. He handed it forward, raising even more dust from the folds of the canvas bag.

Melissa sniffed quickly, reacting from the tiny cloud of dust particles that lifted into the air from her bag. As it tickled at the inside of her nose, she sneezed. At that same moment, the driver's side window and the windshield both shattered.

Melissa dropped down in her seat while Samantha bailed out of the car. She disappeared into the woods, leaving Alex and Melissa hunkered down on the floor of the Firebird.

Another bullet tore through the rear side window, raining shards of tempered glass down on them.

Alex and Melissa faced each other through the gap between the two front seats.

He grimaced. "You still think whoever's out there is trying to help me? Maybe it's somebody from your past?"

Two more bullets pinged off the roof and a third popped one of the tires.

She gave him a serious look. "I've already killed everybody who wants me dead."

Chapter 47

Samantha ran deep into the forest and ducked behind a tree to catch her breath.

Whoever was shooting, was still concentrating their efforts on the car. The shooter had not fired on her as she ran.

Maybe they weren't the target.

Maybe whoever was out there, was after Melissa.

No. That couldn't be it.

It was too much of a coincidence to expect that someone looking for Melissa would find her on the exact same day they arrived.

Coincidences like that just didn't exist.

Whoever it was, had followed her and Alex.

But they hadn't known, moment from moment, where they were headed. She had also been very careful to monitor behind them the entire drive here from Boise. Nobody had followed them. She was sure of it.

There certainly wasn't anybody else on the road when they chased Melissa. Whoever it was, hadn't been following them traditionally. But they had been following. If whoever was following them wasn't using line-of-sight, they had to be doing it electronically.

Could they be using a satellite? It took access to a large organization to commandeer a satellite without being noticed. And she was pretty sure it wasn't somebody from the United States government since they had just killed a police officer.

No. It couldn't be a satellite.

A tracker on the car?

No, they randomly stole that car. There was no way anybody could know for certain that they would steal a car, let alone what car they would take from where.

That left electronic trackers on themselves.

Samantha stripped off her blazer and inspected it.

There!

A small lump under one of the buttons.

There was a tracking device sewn under the button of her blazer.

It couldn't be the only one. If she wanted to track someone, she'd plant more than one device.

She checked the buttons on her slacks and found another tracking device.

She slipped off a shoe and inspected it. The heel had been recently glued back into place. She snapped the heel off against the side of a tree.

Another tracking device.

She dug the tracker out of the heel and inspected it. This was not something put here by Robert. The tiny circuit board had Russian lettering imprinted into it. Was it possible that the Thin Man, after capturing them, had erased their memories and let them go so they could lead him back to…? Where?

To Robert?

That thought chilled her to the bone. If they knew about Robert, or even X-Alpha, the entire operation was in jeopardy.

She stripped down to her panties and bra. She felt around both, but found nothing embedded in them.

Thank God. She did not want to go hiking around the forest naked. It was bad enough she had to do it in her underwear.

Chapter 48

The barrage of bullets had stopped and was replaced by the silence of the forest.

Melissa whispered to him. "Why don't you check to see if your friend is out of bullets?"

Alex was not interested in poking his head up only to have it blown off. "I told you. We have nothing to do with this. Samantha and I are the only two here. I know about one other guy on her team, but he sounded more like a computer geek than a gun nut."

Melissa grunted her disbelief. "I wasn't exaggerating earlier. I've already killed everyone looking for me."

"Maybe you missed one."

"I didn't. This has to be you."

Melissa pointed through the car door left open by the fleeing Samantha. "Your girlfriend's back. And she's naked."

"She's not my... What?"

He craned his neck to see out. Barely visible behind a tree, Samantha was indeed carrying all her clothes in a bundle under one arm and wearing very little. He could just make out the strap to her bra and the high French cut of her panties. Why had she taken off all her clothes?

She made eye contact with him and waved.

This was very strange behavior from her.

He smiled and half-heartedly waved back, sing-speaking to Melissa through clenched teeth. "I think she's lost it."

Samantha shook her head angrily and began to wave again rapidly.

Melissa, not a male, and thus not transfixed by a mostly naked female, was the first to notice. "It's Morse code."

Now that she had pointed it out, it was obvious.

He concentrated on her hand signals as the letters formed into words in his mind.

Take... off... clothes... bugged...

She repeated the same four words again and then stopped.

He and Melissa looked at each other as a mischievous smile spread across her lips. "She wasn't talking to me."

Chapter 49

Alex twisted, pulled, yanked, and twisted some more. It wasn't easy getting undressed in the back seat of a 1970s era muscle car. He remembered it being a lot easier in high school. Of course, he had a different incentive back then and wasn't so focused on trying to stay low enough to avoid getting shot.

When he was down to his boxers and socks, Samantha finally stopped signaling "keep going" with her hands and returned to Morse code.

Fire… Smoke…

They needed to create a smokescreen so they could sneak away from the car out of sight from the sniper. Her plan would work if they had a way to make fire.

He looked to Melissa, crumpled up under the dash of the Firebird. She silently shrugged, neither of them wanting to talk because of the listening devices in his clothing. He knew what she meant. She didn't smoke, so she didn't have a lighter.

A lighter!

Smoking was still cool in the '70s. Every car made back then had a built-in lighter.

He scanned the dashboard and found what he was looking for.

He motioned for Melissa to push down on it. The Firebird would heat the metal coil inside the lighter, he could throw it out into the forest, igniting the dry grass by the side of the road, and create their smokescreen.

Melissa mouthed the word "nope" while shaking her head.

He stabbed two fingers in the direction of the dashboard lighter, silently demanding she push it in.

She shook her head again.

He reached forward to do it himself and she swatted his hand away. Immediately, he lunged between the seats for the lighter. They wrestled, emitting grunts and groans, while still staying low so as to not present a target for the sniper. He twisted one way, and then the next, and finally pushed the lighter down with an elbow.

With his task accomplished, he released Melissa and leaned back, pleased with himself.

Thirty seconds later, it popped and she snatched it out of the dashboard before he could reach for it. She held it just out of reach and whispered harshly, "I won't let you burn the forest down."

He replied in an even harsher whisper, "It's not the whole forest."

"I've been in a forest fire. They move faster than you realize."

"We have to get out of here. This is the only way."

"Find another way."

"There is no other way."

He lashed out and they struggled for control of the red-hot cigarette lighter.

As they grappled, he didn't realize she had already dropped it until the smell of burning fabric assaulted his nostrils.

They both stopped and looked at each other, and then looked down. The carpet was smoldering under the foot pedals and the car was quickly filling with smoke.

They both took a quick breath and held it.

They were about to get their smokescreen.

If they didn't succumb to smoke inhalation first.

Chapter 50

Madina casually reloaded ten rounds of ammunition into the box magazine and slapped it back into the Russian-made Dragunov SVD sniper rifle.

She usually made an effort to carry additional pre-loaded magazines when she was on sniper duty, but she had to make a hasty climb to the top of the mountain when she realized her targets had remained still for too long. She mostly needed the scope on the rifle to see what they were up to.

Using her GPS display as a topographical guide, she had located them earlier through the window of a small cabin at the end of the road.

She hadn't originally planned on firing the Dragunov until she checked in with Umarov and he authorized the termination of the woman who drove the gold colored car away from the cabin.

Unfortunately, the location where the hybrid had stalled out was on the outside of the rifle's serviceable range, and she'd missed the first shot that was supposed to take out the driver.

To give herself time to get closer, she emptied the rest of the magazine in rapid succession, careful to keep the rounds from hitting anywhere close to the occupants in the car. She was still under orders to leave the other two alive.

As soon as she reloaded her rifle, she sighted through the scope, ready to fire two more shots to keep her prey pinned down while she moved closer.

She wasn't prepared for what she saw.

The Firebird was on fire.

When she emptied the magazine, should made sure not to hit anything that might start a fire. In fact, she knew with confidence the fire was not started by anything she had done.

A moment later, smoke engulfed the area around the car.

She could barely make out the car through the scope, and couldn't see anything beyond. They had turned the car into a smoke screen generator by lighting it on fire.

There was now a blind spot where they could run in a straight line without being observed.

She checked the GPS tracker. The dots weren't moving. Both of them were still in the same area as the burning car. She would have to get closer to see if they were near the car, or in it.

Why weren't they running?

She began to worry that she hadn't been as careful as she thought and her actions might have started the fire.

She slung the sniper rifle over one shoulder and began the careful trek through the woods toward the burning car.

With each step, she formulated and practiced her script. She needed to know exactly what to say, and how to say it, when she told Umarov that both targets were killed during the time it was her job to protect them.

She already knew what he would say.

As soon as she hit the road, she withdrew her pistol and slowly approached the car that was now fully engulfed in flames.

She held a hand up to protect her face from the searing heat. The leaves on surrounding trees curled and it looked like the fire might spread.

It was too hot to get close enough to fully see inside the car. If anybody was still in there, they had not survived.

But she needed to determine if her targets had stayed in the car or got out before it was too late. She scanned the road and saw what she was looking for.

She crouched down and traced the outline of footprint. This was not the impression of a textured sole from a shoe. It had individual toe indentations, as if the person who made this was barefoot, or only wearing socks.

She whipped out her GPS locator. It showed the targets were right next to her. In the exact location of the burning car. One by one, the dots on her display winked out as the fire destroyed the tracking devices.

The tracking devices were in the car.

With their clothing.

While her targets went…

She scanned the barefooted marks in the dirt and looked up in the direction they headed.

She didn't need technology to find someone in the forest. Before the wars in her homeland made her into the perfect sniper, she was an excellent hunter.

Chapter 51

Branches and bushes scratched at his legs as he picked his way carefully, but quickly, through the forest. Melissa knew this territory very well, but she was moving with the confidence of someone wearing jeans and a leather jacket. She'd had the foresight to change out of the waitress uniform before driving them to a phone, and since her clothes hadn't been bugged, she'd had the privilege of keeping hers on. She would scout the forest ahead, then pause and wait for them to catch up.

He looked at Samantha's arms and legs. She wasn't doing any better at avoiding every single sharp twig and branch either. They both looked like they'd fallen into a pit of playful kittens.

They caught up to Melissa again, and he leaned against a tree to catch his breath. Even though he had maintained himself physically while in prison, he still hadn't fully prepared himself for this much running after drinking only one cup of tea in the last twenty-four hours.

Who knew that the last two years of prison would actually be easier than the last two days on the outside?

Samantha was also wheezing, and spoke rapidly between breaths.

"Where are we going?"

Melissa pointed into the dense forest ahead of them. "There's a cabin up ahead that doesn't get used much this time of year. You can call Robert from there, and then you can be out of my hair for good."

Alex tried to calm the situation with words of apology.

"We're sorry. We didn't mean to be so much trouble..."

Melissa turned on him, her rage bubbling to the surface. "What?! You've been nothing but trouble. You came into my life an hour ago, and already I've lost my job, lost my car, there's a dead police officer in my yard, and you started a fire that will likely take out half the forest, including my house."

She turned and mumbled loudly as she stalked away through the forest. "Didn't mean to be trouble."

Samantha shot him a withering stare. He grimaced and shrugged his shoulders as if to say "what did I do?"

She shook her head and followed after Melissa.

He picked his way quickly, but carefully, in his stocking feet, trying desperately to avoid the sharp rocks embedded in the forest floor. He was not always successful.

He caught up with them on the porch of an old cabin. It felt good to stand on smooth wooden planks that weren't trying to impale the soles of his feet at any given moment.

He inspected the solid construction of the door frame that stood in stark contrast to the dilapidated walls. "It's gonna take all of us to break through that. Maybe they left the key under the mat."

As he lifted the edge of the mat, Melissa grasped the front door handle, twisted it, and the door swung open.

Alex's mouth fell open. "It's unlocked?"

"Why lock the door of a house nobody's going to find?" Melissa said as she walked inside. He looked around at the surrounding area. There was no road, or even a visible foot path, leading up to the house. It had been built in the middle of the forest with no discernible trail leading to its well-hidden location.

He walked inside and his socks behaved like miniature feather dusters. Instead of tracking muddy footprints across the entryway, he was leaving clean prints in the thick layer of dust on the floor.

Cobwebs and dust covered everything. This house wasn't just ignored during this time of year, it had been abandoned for quite some time. Melissa pointed to a table in the corner. "The phone's over there."

On the table, under a thick layer of dust, sat the same plastic beige-colored touch tone phone that every house in his neighborhood had when he was growing up. The owner of the cabin was probably still paying the monthly fee for this phone to the local phone company.

Samantha wiped away the cobwebs that spread from the phone to the desk. This wasn't looking too promising. Someone who let a place go this far, probably forgot to pay the phone bill too.

Samantha picked up the phone, held it to her ear, and smiled. "We have a dial tone."

Chapter 52

Skyler's head hung low, his chin resting on his chest, as he slept uncomfortably in the hospital recovery room. Maintaining that he was Robert's nephew got him in the recovery room, in a chair, in the corner. He needed to be there when Robert woke up. He had to tell him everything that happened, including the loss of Samantha and Alex.

Robert had to be told about Umarov's plan to assassinate the Russian president and destabilize Eastern Europe. He would know how to proceed. He would know what to do to save the world. Skyler couldn't keep this information to himself, but there was nobody else he could tell.

Robert's cell phone vibrated in his pocket. He had collected it from the nurse upon his arrival.

It shouldn't be ringing. Robert was very careful who had direct access to him. The only other person who had this number, besides himself, was…

His heart jumped into his throat.

Could it be Omega?

It rumbled in his pocket again and he retrieved it. The display showed a number with a United States area code. He didn't know much about Omega, but he didn't think he, or she, was in the United States. He wasn't even sure if Omega was a single person or not.

So who could be calling this phone?

He looked toward Robert, half expecting him to be holding his hand out to take the phone, and its awesome responsibility, away from him. Robert lay peacefully on the bed, his eyes closed. The heart monitor beeped softly to indicate he was in a deep sleep.

The phone vibrated again in his hand. Nobody called this number unless it was important. He couldn't let it go unanswered.

He pushed the answer button and held the cell phone against his ear. "Hello?"

A voice he recognized all too well spoke excitedly through the tiny speaker on the phone. "Skyler?"

He gripped the phone tightly with whitening knuckles. "Samantha?"

Chapter 53

Samantha cupped her hand over the beige mouthpiece on the handset. "It's Skyler."

She returned her attention back to the voice on the other end of the line. "Where's Robert?"

The look on her face dropped and all she said was, "Oh."

It looked like he started to say more because she cut him off. "Don't say anything else. This line is not secure, but we need a way home. Can you arrange something?"

She listened for a moment and then looked at Melissa. "Is Portland the closest major airport?"

Melissa nodded and Samantha confirmed with Skyler on the phone.

"Yes. We have someone who can take us there."

At that comment, Melissa walked out of the cabin. Samantha motioned with her head for Alex to go after her.

He shrugged his shoulders and raised his hands in an "I don't know what to do" gesture. "What do I say?"

She cupped her hand over the receiver. "Say whatever you have to. Don't let her get away."

He rushed out the door and stopped at the edge of the porch. It was so smooth and comfortable under his battered feet. The rocky ground was... not. Rather than step down from the porch, he called out to her.

"Melissa, wait!"

She stopped, but did not turn around. "When I last went to Robert, he couldn't help me. But I still owed him for the first time."

She swiveled slowly in place to face him. "Considering

what it cost me to get you to a phone, tell Robert my debt has been paid."

She turned away.

He had to stop her.

"I'm sorry for what happened. But from what little I know, Robert is in the position to help you again. I'm sure he can get your life back."

She kept her back to him. "There is one thing I would like Robert to do for me."

"Whatever it is, I'm sure he'll do it."

"Tell him to change his phone number."

She moved swiftly and disappeared into the dense forest. He scanned the trees for any sign of movement. It was no use. She was gone.

Samantha was just hanging up the phone when he walked back inside. She looked past him out the door. "Where is she?"

"I couldn't stop her."

She shouldered past Alex and out the door, only to stop at the edge of the smooth wooden planks herself. After stepping on every sharp rock and broken branch to get here, she wasn't so eager to step off the porch again either.

He looked down at his socks and boxers, the only two items of clothing protecting him from the harsh realities of the world. At the very least, they needed footwear. But they also needed something a little more acceptable to wear in public than just their undergarments.

He left Samantha standing quietly on the edge of the porch and crept up the stairs. Maybe whoever abandoned the cabin, left some clothes behind.

Doors creaked on rusted hinges as he peeked into each room at the top of the stairs. The last room had a large hand-carved bed frame, but no mattress. If any of the rooms might still have clothes, it would be a bedroom.

He opened the closet and was rewarded with suits and dresses on hangers. On the floor, were a variety of shoes in both men's and women's styles.

"Jackpot."

Jackpot was an overstatement. The closet was a literal time capsule. As he pawed through the clothes hanging from the cracked wooden hangers, dust lifted from every crease and crevice in the coarse fabric. These must have been the clothes of somebody's grandma and grandpa. They weren't just old, they were antique.

He found a suit with a vest that would fit him okay.

He held up a couple of dresses in the faint light streaming in through the yellowed window. Picturing Samantha's body wasn't too hard, considering he'd seen most of it.

Next were the shoes. Being less of a judge of foot sizes, he grabbed a few pairs of women's shoes for Samantha to try.

As he came down the stairs, shoes and clothing in hand, Samantha walked inside the cabin, closing the door after her.

She looked up at Alex, a worried expression on her face.

"Skyler says he can have a private charter plane waiting for us in Portland that can get us to New York. Once there, he has a contact that can get us passports and credit cards so we can use a commercial airline to get back to London."

He tossed her what he had selected for her from the closet. "Okay. Portland. New York. London. My parole officer's going to have a conniption with all this travel."

She held up the dress in her hands. "What is this?"

He laid out his own dark brown suit on the back of a dusty chair. "I think we found the vacation home of the great Gatsby."

Ten minutes later, he stepped right out of 1930s Americana and onto the front porch. Samantha was right behind him, wearing a faded floral print dress and clunky brown shoes. Standing in front of the dilapidated cabin, they looked like Bonnie and Clyde, ready to wreak havoc on the hapless public.

He looked left, then right. "Which way to Portland?"

Chapter 54

In counterpoint to the faint beeping of Robert's heart monitor, Skyler's heart thumped rapidly in his chest. They were alive! They were both alive!

His elation shifted quickly to worry. He had to get them out of the United States. He had to help them stop whatever was going to happen in Moscow.

But he had destroyed the support structure they needed. Without access to the type of hardware and software he had burned when he sealed the underground vault, they were on their own.

He glanced over at Robert, sleeping peacefully in the hospital bed.

Robert always told him, when you failed to have access to the proper tools to do the job, improvise with what you had. Or find something else.

But before he could do that, he had to find them a plane to take them out of Portland and back into the game.

He looked at Robert's phone. This thing was useless in his hands, but it could do the impossible in Robert's.

He looked over at the frail man sleeping peacefully in the hospital bed.

He had to wake him.

He opened the door to the private room quietly and peeked down the corridor. There was activity down both directions, but nobody was close enough to hear anything coming out of the closed door of this room.

He shut the door and rushed over to the bed. He touched Robert gently on the shoulder and whispered quietly.

"Uncle Robert?"

He didn't stir.

Skyler frowned and lightly slapped him on the cheek.

"Uncle Robert."

Still nothing.

He scanned the room for something, anything, he could use to bring Robert out of his pharmaceutically induced nap. The carafe of water on the counter caught his eye. He poured some of the water into a cup and turned back to the bed.

He made eye contact with an awake Robert and froze.

Robert spoke with a raspy voice. "I hope you're weren't planning to throw that in my face."

Adrenaline coursed through Skyler's veins as his heart skipped a beat. "You're awake!"

Robert sat up uncomfortably on the bed, the tubes protruding from his nose making it difficult to move without them tugging at his nostrils.

"Of course I'm awake. You just got done slapping me awake. How about you help me for change and give me a drink of that water?"

Skyler rushed forward with the cup in his hand and held it to Robert's lips. He sipped it slowly and then settled back into the pillow.

"So, what's been going on?"

Skyler set the cup back on the counter. "You had a mini stroke…"

Robert cut him off. "Not about me. The operation. Did we get the cell phone?"

"No, sir."

"What are you doing here? Why aren't you monitoring the team?"

Skyler lowered his head. How was he going to tell Uncle Robert he had screwed everything up? If they failed this mission, it would be his fault. His fault for destroying the equipment the field agents needed to stay one step ahead of the enemy. His fault for leaving them stranded, and unsupported, in the middle of a mission.

Robert sat up, grunting from the pain of his recent surgery.

"Skyler? What are you not telling me?"

Skyler barely spoke about whisper. "I burned the equipment."

Robert squinted at him. "What did you say?"

He jerked his head up, tears welling up in his eyes. "I was just following protocol. Sam and Alex had been captured, tortured, and most likely..."

He couldn't bring himself to finish the sentence. Robert's eyes reflected understanding.

"I see. But I take it they aren't dead?"

He shook his head. "They just called a few minutes ago. I don't know how they escaped, but now I can't help them. And there's an imminent attack on the President of Russia."

Robert nodded. "Then I suggest you find some new equipment, and fast."

Skyler stood up and snapped to attention. "Yes, sir."

It was good to have Robert back in charge. He held out his cell phone to him.

"Sam and Alex are on their way to Portland and are going to need a plane to New York."

Robert took the phone and smiled. "I know just who to call."

Relief washed over every muscle in Skyler's body. "I knew you would, sir."

Chapter 55

In the middle of the thick Oregon forest, Madina crouched low, pointing the sniper rifle at the dilapidated cabin. She peered through the scope, alternating her view from one window to the next. After ten minutes, she was convinced the place was empty.

She circled the cabin and picked up two distinct trails that led in different directions. Two people had gone one way, and one person another. The most likely scenario? Her targets had stayed together, with the newcomer abandoning them. They probably pleaded with her to help them, but she hadn't felt safe after everything that happened and they went their separate ways.

Madina didn't blame her for her cowardice.

She circled back around to the front of the cabin and watched it for another ten minutes. It was definitely empty.

She left her rifle leaning against a tree and gripped her automatic pistol tightly in one hand as she approached the front door to the cabin.

The floorboards on the porch creaked as she glided across them. She inspected the door frame. No signs of forced entry, so she tried the door handle.

The door swung open, the hinges groaning their protest as she entered the dark interior of the cabin with her pistol on point.

It took less than five minutes to ascertain her targets had been there, made a phone call, and found new clothes.

She only had seven rounds left in her rifle and she was not adequately outfitted for a lengthy campaign on foot. Extraction, and reacquisition of her targets, was her best solution.

She pulled out her cell phone and sent a text to Umarov. Thirty seconds later, his reply left her with very little time to make it to the extraction point.

She opened the front door when the door frame splintered next to her head accompanied by the repeating echo of a gunshot.

She dove backward into the cabin and kicked the door shut with a foot. She scrambled on all fours over to the front window and angled up to peek through the bottom corner. The driver of the gold colored car had shot at her with her own rifle. The woman stepped out from behind a tree and called out, loud enough for her to hear.

"I see why you missed. Your rifle's not properly calibrated for a cold bore shot."

Madina yelled back, loud enough for the woman to hear through the dilapidated walls of the cabin. "What do you want? I'm sure we can work something out."

"Nice accent. Russian? No. Chechen. Yes, that's it. I'm right, aren't I? Now, what is somebody from Chechnya doing running around the back country of Oregon with a sniper rifle?"

Who was this woman?

She double checked the safety on her pistol and verified a bullet was chambered and ready.

The woman outside sure liked to talk a lot.

"And why did you try to kill me? I don't know anybody in Chechnya. Please, don't tell me I was collateral. In the wrong place at the wrong time. That would really piss me off."

She took another quick peak. The woman was leaning around the side of a tree, pointing the sniper rifle at the front door.

The woman was close enough that if she fired through the window, she would either hit her, or send her diving for cover behind the tree, right where Madina wanted her.

Madina popped up and fired three rounds. The first one shattered the window, while the second and third pierced the woman's shoulder, shredding her leather jacket. She went down behind the tree, the sniper rifle flying off to one side.

Madina knew when she had the advantage. And when you had the advantage, you pressed it to keep it. She opened the front door, trained her pistol on the same tree her victim had gone down behind, and stepped out of the cabin.

Movement flash in the corner of her eye.

She looked to her left in time to see the woman, not wearing her leather jacket, swing a thick tree branch at her head.

Chapter 56

After storming away from the cabin, Melissa had doubled back in her footsteps and climbed a tree with a clear view of the cabin.

And waited.

She made sure, when leading the other two to the remote cabin, to break plenty of branches and cut through plenty of bushes. She had left a trail even the least experienced tracker could follow.

Whoever shot at them was most likely following them to finish the job. She had made sure it was easy to follow them.

She sat silently in the tree when she watched Alex and Samantha leave the cabin in 80-year-old clothes. Not just clothes that were eighty years old, but clothes only an 80-year-old would wear. If they planned to go where there were other people, despite the funny looks they would get, it was still better than walking around in their underwear.

She had underestimated who was following them and almost yelped involuntarily when she suddenly noticed a woman with a sniper rifle crouched down behind the very same tree she was hiding in. She hadn't even heard her approach.

She watched the woman, while the woman watched the cabin.

She stayed perfectly still when the women circled around to the other side of the cabin and then slowly returned back to her tree.

When the woman finally made her move toward the cabin, Melissa almost laughed out loud when she watched her leave the rifle at the base of her tree.

Once the woman was inside, Melissa dropped silently from the tree and prepared her trap.

It would involve a missed shot, stuffing her leather jacket full of leaves and propping it against a tree, and balancing the rifle on sticks that matched the same color as the tree trunk.

Her plan had worked beautifully, and now the hunter lay unconscious at her feet.

She wasn't as interested in helping Robert's associates as much as she really didn't like getting shot at. When the sniper woke back up, she would have a nice heart-to-heart with her and determine if this was something personal, or if she had merely been caught up in something that did not concern her.

It was an added bonus that, holding the sniper prisoner for a while, gave Alex and Samantha the chance to make a clean getaway.

Chapter 57

Using the position of the sun to keep them headed in the same general direction, Alex and Samantha finally found the main road. Several times, as they traveled through the forest, they had to take a wide circular path to avoid the increased level of police activity and fire patrols that were dealing with the blaze set by Melissa's Firebird.

If the two of them were spotted walking around without a car this far from town, let alone wearing turn of the last century clothing and lacking any ID, they would immediately be detained. Any police officer worth his weight in salt would be a fool not to detain someone like that. And once in custody, they would quickly be identified as the couple from Boise wanted on burglary and assault charges.

They had to steer clear of anybody, and everybody, in a position of authority.

As they walked along the road, anytime they heard a car engine, they ducked into the woods and waited to see if it was a police car, a fire engine, or any other state or city vehicle. When it wasn't, by the time they made it back to the road, it was too late to flag the car down for a ride.

They needed to find a place where they could see farther down the road and that would give passing cars enough time to see them to and, hopefully, stop.

And they had to do it soon. There were only a few hours of daylight left and nobody would see them in the dark.

They finally found a place that gave them an extended view of the road in both directions. If they were going to find a way to hitchhike without being picked up by the authorities, this would be the place.

Alex crossed to the other side of the street from Samantha and hid amongst the trees. Nobody was going to stop for two people by the side of the road, especially if one of them was a six-foot tall male. But they might stop for a woman stranded all by herself on the side of the road.

She waved at two passing cars as they sped by, but only got a honk from one and nothing from the other. The sun was starting to set, and she needed to change her tactics.

After confirming the next car was not a police car, or any other emergency vehicle, she stepped out in the middle of the road, shoes in hand, and waved the car to a stop.

As the driver, a young college-aged boy, rolled down the passenger side window, she acted exhausted and beat, even though she really didn't have to act too much. She placed her arms on the edge of the door and leaned into the car.

"Thanks for stopping. My car broke down and it feels like I've been walking for hours."

"I guess I could give you a ride into town."

"How about a ride to Portland?"

"I'm sorry. I'm not going to Portland."

"You are now."

She motioned behind him. When he turned around, Alex tapped on the driver's side window with the gun and smiled.

Chapter 58

Melissa took full opportunity of the downtime while her captive, tied to the old rocking chair in the tiny living room of the cabin, slept off the blow to her head. She had meticulously field stripped the Dragunov sniper rifle and the woman's cell phone. Both lay in pieces, arranged on the floor in front of her. The pistol she had saved from the dismantling process subjected to its peers. It rested by her side, with a round in the chamber, should the women prove more difficult to subdue than she hoped. She didn't want to use it, but would if she had to.

She stared at the miscellaneous parts of the sniper rifle on the floor in front of her. None of them gave up much information as to who employed the sniper, or who she was after. The cell phone, however, had provided a little insight, if not generating its own flurry of questions, as to how connected the sniper's employer was.

Even though the phone was no bigger than the ones you could buy at any name-brand authorized dealer, it was a satellite phone masquerading as your average everyday touchscreen smartphone. Even after removing the battery, she wasn't convinced the phone was completely disabled. She noticed the SIM card was thicker than normal. Upon closer inspection, she quickly realized it had its own integrated battery, and most likely continued to transmit its GPS location to whoever cared to listen. There was only one person who had access to cutting-edge technology like that.

She ground the SIM card under the heel of her boot as she stared at the sniper, still unconscious in the rocking chair, and wondered if Hannah had sent her to kill one of the few people who knew that Hannah was alive and well, plying her trade to those with the deepest pockets.

It was time to find out.

She stuck a cup under the faucet in the kitchen sink. After a few coughs and sputters from the numerous air pockets that had settled in the unused water lines, the cup slowly filled with murky water. It really didn't matter about the quality of the water. She wasn't going to make her drink it. Just wake her up with it.

She could've woken her with some light slaps to the face, or even gently shaking her shoulder. But the psychological effect of having water thrown in your face, while tied to a chair, would quickly establish who was in charge.

She turned away from the sink, with the murky water in hand, and found herself staring into the dark eyes of the sniper.

The sniper regarded the glass in her hand. "Please don't tell me you were going to throw that disgusting sludge in my face."

She smiled. "The thought had crossed my mind."

The sniper struggled against the ropes that bound her tightly to the rocking chair. "Untie me right now."

"Or what?"

"I am not alone. The others I am with will find me."

She shook her head and snorted a small laugh.

"I already found the GPS unit built into the SIM card. Nobody knows where you are."

A small black object clipped the broken window pane, chipping off a piece of glass, as it tumbled into the living room after having been tossed by someone from outside the cabin. Melissa instinctively yelled, "Grenade!" and dove into the kitchen, covering her ears and squinting her eyes against the impending concussive blast.

Instead of exploding, the grenade emitted a series of melodic tones, like someone playing a quick tune on a wooden xylophone.

As the song repeated itself, she peeked around the edge of the couch and saw the military spec cell phone resting in the middle of the living room. She quickly glanced at the sniper, who was smiling. "That would be the others I was telling you about. If you want to live, I suggest you don't let that go to voicemail."

She crawled forward, staying low and snatched up the phone.

"Hello?"

The voice on the other end should not have taken her by surprise, but it did anyway.

"Why have you chosen to interfere?"

"Why did you send a sniper to kill me?"

There was a slight pause before Hannah replied. "That was not my intent."

"Don't tell me I was in the wrong place at the wrong time."

"I have every intention of waiting, however long it takes, for you to come back to me on your own."

"I just want to live my life in peace."

"It would appear fate has other plans for you."

She glanced over at the sniper, still tied to the chair. "What about you Hannah? What are your plans for me?"

"Send the woman out unharmed, and you and I will discuss this another time."

"And if I don't?"

"She's not one of mine, she belongs to a client. I'm

giving you as much leeway as I possibly can. But if you interfere with my business, I will have no choice but to deal harshly with you. And neither of us wants that."

"So, if I let her go, you will let me go."

"I believe that is the deal on the table."

"How do I know you won't send someone else after me?"

"I am the only reason you did not die in the middle of the jungle. I am the only reason you did not die at the bottom of a collapsed building. I gave you a new life, a new name, and a new face. I have too much invested in you to write you off. My only interest with you now is to give you the space and the time you need to decide to come back to me."

She closed her eyes and pressed the phone to her ear. Her mind raced through the possibilities of where she could go to be beyond Hannah's reach.

Nothing came to mind.

It was nearly a minute before Hannah spoke again. "Melissa?"

She stood up and strode toward the sniper, snatching a knife off the dining room table. "Tell your men outside to stand down. She's coming out."

Chapter 59

Madina dabbed a dirty towel against her split lip. The wound opened from the pressure and blood seeped out again as she inspected her swollen face in tiny cabin's dingy bathroom mirror. The red puffy line across her face was a perfect representation of the tree branch the woman had used to subdue her.

The rotor wash from the helicopter sent to collect her kicked up leaves and dust, and blew them through the shattered windows of the abandoned cabin.

The woman still held her own pistol pointed at her. "I believe your ride's here."

She stared hard at the woman. "This is not over, between us."

The woman smirked. "You started it. Just be glad I didn't finish it, or we wouldn't be having this conversation."

She tossed the dirty rag on the floor at her feet and walked out of the cabin with her head held high. There was no way she was going to let her prey see her as weak.

And she was her prey.

Madina was not done hunting.

She walked out the front door and up to the nylon rope that dangled from the helicopter hovering overhead. This was her originally planned exfiltration method, so she already had the appropriate harness integrated into her tactical suit. She clipped herself to the nylon rope and let it draw her up through the air toward the helicopter.

She watched her prey recede back into the cabin just as the motorized pulley jerked to a stop and she placed a foot into the open doorway of the helicopter.

She unclipped herself from the rope and forced her way to the cockpit.

Pointing out the front windshield, she hollered over the noise of the twin rotors. "Destroy that cabin immediately."

The pilot looked sideways at her with a shocked expression on his face. "My orders are to…"

She reached past him, flipping several switches on the control panel with one hand, while grabbing the flight stick with the other. Before the pilot even had time to react, she tilted the helicopter forward just enough for the targeting systems to engage and pulled the trigger. Several missiles shot from the pods mounted on both sides of the helicopter.

The decades-old cabin never stood a chance. It disappeared in a ball of fire while black smoke rolled upward into the sky. The high-yield explosives evaporated the dilapidated wood, reducing it to splinters that rained back down into the forest, hundreds of feet in every direction.

The soldiers that had taken up strategic positions around the cabin picked themselves up as their angered insults burst through the static of the helicopter's comm system. She snatched a spare pair of headphones from the hook where they hung along the cockpit ceiling and spoke rapidly into the mic.

"Search the debris for her body."

As more insults came across the comm, she pressed the talk override button. "A ten thousand dollar bonus to the first one with proof that the woman inside the cabin is dead."

The comm quickly fell silent. Peering out the front windshield, she saw several soldiers already rushing in to the still burning crater where the cabin used to be.

She placed the headphones properly on her head and leaned in to the communications officer. "Patch me through to Umarov. On my headset only."

"Yes ma'am!"

The officer focused on his equipment, glad to be given something to do while she was in another one of her moods.

She had taken great care to foster the belief that she was unstable and unpredictable. But she was exactly the opposite. Everything she did, she did for a purpose. Umarov taught her that.

While she waited to be connected, she looked out the window at the soldiers as they picked their way through the debris. Their haphazard search was disorganized, one of the unfortunate results of hastily hiring mercenaries who had never worked with each other before. This group of hired soldiers had been thrown together and did the best they could to form a cohesive group less than an hour after meeting each other for the first time. But the mixture of men and women that made up the new group all shared one thing in common; the desire for a free Chechnya.

One of the female merc's voice broke through the open comm static and drew Madina's attention to where she was clearing debris away from a square hole in the ground.

"This is Karina. I've located an underground passage."

Madina leaned forward and peered out the front windshield of the helicopter. "Have you found the body?"

"No ma'am. She may have escaped through this tunnel."

"Go down and check."

The mercenary looked up at the helicopter. "Yes ma'am."

Chapter 60

Down on the ground, surrounded by smoldering debris, Karina caught the eye of another mercenary. They all wore the same uniform, complete with helmet, goggles, and balaclava that hid their features. The only way to tell the men from the women were the broader shoulders of the men.

She called over to the male mercenary closest to her. "You stand guard while I check the tunnel."

He stepped carefully through the still burning debris. "What's in it for me?"

"If I find the body, I'll split the bounty with you fifty-fifty."

"Sixty-forty."

"I'll find someone else."

"Okay, fifty-fifty. You go. I'll watch."

She took several steps down into the darkened tunnel and switched on the light mounted to the side of her AK-104 carbine with attached sound suppressor. The smoke was thick, and her light barely penetrated the haze beyond several feet in front of her. Fortunately, the tunnel was only three feet wide with smooth dirt walls on either side. There would be no place for the woman to hide if she was down here.

She pressed the talk button on her comm unit. "This is Karina, I'm going in."

Her comm hissed with static, but there was no response from anyone. She pushed the button again.

"This is Karina, can anyone hear me?"

Static was the only reply. She slowly backed out of the

tunnel to the bottom of the stairs carved into the packed dirt. She pushed her comm button again.

"This is Karina, does anyone read?"

Madina's voice cut through the hiss of static. "This is Madina. Did you find the body?"

"Not yet ma'am. The tunnel seems to be interfering with the comm unit. I had to return to the entrance to be able to communicate."

"Stop wasting my time soldier! Get down there and find her!"

"Yes ma'am."

Karina pressed the AK-104 carbine's polymer butt stock into her shoulder as she walked in a half-crouch deeper into the dark and smoky tunnel. The tunnel was tall enough that she could stand without a problem, but crouching slightly steadied her rifle and quieted her footsteps.

Up ahead, she thought she heard a noise and switched off the flashlight, letting the darkness expand around her.

In the blackness, her other senses heightened. She turned her head to one side and listened intently. The sole of a shoe scraped against the dirt floor just a few feet in front of her. She sighted her rifle blindly in the direction of the sound, and fired.

Mikhail stood at the edge of the underground tunnel Karina had disappeared down fifteen minutes before. Smoke had started to billow out of the opening several minutes ago, and then dissipated as quickly as it had started.

He heard scuffling sounds coming from the inky blackness and pointed his own AK-104, with attached sound suppressor, into the opening.

And waited.

The scuffling resolved into the sound of something big and heavy being dragged. A dark shape materialized through the smoke and he tightened his grip on the carbine.

As soon as the dark shape reached the bottom of the stairs, he recognized the black uniform they all wore. Karina had her back to him, and was dragging something out of the tunnel.

She craned her neck around and looked up at him.

"Are you going to help me, or do I keep the whole bounty for myself?"

Madina disconnected from her call with Umarov and rappelled down the rope out of the helicopter. She landed softly in the small clearing, just south of where the old cabin used to stand. The rotor wash from the helicopter bent the dry grass into a flat circle all around her.

She approached the two mercenaries who had found her prey. She bent down over the body between them and inspected it closely. The face was badly burned and missing the lower half of the jaw. The clothing was also badly burned.

She stood back up and inspected the two mercenaries. With their identical uniforms, helmets, goggles, and balaclava, the only way to know who they were was the name badge sewn over the front left pocket of their tactical vest.

"Is this the condition you found the body?"

Karina was the first to respond. "No ma'am. She was apparently about to throw some form of accelerant on me when I shot her. She fell backward and lit herself on fire instead. I did the best I could to get the fire out as quickly as possible, knowing you would want proof."

Madina bent down and stared at the charred corpse. "There's not much of her left."

Mikhail spoke up. "Do we still get the reward?"

That was the problem with mercenaries. You hoped and prayed that they believed in the same ideals you did. But in the end, they were still hired guns willing to put their lives on the line for money.

She couldn't blame them, and let out an exasperated breath.

"Yes. You get the reward."

Madina unsheathed her combat blade and, with a single motion, chopped off the hand of the dead woman. She stood and tossed the hand to a soldier standing near her.

"Run the fingerprints through every database on the network. I want to know who this woman was."

The soldier fumbled the hand as he tried to catch it. He looked relieved when he got it under control without dropping it. "Yes ma'am."

She took a big breath and recomposed herself. "We've wasted enough time on this diversion. Gather your men…"

Karina interrupted her with a sharp clearing of her throat. Madina acknowledged her with a slight nod of her head. "And women. We still have a mission to complete."

Karina stepped forward. "What's the mission?"

Madina smiled. "An associate of our employer was just hired to pilot a private charter out of Portland. We have a plane to catch."

Chapter 61

Gripping the steering wheel, Samantha sped the gray sedan past the sign showing that the Portland International Airport was the next exit. Alex sat in the back seat with the owner of the sedan while she drove them to the plane Skyler had promised would be waiting for them. They would be meeting the private jet by the charter hanger, thereby avoiding the necessity of proper identification required in the main terminal, of which neither of them had.

It had become clear, early on in their impromptu road trip, that the driver would be giving them no trouble. Especially after Alex had let slip that they were secret agents on a mission. It turned out, the driver was a big fan of James Bond and was more than eager to help in their cloak and dagger activities. In fact, he had been offering them hundreds of hostage disposition suggestions the entire time, and insisted they call him Nate, now that they were friends.

"You could handcuff my hands together around the steering wheel and leave me the key on the dashboard. The time it would take me to reach the key with my foot would give you plenty of time to escape."

Alex pinched his nose. "I told you kid," he said through gritted teeth. "We don't have any handcuffs."

"Oh, right, right."

Nate frowned, lost in thought. Suddenly his finger shot up to point at the roof.

"I've got it! You could lock me in the trunk, and then make an anonymous call right before getting on the plane. By the time they found me, you'd be long gone."

Samantha offered her response from the front. "There's

an emergency release switch in the boot of every car these days."

Nate shook his head and laughed. "You guys think of everything."

Alex placed his hand on the kid's shoulder. "Tell you what. Why don't you just drop us off at the airport and go back to whatever it was you were doing. In fact, if you give us your address, we'll send you money for gas."

Nate's face brightened. "That sounds awesome."

He dug through the debris on the back floor of his messy car, produced a ballpoint pen and scrap of paper, and began scribbling on it.

"Here's my address, phone number, and email. If you guys ever need anything, anything at all, you let me know."

Alex took the paper from him and inspected it, his eyes bulging in surprise. "Wait a minute. You live in Boise, Idaho?"

"Yeah, with my grandma."

"What were you doing in Oregon?"

Nate shrugged his shoulders. "Visiting my cousin in Bend. You caught me on my way home."

A wrinkle in their hastily thought out plan developed in the back of Samantha's mind. "Is there going to be a problem with you getting home late?"

"Nah. I'll just tell her I got tired and pulled over to take a nap."

"And she'll believe that?"

"Look, even if I told her I'd been kidnapped by spies and dragged halfway across Oregon to help them escape, all that she'd say was, 'That's nice dear,' and bake me some chocolate chip cookies. Yeah, she won't be a problem."

Samantha steered the car onto the exit and followed the

signs to the private charter hanger.

A private jet sat on the tarmac. An older man, dressed in a pilot's uniform, stood near it and watched them approach. She stopped the car twenty feet from the plane, but left the engine idling. She got out as the man approached, and as he got closer, he smiled. "You Samantha?"

She returned his warm smile. "Yes."

He jabbed a thumb over his shoulder at the plane sitting on the tarmac. "She's fueled up and ready to go whenever you are."

Alex opened the back door and joined in on the conversation. "How long until we get to New York?"

"I'm not taking you to New York. We'll have one refueling stop in Maine, and then it's off to the U.K. for your debriefing, courtesy of the extended range of the Citation Sovereign private jet."

Samantha's heart skipped a beat. How much did this pilot know about them?

The pilot saw the look on her face and gave her a wink. "Robert and I go way back to another time; another era. We keep very few secrets from each other."

Alex squinted his eyes at the plane. "You wouldn't happen to have any food on that thing would you?"

The pilot smiled. "I was told the two of you had a rough day, so I made sure to stock the fridge."

Alex pointed at the pilot with a huge grin on his face. "You sir, are my hero."

Nate climbed between the front seats and settled in behind the steering wheel. He looked up at Samantha with his hand on the open door. "I really mean it. If you're ever in the neighborhood again and you need anything, Alex has my info."

She smiled at him. "Thanks. We'll send you money for gas, I promise."

He shook his head. "Don't worry about it. I'll just turn it in as a business expense."

"What business are you in?"

He gave her a half smile. "It's better you don't know."

He shut the door and reversed the gray sedan across the tarmac, away from the plane.

Alex was already headed up the stairs built into the lowered door when he paused and called out to her. "Shouldn't we get going?"

He disappeared into the plane, and she rushed up the steps after him. "What's your hurry? We're going to make it to London ahead of schedule and…"

The rest of her words caught in her throat as she stared down the barrels of two assault rifles pointed at her. A third black-clad soldier held an assault rifle pointed at Alex, who was already seated at the back of the small plane.

The soldier closest to her lowered his assault rifle and grabbed her roughly by the shoulder. He forced her down the aisle and shoved her into the seat next to Alex.

As soon as she was buckled in, he pressed against the throat mic around his neck and spoke in his guttural Russian accent. "This is Mikhail. The packages are secure."

Chapter 62

Skyler sat in a pub overlooking the Thames, the longest river in England that also cut right through central London. In the distance, from the vantage point of his table in the corner of the pub, he could see Vauxhall Cross, the headquarters of Britain's Secret Intelligence Service MI6 division. He was able to see the street in front of the pub through the windows, and keep an eye on both the front and kitchen doors from his table.

He wasn't usually this paranoid when selecting a place to sit in public, but this time was different. This time, he was waiting for someone to deliver a counterfeit badge to gain access to MI6. While he was still technically an employee with MI6, he was also technically on administrative leave, while on loan to Uncle Robert. His official cover was that he was helping optimize the secured virtual network for a division within the United Nations. As such, his security badge had been lowered to grant access only to the public space at MI6 headquarters.

He could effectively get into the lobby, but could go no farther. Not without higher clearance.

And so, with one leg bouncing up and down rapidly under the table, he waited for that badge. He'd been sitting there for so long, the head on his ale had dissipated. It didn't matter. He had no intention of drinking right before breaking in to one of the most secure areas in the British government. He needed to be at one hundred percent capacity of his brain function if he planned to pull this off. And he was such a lightweight, a couple of sips would be enough to put the entire operation at risk, even if he didn't have multiple doses of painkillers swimming through his bloodstream right now. If he got caught, Robert would disavow any knowledge of his actions. Robert would, most likely, deny ever knowing him at all. He didn't want to get caught, so the ale sat, untouched, on the table.

He watched the main entrance to the pub, periodically glancing at the kitchen door to keep anyone from sneaking up on him from that direction. He had been diligent in maintaining awareness of his surroundings, so it surprised him when someone sat down at his table.

The man had short dark hair, and the perpetual five o'clock shadow that had become increasingly popular for spies in Hollywood action movies. The man looked at Skyler's untouched ale before snatching up and raising it to his lips. "It'd be a shame to let a good ale go to waste."

He didn't look, or act, like someone from MI6. And his Midwestern American accent confirmed it before he downed half the glass of ale in one go.

In a state of shock, Skyler stammered out, "I'm sorry, I'm saving this seat for someone."

The American winked at him. "With how long you've been sitting here, I believe you've been stood up."

"What makes you say that?"

"The head on your ale was nearly gone. You also spent a lot of time watching the front door with an occasional glance toward the kitchen. Since there's only two ways in to this pub, the front door and the loading dock in the back, that tells me you are waiting for someone. But you're not sure which way your companion will choose. And who, in their right mind, would enter a pub through the kitchen unless they were coming here for something other than a stout ale?"

The man raised the glass to his lips again. "And who orders a pint of Britain's finest without drinking it?"

Could it be that he had been compromised? Robert said he would contact someone to get him into MI6. But how had this brutish American found out about it? And what had he done with Robert's contact?

The American finished the drink and smacked the empty glass on the table.

"Name's Jake. I work for the Agency, with the occasional freelance on the side."

Jake laughed loudly as if Skyler had just said something funny. At that same moment, something bumped up against his leg under the table, the scuffing sound it made as it was pushed across the floor by the man's foot was masked by his outburst of laughter. Jake leaned in close and continued talking as if they were mates having a drink in the local pub, and nothing more.

"In the bag is everything you need to get into MI6. There's an access card that will let you into every room in the building, even the Dungeon, and a small case with contact lenses to get you past the retinal scanners. There's also a ceramic gun with integrated silencer and caseless subsonic rubber bullets, the nonlethal kind, just in case you need it. There's not a single metal piece anywhere in the gun, it won't be detected as you enter the building."

This was the man Robert had sent after all, but all he needed was to gain access to the server rooms in the basement. He wasn't going to shoot anyone.

"I won't need the gun."

"Never say never, my boy. Do you know how to shoot?"

"I was third in my class on the range."

"Then definitely take it. But when this is all over, I will

need that back. The CIA doesn't even know the Glass Gun prototype is missing. I'd like to return it before anyone notices. Even if they do, they won't create much of a public stink about it, since this thing doesn't officially exist. But all the same, I'd rather not draw undue attention to myself."

Jake glanced around the pub before looking him square in the eyes. "You have about twenty-four hours before they start looking for the guy whose security badge you have. I suggest you get whatever it is you need, and get out of there as fast as possible."

"I'm not…"

Jake held up a hand. "I don't want to know what you're up to. I was asked to give you a way in along with a weapon you could sneak past security, and I did. That's as far as my involvement goes. Good luck kid."

Jake stood and quickly disappeared through the door leading to the kitchen. Skyler had expected someone from MI6 to help. Why had Robert contacted the CIA for this? Had he already tried someone within British Intelligence and was turned down? Or did he go directly to an outside source knowing that, what they were about to do, would never be condoned by the British government or the Crown?

He reached under the table and grabbed the bag.

He needed to get inside MI6 and reestablish contact with Samantha.

And he had to do it sooner, rather than later.

Chapter 63

One hour later, Skyler stood across the street from Vauxhall Cross. He wiped his sweaty palms on the silk slacks of his £3,000 suit, the camouflage necessary to look like he belonged at Britain's premier intelligence hub. He'd already hacked the building security database to show his picture on the guard's monitor when he swiped the stolen security badge at the entrance. Unless the guard knew Arthur Wells personally, he would get through without a problem.

The CIA's Glass Gun was nestled into the small of his back, held in place by medical tape, and his eyes blinked from the intrusion of the contact lenses that would get him through the retinal scanner.

He would've been here sooner, but he had to make a quick stop at the local chemist to get contact lens wetting solution to soothe his perpetually drying eyes.

He tilted his head back and flooded both eyes with solution again. It ran down the sides of his face, making him look more like he'd been crying rather than relieving the discomfort that seemed to be getting worse, not better. Once inside, he would yank those suckers off of his eyes. There was no way he could work like this. All he had to do was get through security. And he had to do it before he could no longer see.

He pocketed the now half-empty bottle of solution and headed for the entrance, his eyes blinking rapidly.

He pushed his way through the front doors and smiled as he approached the security clearance area just inside the entrance. He tried not to look as uncomfortable as he felt.

The security guard gave him a cursory glance and silently indicated the plastic tray on the table next to the metal detector. Skyler emptied his pockets, placing his keys, wallet, tiny bottle of rewetting solution, and BlackBerry cell phone into the small plastic tray. He paused in front of the metal detector. The guard slid the tray across the table to his side and scanned the contents with his eyes before waving Skyler forward through the metal detector.

Skyler held his breath and stepped forward.

The metal detector buzzed loudly and the green lights on both sides flashed to red.

The guard quickly held up a hand, stopping him in the middle of the metal detection unit. "Step back please."

Skyler stepped back, and the unit reset itself. His heart pounded in his ears and both his mouth and his eyes went dry. He could still talk with a dry mouth, but every time he blinked, the contact lenses shifted slightly, threatening to pop out on their own.

The guard looked in the small plastic tray again and then looked back up at him. "Your badge."

Skyler swallowed dryly. "Excuse me?"

"You forgot to set your badge in the tray."

Of course. The electronics in the badge would be enough to set off the magnetometer in the metal detector. He unclipped the security badge from his front jacket pocket and placed it in the tray the guard had slid back over for him.

The guard waved him through the metal detector again.

This time, the lights stayed green.

The guard removed each item from the plastic tray and handed them to him one at a time, pausing at the cell phone. The guard pressed the power button several times on the

BlackBerry.

"Your phone won't turn on."

The contact lenses felt like they were two inches thick. He blinked several times, trying to force his body's natural tears to bring relief to his eyes. But no relief came. He didn't need to be delayed because a cell phone wouldn't turn on.

"My battery died. The charger's in my office."

The guard shrugged and held out the dead cell phone to him without further comment. Skyler forced himself to not blink too much as he smiled at the guard and took the phone, shoving it back into his pocket to join his wallet and keys, as he made his way to the second security checkpoint.

He resisted the urge to flood his eyes with the rest of the rewetting solution. He did not want to get caught wearing contact lenses with someone else's retinal pattern printed on them. He would just have to suffer through the pain until he was past security.

He willed himself to blink less as he approached the checkpoint.

He swiped the security badge for the reader and the guard's station monitor beeped. The guard glanced at the monitor and then back to him as he swung out the retinal scanner. "Welcome back, Mr. Wells."

Skyler leaned forward into the retinal scanner and blinked. He thought he felt the contact lens shift slightly just as the red scanning light swept across his eye.

The scanner emitted a double tone, indicating failure.

The guard pressed a finger against his touchscreen monitor. "Please try again."

Skyler blinked rapidly a couple more times, but the contact refused to shift back to the center of his eye. If the contact shifted too far, the system would read his own retina, and would not only fail to match the badge he had used, it would show an employee on temporary leave, trying to gain access with a stolen badge. It would get worse when they discovered the retinal printed contact lenses in his eyes and the ceramic gun taped to the small of his back.

He had to do something to get that contact lens centered.

The red light of the scanner swept across his cornea and emitted the double tone again.

He could feel sweat forming along his brow.

The guard swung back the scanner and produced a soft cloth. He proceeded to wipe the lens of the scanner. "Sorry about this Mr. Wells. We've been having problems with the scanner for about a month."

With the guard distracted, Skyler closed his eye and pressed on his eyelid with a finger, forcing the contact lens back into position.

The guard swung the retina scanner back. "Okay, try it now."

Skyler blinked again and the contact finally settled.

Leaning forward, he let the low-powered micro laser sweep across his eye. The scanner emitted a single beep and the magnetic lock on the gate disengaged with a clunk.

He was in.

Chapter 64

Skyler decided quickly that his first stop inside the building was the restroom. He had to get those infernal curved discs out of his eyes.

Prior to entering the building, his biggest fear was running into someone who knew who he really was. Now, his biggest fear was drawing attention to himself, no matter who somebody thought he was.

His eyes blinked rapidly as he made his way down the hall to the bathrooms at the other end. Just as he reached the alcove that would take him to the entrance to both the men's and women's bathroom doors, he was stopped short by a woman in a custodial outfit placing a yellow wet floor sign in the middle of the alcove.

She looked up at him and smiled. "Sorry love, it'll be about ten minutes."

He blinked at her in surprise, which was the worst thing he could have done. One of the lenses popped right out of his eye. His emotions ran the full gamut in a half second between relief for that one eye to abject terror should someone else discover the contact lens.

He immediately dropped to his knees and started sweeping his hand across the floor.

The custodian gaped at him in surprise. "Are you all right sir?"

He responded without looking up, devoting his full attention to the floor around him. "Yes. Just lost my contact lens."

"Oh dear," she exclaimed and dropped to her hands and knees. She began scanning the floor in front of her. "Let me help you."

He couldn't let her find the contact lens. "No. No. That's okay. I can find it on my own."

She continued sweeping her eyes across the floor. "No worries. My sister loses hers all the time. I've gotten quite good at... here it is."

She let out an audible gasp. "It looks shattered."

He scrambled over and scooped it up before she could inspect it further.

A confused expression formed on her face. "How did it shatter?"

He tried to smile reassuringly, but it probably looked more like he was trying too hard. "These are special lenses. When they dry out, a pattern forms on the surface so I can find it more easily. I paid extra for that. I guess it works."

He stood up quickly. "I've got to get to the other bathrooms before it dries out even more."

The custodian stood up just as quickly. "Go ahead and use this one. I'll wait."

He thanked her and pushed his way into the bathroom. He was thankful to be out of sight and, because of the yellow cone outside, no one would be interrupting him while he removed the other one.

Easier said than done. The first contact lens had popped out of its own accord, but the other one was shifting around his eyeball, unwilling to come out.

He stared closely at himself in the mirror again as he tried to pinch and grab the contact lens, his eye turning redder with each failed attempt.

The custodian's voice echoed through the closed door. "Is everything alright in there?"

His fingertips snagged the lens and peeled it off of his

eye. The same relief his eye felt washed over his entire body. He let out a long breath. "I'll be right out."

He rinsed his face off in the sink and used the mirror to make himself look a little more presentable. His one eye was red and puffy, like he'd been out drinking all night. There wasn't much he could do about that.

He walked briskly out of the bathroom, nodding at the custodian and thanking her for her patience, and headed for the elevator.

He was glad to be the only one waiting at the elevator bank, and even more so when the first set of doors to chime opened to reveal an empty car. He slipped in and pushed the button for the lower basement.

From down the hallway he heard a deep male voice, "Hold the elevator, please."

He pressed the force-close button rapidly in succession like it was a button on an 80's arcade video game cabinet.

He heard the heavy footsteps of the man break into a run as the doors began to close. Whoever it was, he was determined to make this elevator as he called out again, "Hold the doors!"

The running man reached the elevator just as the doors snapped shut. Skyler heard muffled curses as the elevator dropped away from the main floor.

That was too close for comfort. He could feel himself sweating through the armpits of his £800 shirt. He was a tech guy. He did not have the personality to handle the job of a field operative. As it was now, he was about ready to faint. And he hadn't even come across any real opposition getting inside the building. Just the minor, everyday issues that plagued someone on their way in to another day at the office.

His stomach flipped as the elevator stopped abruptly. The doors opened to reveal the concrete hallway of the lower basement, the location of the secured network room. The room everyone called the Dungeon. From the Dungeon, he would be able to regain all the capabilities he had before he burned his equipment when he thought he'd lost Samantha.

The hum of air-conditioning vibrated through every cell of his body as he got closer to the server room.

He swiped the stolen security badge and the lock clicked open.

He slipped inside and the door automatically relocked. He made his way past rows of servers that went from floor to ceiling and stretched all the way from front to back of the gymnasium sized room. The special room he wanted was located dead center in the massive server room and had its own security access level restrictions. Access that Arthur Wells, and only eleven other people in MI6, had.

Arthur Wells was one of the Digital Dozen. A select group of computer espionage professionals who had access to the one-of-a-kind computer system that could destabilize entire nations with a few keystrokes.

When he was still active at MI6, Skyler had submitted his transfer request into the Digital Dozen when a position had opened up. He recalled, with a sense of irony, he had lost his bid for inclusion into the exclusive MI6 hackers group by a fraction of a point.

The person he had lost to?

Arthur Wells.

And right now, he had Arthur's security badge; courtesy of a CIA agent who seemed to have no problem freelancing for Uncle Robert and handing it over to some kid he just met in a pub. He wondered if, had he gotten the job instead of being recruited into the Peacekeepers X-Alpha program, would it be his badge being used right now?

He made his way through the maze of servers and arrived in the center of the room. Before him stood the circular titanium-walled office that was set apart from the rest of the equipment in the center of the server room. To protect its state-of-the-art equipment, the room could be sealed off from the outside world, creating a nearly impenetrable fortress to protect the unique systems inside.

England was famous for its dungeons. But the one it should have been most famous for, was the one that no one knew about, save for a select few. Just about everyone outside of MI6 whispered rumors of the Dungeon to each other, but less than one percent of the public knew that such a place actually existed.

What looked like a ten-foot tall circular room in the middle of the larger server room was actually a fifty-foot tall silo. The foot-thick titanium walls continued down another forty feet, protecting the sensitive equipment and connections to the outside world.

The Digital Dozen could perform their electronic miracles inside the Dungeon without concern for interference from the outside world, even if that intrusion was a nuclear bomb dropped onto Vauxhall Cross.

Even though twelve people had continual access to this room, he knew they rarely used it. It was the digital equivalent of a bomb shelter, to be used during a major cyber-attack that crippled the rest of the United Kingdom. Its connections were hard-lined directly to the subsea fiber-optic cables that stretched along the bottom of the ocean toward Europe and the Americas. The communications system in the tiny, circular, room also maintained permanent uplink connections with satellites all around the globe. The only way to cut the Digital Dozen's access to the outside world, was to eliminate the outside world.

Skyler was but a single card swipe away from gaining access to this very special room.

He crossed the open space that surrounded the building, noting the eight concentric circles of polished brass embedded in the concrete floor around the building in the center. The cylindrical shaped building had the number nine etched in the titanium above the only door.

So the rumors were true.

This room had been designated as the ninth circle of Hell. The Hell of treachery and traitors.

Stamped into the metal, just below the number, was the modification of the phrase seen by those entering the gates of Hell as envisioned by Dante Alighieri in his epic poem, Divine Comedy. But instead of being a warning, it was a commandment to everyone who stood before this door.

"Restore all hope, ye who enter here."

This room was designed to protect Britain's interests all over the world from every kind of digital treachery. Skyler had to remind himself that he was not being a traitor to Queen and Country as he swiped the stolen badge across the card reader that would give him access to one of the seven great world powers' digital version of a genie in a bottle.

Inside this room, your wish, any wish within the digital realm, was its command.

There was a faint click from the door's locking mechanism right before the door rotated silently around inside the wall, in its own concentric circle, until it revealed the opening.

Skyler had just stepped across the threshold when a voice echoed out to him from what should have been an empty room.

"Hello?"

Skyler reached behind him, tugging up the tails on his expensive silk shirt, and exposed the gun taped to his back.

It looked like he would be needing it after all.

Chapter 65

Skyler slipped the gun quietly out of the impromptu holster that was hastily formed out of medical tape on his back. He held the gun behind his leg, out of sight from the direction of footsteps echoing behind another row of servers in the room, and put on his warmest smile as someone came into view, talking as he approached.

"It's about time Elise, we've been…"

The man froze and gawked at Skyler.

"Who are you?"

There wasn't supposed to be anyone in this room, so he never thought of a suitable cover beforehand.

"I, uh…"

The man noticed Skyler's arm tucked behind him, hiding something, and immediately reacted by spinning around, breaking into a full run, and disappearing back around the row of servers.

Shit!

He took off after the man, gun raised.

He ran to the edge of the server stack and peeked quickly around the corner. The man was sitting at the main workstation console, furiously typing.

He was locking down the workstation.

If he was able to finish, Skyler's entire trip into MI6 would be wasted.

Skyler came around the corner, pointing the ceramic pistol at the man's back. "Move away or I'll shoot."

The man ignored him and continued typing furiously. He couldn't let the man finish. He squeezed the trigger, and the silenced pistol spat like an angry cat.

The rubber bullet caught the man square between the shoulder blades, its kinetic force shoving him face first into the console. His head connected with a wet smack against the edge of the monitor and he slid sideways across the counter before falling to the floor.

Skyler held the gun on the still form of the man as he approached the workstation and scanned the monitor for signs he had finished his task. The screen still showed the beginning of his attempt to lock the workstation. But the end of the command string was a garbled mess of random characters where his hands had swiped erratically across the keyboard when he collapsed to the floor.

The workstation was still open, and all its magical capabilities were fully accessible. He leaned down and held two fingers against the side of the man's neck.

Skyler breathed a sigh of relief. His pulse was strong.

He had gained access to the room that would reconnect him with Samantha, and he had done it without killing anyone.

He sat in the chair and began deleting the commands the man had typed in, but thankfully, never finished.

A woman's voice from behind startled him. "Basil? You left the door open again."

He grabbed the pistol off the desk and spun around, pointing it at her. Her eyes zeroed in on it and she drew in a sharp breath of surprise.

It was then Skyler realized that when the man spoke moments earlier, he had said "we". The very room he had expected to be empty was filled with an unknown number of MI6 operatives. He stood up from the chair, keeping the gun pointed at her.

"How many more employees are down here?"

A moan at his feet drew her eyes away from the gun. When she saw her colleague sprawled on the floor, she dropped the cardboard tray of Starbucks coffees she was carrying and bolted.

He called after her. "Stop!"

She didn't.

He fired, but the rubber bullet bounced off the corner of a server rack as she disappeared behind it. By the time he rounded the same corner, she was already out the door. By the time he reached the door, she had disappeared amongst the server racks.

It was useless to follow her. The massive server farm outside the short circular building was a veritable maze. A maze she was most likely familiar with.

Besides, there was still a third employee hiding somewhere in this room. There had been three cups tucked into the holders of the little cardboard tray she had dropped, and most people ordered a larger cup before buying a second coffee.

He knew breaking into MI6 wasn't going to be easy, but it wasn't supposed to be this hard.

The faint hissing sound of someone whispering perked his ears. He inched quietly along the edge of the server rack and peeked around it. The third employee was crouched over the first man he'd already shot.

The whispering was a little more pronounced, now that he was closer. "Basil. Basil, get up."

Basil rolled on the ground at the other man's feet, unable to respond beyond a faint moaning sound. He was suffering from whiplash, and blunt tissue damage to his back and forehead. He wasn't going to be getting up anytime soon without help.

Skyler stepped out into the open, his pistol pointed at the man. "Don't move."

The man's head snapped over to look at him, and he froze.

Skyler motioned to Basil with the pistol. "If you can get him to his feet, I'll let you both walk out of here."

The man hesitated.

Skyler lowered the pistol. "I don't want to hurt anyone. In fact, I thought this place would be empty."

The man shook his head slightly. "It's rare that there's any less than two employees in this room at any given time."

Skyler shrugged. "Huh. I guess things have changed since I left."

The man's brow furrowed. "Who are you?"

"Doesn't matter. If you want to get out, you have to go before…"

Alarm klaxons sounded, cutting him off. The lights dimmed and switched to a strobing red color.

Between the sounds of the pulsating alarm, he heard the sound of the main door rotating within the walls. He turned around, just in time to see the entry to the circular room seal up.

Bollocks!

Now he had hostages.

He turned back, just as the third employee tackled him, knocking the gun from his grip and slamming him to the ground. The gun skittered across the floor as they wrestled with each other.

Skyler was a tech geek, not a ground level combat fighter. Fortunately, the same was true of his opponent.

They grappled awkwardly on the floor, neither getting the upper hand on the other. Skyler's problem was, he did not want to kill anyone, let alone an MI6 operative. But when the employee got an arm around his neck and squeezed, it appeared he didn't have the same reservations.

If Skyler wanted to win, he would have to make the tough decisions. Even if that meant killing one of the good guys.

He had to think of the greater good and couldn't let his loyalty to the British government cloud his judgment. As the life was choked out of him, his brain zeroed in on the Peacekeepers X-Alpha motto.

Allegiance to all, obligation to none.

Whether this MI6 agent knew it or not, Skyler was on a mission that affected the entire world, including Britain.

And he would not fail.

Skyler grabbed the agent's thumb with his hand and twisted until he heard the joints snap. The agent roared in pain and his grip loosened from around Skyler's neck.

That was all the opening he needed.

Still gripping the agent's thumb, he twisted even farther until he pulled the agent's arm fully away from his neck. Once completely free, he shoved the agent away from him and scrambled for the gun.

He slid across the floor, snatching up the gun, and rolled onto his back as the agent charged at him again.

He aimed low and fired.

The rubber bullet hit the agent in the shin. The force of the impact sent his leg backward at an awkward angle and somersaulted him face first to the floor.

The agent landed with a sickening thud; and didn't move.

Skyler got to his feet and slowly approached the second person he'd ever shot in his life. It didn't matter that he'd used nonlethal ammunition. Both times had resulted in a bloody resolution for his targets.

He held the gun study as he leaned over the agent who lay face down on the floor, blood seeping out from around his head.

He felt for a pulse. It was slow, but strong.

He breathed a second sigh of relief for the fact that he had still not killed anyone.

He angled the agent onto his side and noted the swelling of the nose, indicating he had broken it when he smacked face first onto the floor.

He had taken only one class of emergency first aid, long ago. But he felt he still knew enough to minimize the permanent damage to the agent if he acted quickly.

During his struggle for survival, he'd stopped being aware of the blaring alarm sounds that echoed in the room. But he became instantly aware of the moment they went silent.

He had thirty seconds to act before the door to the room opened and a squad of soldiers, armed with automatic rifles, assaulted the room and killed him.

He ignored the first moaning employee and scooted the chair back in front of the computer terminal and sat down.

That used up five seconds.

Twenty-five seconds left to do something that took the average computer user over a minute.

Fortunately, Skyler was not your average computer user.

His fingers flew over the keyboard, a portion of his brain counting down the remaining seconds before the external lock override mechanism opened the door and allowed entry for the assault team waiting outside.

Even though he had not been given any indication, other than the alarm being turned off, that there was anyone outside the room, protocol dictated that they were there. And they were most likely eager to rush in for the kill. If it were him, he knew he would be.

He silently counted down into the single digits as he initiated the raven protocol.

It was the final failsafe should Vauxhall Cross ever be infiltrated by enemies of the state. It would seal the door to this room and destroy the motors that enabled the door to open of its own volition. The foot-thick wall of titanium would take more than thirty-six hours for someone on the outside to cut through. More than enough time for British forces to regain control of the building before anyone gained access to this room.

There were only five seconds before the lock override outside would open the door. That left five seconds for him to destroy the motors so that couldn't happen.

Four seconds.

Three seconds.

Two seconds.

"Quote the raven, nevermore," he said out loud as he pressed the return key on the keyboard.

There was a series of popping sounds in rapid succession around the building as motors melted under the sudden intense heat of their self-destruct units.

He was now locked in this room for at least thirty-six hours, even if they began cutting right away. He glanced over at the three cups laying sideways in a spreading pool of coffee. It would've been nice if at least one of them had survived.

He located plastic locking cable ties and secured his two hostages to server racks that were bolted to the floor and ceiling. They were where he could keep an eye on them, but they were still far enough away to not interfere with his tasks.

He split his BlackBerry cell phone in half and extracted the USB thumb drive that had replaced the inner workings of the phone.

He disabled all the security protocols in the computer terminal and plugged the thumb drive into an available port.

The thumb drive was more than just storage. It quickly scanned the system it was plugged into and begin configuring everything to pick up right where he had left off.

Since the progress indicator estimated another ten minutes before he could begin using the system, he checked the other rooms inside the building, looking for food and water. He hoped to find enough to last the three of them until the assault team breached the titanium wall in a day and a half. He was pleasantly surprised when he found a mini-fridge in the break room stocked with sodas and candy bars. While not very nutritious, it would still prevent starvation and dehydration while his hostages waited for rescue, and he waited for death.

He dropped piles of snack food next to his hostages.

"Try not to eat it all at once. It has to last you a while."

Basil had regained his senses and stared at the candy bars before looking up at him with disdain. "What are you going to do with us?"

"I'm gonna do my best to keep you fed and maintain a reasonable bathroom schedule."

"And after that?"

"We'll cross that bridge when we get to it, okay?"

"They'll kill you. You know that don't you?"

Skyler nodded. "I know. And I've planned for that."

"What is it you want?"

"I want to help my friends."

"I've never heard a terrorist refer to other terrorists as friends."

Skyler smiled at him. "That's because we're not terrorists."

The computer beeped behind him, signaling it was ready.

"When your friend wakes up, let him know the first bathroom break is in a couple hours. And do try to keep it down over here. I need to concentrate."

He returned to the computer, sat down, and cracked his knuckles. The first thing he need to do, was commandeer a satellite.

His mind raced through the list of commercial and military satellites that met his criteria. Just as quickly as he thought of one, he crossed it off his mental list. Grabbing a military satellite might create an international incident if it was discovered that it was the computer systems inside MI6's Dungeon that had taken it. That went against everything Uncle Robert and his Peacekeepers X-Alpha initiative stood for. Their goal was to prevent worldwide destabilization, not add to it.

Unfortunately, grabbing a commercial satellite would instantly affect millions. Who knew what kind of worldwide chaos would ensue when everyone suddenly lost their satellite television signal.

He kept thinking of fewer and fewer satellites, yet still crossing them off his list. He needed one that would affect as few people as possible. One that, if it unexpectedly went off-line, would not necessarily surprise the people who owned it.

His list was quickly pared down to one final name.

Alexander.

He was perfect.

Alexander was NASA's latest experiment in getting the most bang for taxpayer dollars. Alexander was a PhoneSat; a small, low-cost, satellite that used an unmodified consumer-grade off-the-shelf smartphone as its hardware base and was launched into Low Earth Orbit.

Smartphones proved to be the perfect starting point for NASA's Small Spacecraft Technology Program. Modern smartphones had a fast CPU, integrated lithium-ion battery, built-in camera, multiple acceleration and rotation sensors, a compass, a GPS receiver, and multiple wireless band radios. And because manufacturers were competing against each other to include all of these technologies in the smallest form factor, at the lowest price, to a worldwide phone buying market, NASA had everything it needed to build a complete satellite for less than $7,000.

Someone might escalate the problem quickly when a hundred million dollar satellite went missing. But when a $7,000 satellite goes off-line, it's not as much cause for concern. It's almost as if they were expecting it.

Skyler should've put Alexander at the top of his list from the very start. He was the only PhoneSat built by NASA with a two-way S-band radio. Part of the "S" band was reserved for unlicensed spectrum devices such as cordless phones, wireless headphones, and the ever popular Bluetooth protocol. It was within this same spectrum that the communication devices placed over the back molars of Samantha and Alex operated.

While he began programming his intercept software to take control of Alexander, he prayed silently that the same electrical current that had been used to torture Alex, but not kill him, had only temporarily knocked out the communications device, rather than short it out completely.

But, the only way to find out, was to get the PhoneSat directly overhead. The nanosatellite's S-band transceiver was powerful enough to communicate with the low-powered tooth comms, and was not subjected to the same range limitations of the transceiver built into Samantha's Aston Martin. The Aston Martin's communications transceiver was designed to hide its signals amongst the clutter of other S-band traffic. At this point, Skyler didn't care about the increased, and thus more easily detectable, signal boost from the PhoneSat. He just wanted to regain contact with Samantha.

It took him nearly an hour and a half to secure the satellite, but he finally did it. With his first task complete, all he had to do was locate the plane that Samantha and Alex were on and move the satellite overhead. Then he would send the initialization commands to Samantha and Alex's tooth comms, and pray they were still functioning.

By now, they were well on their way to New York and he could track them with the plane's transponder after he hacked into the United States' Federal Aviation Administration's air traffic control system.

That took him another thirty minutes.

Once in, he spent the next twenty minutes scanning the records of all planes heading eastward across the United States. He double checked, and triple checked, the list of planes, both publicly available and privately listed. The plane he was looking for, was not there.

He accessed the departure records of all planes that took off from the Portland airport over the past several hours.

The plane that Samantha and Alex were supposed to be

on had taken off as scheduled. It couldn't have just disappeared. A quick database search of all plane landing records in the United States over the past few hours reflected that the plane was still in the air.

But where was it?

Chapter 66

Alex peeked out the window of the private jet. Below him, he could just make out the familiar shape of the Alaskan coastline as they shot out over the open ocean at over eight-hundred kilometers per hour.

Prior to his release from prison, his original parole officer, most likely his only parole officer, had given him explicit instructions. It all boiled down to not even thinking about leaving the small town where he had found him a job and a place to stay. He wondered what that guy would have to say about him leaving the country.

It's not like Alex had any say in the matter. Samantha had picked him up outside the gates of the prison complex before he even made it to the apartment that taxpayers were subsidizing on his behalf. And how was he supposed to get back? With no passport, and the heavy travel restrictions placed on felons out on parole, he saw nothing but trouble along the road ahead.

This was presented as a temporary gig, with only a couple days of easy travel for a sizable payout. He hoped, with his actions over the past couple of days, he had impressed Samantha and her employers enough to make it a more permanent position.

This was what he was trained to do. This was what he was good at, and he hoped Samantha saw it too.

When they finished the current mission, or more importantly, if they lived through it, he would get Samantha to convince her superiors to bring him on full time.

Besides, there was no way he could accomplish his life's goal flipping burgers in a dead-end job in the middle of

America.

Then again, it was probably better than being held prisoner by three mercenaries, two men and one woman by the looks of it, in a plane bound for parts unknown.

Speaking of where they were going, he took his attention away from the window and looked at the larger of the mercenaries, the one who referred to himself as Mikhail. With the exception of a few brief exchanges, nobody had said a word since they took off from Portland. It was getting a little too quiet for Alex's liking. He would have to rectify that.

"I see we are leaving U.S. airspace. Where are we going?"

Mikhail glanced at his watch and gave him a disapproving look. "How did America become such a powerful nation? None of you can stay quiet for more than an hour."

"I just want to know where we're going."

"And I will tell you the same thing I told you the last three times." Mikhail leaned in closer, his lip curling up in a sneer. "No questions."

Alex pressed further. "There are three of you, armed to the teeth, and only two of us. What's the harm in telling us where we're going?"

Mikhail squinted his eyes, a thick vein pulsated in his forehead. "Shut up, or I will shut you up."

"Why can't you tell us where..."

Mikhail leapt up from his seat and drew the pistol from his thigh holster in a single motion. With his free hand, he twisted Alex's shirt in his fist and pressed him deeper into the leather seat. He held the pistol barrel against Alex's closed mouth.

"If that opens again, I put a bullet in it. Do you

understand?"

Alex nodded his head and Mikhail backed off, holstering his pistol.

As Mikhail sat back down, he pointed a stubby finger at Alex to punctuate he meant it.

Alex, with one hand, mimicked zipping his lips shut, locking them, and tossing away the key.

His other hand used the distraction to tuck the serrated combat knife he had liberated from the mercenary under his leg. It was always important that the left hand knew what the right hand was doing so they could coordinate their efforts.

Now that he was armed, he felt a little more comfortable that the odds were swinging back in his favor.

The pilot emerged from the cockpit and approached Mikhail. He spoke quietly, but in the small plane, Alex could still hear what he said.

"I just received the weather report, and the winds are a little high. We should be landing within the hour, but it's going to get a bit bumpy on approach, so everyone should buckle in."

Mikhail grunted his approval and called over to the other two mercenaries sitting at the front of the plane. "Buckle in, we're landing."

Alex and Samantha both silently secured their seat belts as well.

Mikhail leaned over to Alex, reached out and triggered the lock release on his belt. "Not you."

Alex couldn't hold his tongue any longer. "Do you think your employer will mind if I get injured?"

Mikhail sneered at him. "I don't think so. My orders are to kill you when we land."

Chapter 67

Inside the Dungeon, deep down in the bowels of MI6, a tone emitted from Skyler's terminal at the same moment one of the windows on his screen began flashing. His dynamic monitoring program, known in the hacker world as a computer worm, was running within ACARS, the Aircraft Communications Addressing and Reporting System.

His worm had flagged a weather request from the plane he was looking for. The ACARS system automatically generated the weather report and transmitted it back to the requesting plane while Skyler's worm logged the approximate location of the plane, based on the VHF ground radio stations communicating with it, and sent that data to his terminal. He had already set up that data feed to show the plane's location in another window where Google Earth was running. A red dot blinked to life over the Pacific Ocean, between Alaska and the easternmost coast of Russia.

No wonder he couldn't find the plane.

He had been searching in the opposite direction.

He didn't have time to wonder why the plane was headed toward Russia instead of New York. It made sense, since they needed to go to Moscow anyway to prevent the assassination of the President of Russia. But how had they known?

He didn't have time to worry about that. Somehow they had found out, and that was good enough for him.

His fingers flashed furiously across the keyboard as he programmed the satellite with its new course.

Behind him, a voice called out, breaking his concentration.

"You promised us a bathroom break?"

Chapter 68

Outside the window of the private jet, St. Lawrence Island crawled by underneath. While the island was considered part of Alaska, it was still closer to Siberia than to the Alaskan mainland. It also meant they would soon be leaving the comfort of U.S. airspace.

The large mercenary had assured Alex he would be dead soon, and in the confined space of the private jet's passenger compartment, it would be difficult to get the upper hand on all three mercenaries. But he did have the combat knife, and that was all he needed to have a fighting chance.

Since he was dead already, he decided to engage the large mercenary again.

But something stopped him.

It was a little voice inside his head.

"Samantha. Alex. Can you hear me?"

His head snapped over to Samantha to see if she had heard it too. Her look told him everything he needed to know. The comm unit built into the false tooth over his back molar had been reactivated.

Samantha's eyes bored into his as she nodded her head in the direction of the mercenary. He knew exactly what she wanted him to do. He had to create a distraction so that nobody would hear her respond to the voice in their heads.

He leaned forward toward the large mercenary. "Hey ugly. Since I'm going to die anyway, there is something I have to confess to you."

"Yeah? What is it?"

He focused to remember the insult correctly as he spoke

in Russian. "Vasha mama sosala menya."

For a brief moment, Mikhail's face remained frozen and he was concerned he had not said "Your mom sucked me off" properly.

Then the merc's face darkened. "Ahueyet?!"

That was slang for "What the fuck?!"

Good. He had remembered it correctly.

Mikhail forgot about being buckled in as he tried to stand up unsuccessfully. Alex took advantage of being the only one not imprisoned in the luxurious leather seats, stood up quickly, and punched Mikhail square in the face; blood exploding from his nose.

He leapt behind Mikhail's seat and pressed the combat blade against his neck just as the other two mercs unbuckled themselves, jumped to the aisle, and raised their assault rifles.

"Shoot him! Shoot the motherfucker!" Mikhail roared, ignoring the serrated blade cutting into the flesh of his neck.

Alex had his retort ready. "If you shoot, the bullets will rip through the fuselage and we'll crash into the ocean. None of us will survive."

The two mercs looked at each other, then back to him.

"Shoot him now!" Mikhail bellowed.

The mercs hesitated, unsure of what to do. Alex was more than happy to let them remain undecided. He glanced over at Samantha and saw her silently relaying their predicament to Skyler.

He returned his attention back to the front of the plane in time to see the pilot step out of the cockpit and freeze.

It was time to regain control of the situation.

He gripped Mikhail's hair, pulled his head back, and pressed the knife farther into the skin of his neck.

"This is how this is going down. Drop your weapons and buckle yourselves back in. You, pilot, turn this plane around and take us back to the good old US of A."

The pilot nodded and disappeared back through the cockpit door. The mercs were still undecided as to whether to shoot him, or comply with disarming themselves, when the plane did a barrel roll.

Alex and the two mercs tumbled along the walls and ceiling of the plane like shoes in a dryer.

The plane finished its roll and leveled out. Alex somersaulted back down the other wall and sprawled on the floor at Mikhail's feet.

Mikhail was out of his seat in a flash and knelt over Alex, pressing his pistol into Alex's temple.

"You don't get any last words," Mikhail said as he thumbed back the hammer.

One of the other mercs, the female one, was instantly at his side. "Mikhail wait!"

The blood in his eyes was almost as red as the blood that ran down his face. "Why should I?"

"She said he must die on Russian soil."

"What difference does it make if I shoot him now or in half an hour?"

"The difference is whether or not you explicitly followed Madina's direct order."

He mulled that over for a while before he pulled the gun away from Alex's head and lowered the hammer slowly.

"I want to be the one to kill him."

The female merc smiled. "And you will. As soon as we land, we will take him together to a secluded area of the airport and I will enjoy watching you put a bullet through his brain."

Chapter 69

Mikhail's nose finally stopped bleeding as the plane settled into its final approach to the Provideniya Bay airport, the closest airport to the United States in the Russian Far East. It would feel good to place his feet back on Russian soil, even if it was one of the lesser populated autonomous districts. He had been gone for far too long.

When he had been kicked out the military because of his temper, he hired himself out as a mercenary to whoever had the money. Unfortunately, that meant he spent the majority of his time in other parts of the world, and he missed home, even if just a little bit.

While Provideniya Bay was technically within Russia's borders, he was still farther away from home, from Moscow, then when he had sold his services to governments, and rebels, during the past nine years.

But all that was about to change.

He looked over at the smug, and incredibly stupid American, who had taken advantage of a rare opportunity to actually land a punch; and broke his nose. As soon as he disposed of this piece of shit, he would board a MiG-29 jet fighter, and be back in Moscow in a few hours after being away for nearly a decade.

The American smiled at him. "How's the nose?"

That was the problem with Americans. It didn't matter if they greeted you in friendship, or stabbed you in the back. They were always smiling. No doubt, when he shot this one in the head, he would die with a smile on his face.

Everyone jerked slightly as the plane touched down with a double bounce. While the plane taxied slowly down the runway, Karina appeared at his side.

"You've waited long enough Mikhail. We are on Russian soil. Let's kill this bastard, collect the reward, and go home."

He looked up at her. She was still suited up in full combat gear, ready for action. As much as he hated to admit it to himself, because he was such a tough guy on the outside, he admired her for that. The other merc had removed his helmet and balaclava, and had even unclipped his tactical vest to be more comfortable, even though they still had two prisoners on the plane.

One should never relax that much in the middle of an operation.

Never.

Karina's combat gear had remained secured and her balaclava hid all but her eyes. Her ever alert eyes. She had stayed vigilant for the entire flight, and now as the plane slowed to a stop, she was still ready for anything.

He wondered if she maintained this same level of focus and intensity in the bedroom. Maybe, after they had completed this mission and collected the reward, they would check into the most expensive suite in Moscow's finest hotel and find out.

But the mission wasn't over yet. They still had to dispose of the man and deliver the woman to Madina, who would be waiting for them in Moscow.

He didn't like working for known Chechen terrorists, especially against Russia. But then again, Mother Russia had turned her back on him when she dishonorably discharged him from the military.

Money was money. And terrorists' money was as good as anybody's. You needed money to survive in today's world. And soon, he would have more money than he knew what to do with.

But before that happened, he had to get the British woman to Moscow and kill the American. Not necessarily in that order.

He stood up and looked over at the sloppy merc. He had proved himself to be very capable when the shooting started, but the downtime in between left a lot to be desired in a soldier.

"What's your name, boy?"

The merc stood up and snapped to attention when he realized he was being addressed by his superior.

"Kolya sir."

"I want you and Karina to watch the American and hold him here. Do nothing until I get back. He is mine."

"Yes sir."

He started to turn away before stopping himself.

"And Kolya?"

"Yes sir?"

"I never want to see you out of uniform during an active operation again."

Kolya began clipping his tactical vest closed. "Sorry sir. Never again."

Mikhail drew his pistol and pointed it at the British woman. "Let's go."

Chapter 70

Alex watched Samantha head down the aisle with Mikhail right behind her. She paused for a moment at the door and looked back at him, the look on her face saying what they both knew.

They would not be seeing each other again.

The voice in his head echoed through the bones in his skull. "What's going on? Will somebody talk to me?"

"Not now Skyler," Alex mumbled quietly.

Ever since Samantha had picked him up at the prison gate, it seemed her, and her group, had been two steps behind the people they claimed they were trying to stop. They had been outnumbered, outgunned, and apparently outclassed, every step of the way. And now he was about to be killed.

Mikhail paused at the door, after Samantha had gone through, and smiled back at him. It was not a warm smile, but one of satisfaction. "I will be back in five minutes."

He glanced out the side window and watched Samantha being led at gunpoint toward four Russian MiGs waiting on the other side of the tarmac. It didn't take a math genius to calculate that, while five of them had landed at the airport, only four of them would be leaving.

His only regret was that he had failed those who had been counting on him. His mission had only just begun, and he had not been successful in the least.

The female merc, the one Mikhail had called Karina, pointed her assault rifle at him.

"Take off your clothes."

The other merc barked out a laugh. "Good. I like it.

Death is not enough for this American pig. Let's humiliate him too."

Karina responded by swinging the assault rifle around and pointing it at him.

"You too."

Chapter 71

Mikhail had just secured Samantha into the rear seat of the two-cockpit MiG-29UB jet fighter, when gunfire erupted behind him.

He spun around in time to see the American running down the steps of the private jet on the other side of the tarmac. From this distance, he could just make out that the American had an assault rifle in his hands. He watched in shock as the American paused at the bottom, spun around, and fired another volley of bullets into the side of the plane.

The American turned and started sprinting toward him. Mikhail drew his pistol, but they were still well out of range of each other.

Karina appeared at the door of the plane and shot several rounds into the back of the fleeing American, taking him down.

The American skidded across the tarmac, leaving a smeared trail of blood like the slime trail left behind by a snail.

Karina rushed up to the body, kicked away the assault rifle, and fired two more rounds into the back of the American's head.

Mikhail was furious as he ran up to her and stared down at what should've been his prize.

He looked at her, questioning her silently about her actions.

Karina was huffing and puffing rapidly. "He got the drop on Kolya. Knocked him out and took his rifle before I could react."

Mikhail kicked the bloody and lifeless form on the

tarmac repeatedly in frustration. "You were my kill! Mine!"

He swung around and backhanded Karina across the face, scraping the skin off his knuckles along the edge of her helmet.

"How could you be so stupid? What happened in there?!"

Karina massaged the bruise that was no doubt forming underneath her balaclava and stared hard at him. "Why don't you ask Kolya?"

How dare she allow the look of defiance to creep into her eyes? He contemplated hitting her again for the insubordinate thoughts in her head.

This was why you never let women into the military, or even private mercenary troops. But there was hardly anything he could say about it, when his superior was a woman. He suppressed the rage and regained control of his emotions.

"Where is Kolya?"

She looked back toward the bullet-riddled private jet. "He's still out cold."

He wanted to administer a swift, and just, punishment to Kolya, but a sudden roar behind him brought his attention back to the MiG, the one that contained the British woman, as it taxied out onto the runway. There were more important matters he had to attend to. He would have to delay his special form of justice.

He turned back to Karina.

"Get Kolya into a MiG. I will deal with him in Moscow."

"Yes sir."

Karina trotted back to the private jet.

Mikhail headed to one of the three remaining MiGs as the first one took to the skies in a mighty roar.

As he strapped himself in to the rear seat of the cockpit, he glanced over to see Karina supporting, but more like half-carrying, a still stunned and groggy Kolya down the stairs of the private jet.

He would have to talk to Madina about maintaining her standards of recruitment despite the sudden growth of her organization.

He watched them limp toward the other MiGs as the one he was in taxied down the runway. He was pressed into his seat as the fighter jet accelerated before lifting into the air.

A tone sounded in the headphones built into the helmet and the pilot's voice echoed in his ear.

"I have a communication for you from Madina, hold while I patch it through."

Why was Madina calling him now? What was so important that it couldn't wait the few hours it would take for him to fly to Moscow at Mach 2? What could he possibly do with whatever she had to tell him now?

The static in his headset popped and crackled before Madina's voice came in loud and clear.

"Mikhail?"

"Yes ma'am, I can hear you. What is it?"

"I just confirmed the identity of the body you pulled out of the tunnel from under the cabin."

This would be interesting. They all secretly wanted to know the identity of the woman who'd managed to get the drop on their commander.

It had to be somebody big.

Somebody known throughout the mercenary community, if she was calling to tell him now. It had to be somebody so important, she couldn't wait.

"Was it someone we knew?"

"Yes. Yes it was."

"So who was it?"

"It was Karina."

Chapter 72

Melissa Stone supported Alex as they pretended to hobble across the tarmac toward the waiting MiGs. Alex kept one hand on the belt of Kolya's ill-fitting uniform. At gunpoint, Melissa had forced Kolya to put on Alex's clothes and then handed him back his assault rifle with the safety on. She had told him, if he flipped the safety off before exiting the plane, she would kill him.

He hadn't been paying attention, or thought she was bluffing, because he immediately switched the fire selector to full auto, forcing her to shoot into the back of the seats near him, driving him out of the plane. The rested had played out exactly as she had hoped and Mikhail was none the wiser about the switch.

When they were only halfway across the tarmac, the two MiGs they were headed for fired up their engines, taxied onto the runway while their canopies were still lowering, and took off.

Not really needing the support, Alex stood up fully as they both watched the fighter jets rocket off into the sky without them.

He looked at her, confusion written on his face. "What just happened?"

She scanned the sky, looking for trouble. "They just figured out who I am."

"How did they do that?"

"Well, technically, they didn't figure out who I am. But they know who I'm not."

"That's really not telling me much."

She spotted the pinpoint dot that she had been looking

for in the sky. The dot expanded quickly until it resolved itself into the dark outline of a fighter plane. But instead of seeing it from the perspective of a side profile view, she could make out both wings poking out to either side of the center fuselage.

It was coming straight for them.

She heard the faint sound of a buzz saw in the distance right before the ground exploded chunks of concrete into the air. The storm of bullets tore up the tarmac in erupting parallel lines around them as the fighter strafed their position.

The jet screamed overhead and banked sharply, preparing for a second run. Deep in the sky, the other two jet fighters split apart from each other in preparation for strafing runs of their own.

She didn't think she needed to say it, but she said it anyway. "Run!"

Chapter 73

Skyler held his gun on Basil, while Basil did his best to ignore him from the toilet in the open stall. He tried to get his hostages to wait until Samantha and Alex had taken off again from the airport on the East Coast of Russia, but they were insistent that it was time for another bathroom break.

Through Alex's tooth communication transponder, Skyler learned that Melissa Stone was not only still alive, but had come up with a plan to get both of them onto the waiting jet fighters. Through the camera built into the PhoneSat, he had watched Samantha being loaded onto a MiG. Now, with Melissa and Alex replacing the other two mercenaries, they would have the remaining merc outnumbered three to one. Those odds were much better, and it finally looked like they were catching a break.

But instead of watching his seemingly expanding team of operatives climb into their respective jet fighters, he was watching one of his hostages sitting on a toilet doing nothing. As soon as he got back to the workstation, he would reposition the nanosatellite over Moscow and reacquire their signal once they arrived.

Basil looked around the stall uncomfortably before making eye contact with Skyler again.

"This is really hard to do with you staring at me."

Skyler shrugged. "Sorry. I can't risk you obtaining a weapon."

Basil looked around him at the empty stall. "And just where are all these weapons you speak of?"

"The toilet seat, the handicap grab bars, even the bolts from the door. We both attended the same training courses.

What around you is not a weapon?"

The look on Basil's face changed to one of slight amusement. "I see your point."

He tilted his head at Skyler.

"Why are you doing this? Why are you here?"

"You need to use the bathroom, and I need to maintain control of the situation."

"That's not what I meant. Why are you down here in the Dungeon?"

"I'm afraid the answer to that is way above your pay grade."

"I couldn't help but overhear your conversation earlier. The woman on the other end of your line was also British, and she spoke using the same jargon we use during active missions. But this isn't an SIS operation; otherwise you would have requisitioned our help through proper channels rather than break into the Dungeon all by yourself."

Skyler didn't have time to get into a discussion, philosophical or otherwise, with a hostage. He needed to send the reposition orders to the PhoneSat so that it would be in position by the time his team reached Moscow. He had to get back to the workstation.

He studied Basil, sitting on the toilet. Basil studied him back.

It didn't look like Basil was concentrating on using the toilet. It seemed more like he was just wasting his time.

"Are you done? Because you sound done," Skyler commented aloud.

"Why are you here?" Basil asked again.

Skyler suddenly realized what Basil was doing. He did not have to go to the bathroom. Instead, he was keeping him away from the terminal, and preventing him from doing what he needed to do. He angled the pistol so it was pointing directly at Basil again. "Yep. You're done."

He stayed back far enough to prevent Basil from attempting to rush at him. He'd had the forethought to encircle the wrists and ankles of his two hostages with locking plastic zip ties, much like bracelets and anklets. The zip ties of each hand, and each foot, we're connected to each other with a locking zip-tie of their own, forming improvised handcuffs. He used the bridge between the bracelets to secure them to the server rack with yet another locking zip-tie. At no time were his two charges ever unshackled.

He led Basil back into the main room, tossing him two zip ties. "Secure yourself to the rack."

Once Basil had relocked himself to the server rack, Skyler took another step back and, gripping his pistol with both hands, sighted down the barrel at them.

"Both of you tug on your restraints as hard as you can."

Both MI6 agents pulled on the zip ties, proving none of them had worked loose, and they were both securely attached to the server rack.

He relaxed his grip on the pistol and let out a calming breath. The most critical time was when his hostages were mobile. If either of them had plans to try anything stupid, they would do it when they were not tied to an immovable object.

A faint, high-pitched, whine began vibrating through the walls. The MI6 agents looked at each other, and then back at him with wide smiles spread across their faces. They were all thinking the exact same thing.

The countdown had begun.

In thirty-six hours, an assault team would breach the wall

and come in guns blazing. The thought of a squad of soldiers, each one trained to kill with only one shot, all gunning for him, unnerved him to no end. But he couldn't let that interfere with the time he had left.

He still had thirty-six hours. Plenty of time for his team on the ground to prevent the assassination of the Russian president.

Speaking of his team on the ground, Melissa and Alex should have boarded the jet fighters by now.

As he approached the workstation, one of the windows on the monitor, the window that showed the live camera feed from the PhoneSat, showed the aftermath of a war zone. There were craters, smoke, rubble, and fire everywhere. It took a moment to register that he was looking at what used to be the runway of the Provideniya Bay airport.

"What the...?!"

He shoved the chair aside and typed furiously, the image zooming out to show a wider view of the airport. The destruction was not limited to the runway. Everything at the airport had been targeted. Buildings, cars, even the private jet his team had arrived on were nothing more than smoldering heaps. The small group of helicopters, off to one side of what remained of the main airport building, had all been destroyed; most of them still on fire and belching black smoke into the air.

He'd only been away, at most, five minutes. What had happened in that time? And why had the mercenaries destroyed the airport?

He keyed in the comm channel and yanked the microphone toward his mouth.

"Alex? Can you hear me?"

There was no reply.

"Alex! Do you read?"

Still silence.

He pulled the chair over and sat down heavily in it. Looking at what remained of the airport, there was no way either of them could have survived if they were on the ground when the jet fighters rained a firestorm down on the area.

That left Samantha the only operative left on the ground, in a manner of speaking. She wasn't technically on the ground. Instead, she was in a jet fighter bound for Moscow. He had to get his nanosatellite in position to pick up her signal when she landed.

He was reaching for the keyboard to switch his active window from the comm station to the satellite navigation program when a loud gasp for air echoed through the computer terminal's speakers. It was immediately followed by Alex's breathless voice.

"Where the hell have you been?!"

Chapter 74

Alex bobbed in the frigid lake that was little more than a glorified pond just off the edge of the runway. Melissa broke the surface of the water a few feet away from him and gulped at the air.

While not exceptionally deep, it had been deep enough to slow and deflect the bullets that had followed them into the lake. They both scanned the skies, looking for any sign of an impending attack, while he updated Skyler.

After he was done explaining the situation, Skyler said to give him a few moments to check on something and then he disappeared from inside his head. Despite the fact he was gone right now, the very thought of Skyler being able to return any time he wanted stripped away all illusions of privacy for Alex. He would have to be careful what he said, and who he said it to, as long as there was a transmitter stuck on his back molar.

Melissa splashed over to him. "I don't think they're coming back."

He could see her lips trembling from the freezing water. He grabbed her tactical vest and pushed her toward the edge of the pond. "We need to get out of this water, and into dry clothes, before hypothermia sets in."

She responded by swimming for shore. They both crawled out of the pond and flopped onto their backs. It was not easy swimming in full tactical combat gear through ice cold water, and they were exhausted, from having to dodge incoming bullets and rockets, before they even jumped into the tiny lake.

He lay on his back, staring up at the sky, when a ring of

gun barrels entered his peripheral vision, all pointed at him.

"Ni s mesta!" someone demanded in Russian.

Alex tilted his head and looked at the one who spoke, replying in English.

"Don't worry. I'm too tired to move."

Rough hands reached down and yanked him to his feet. He and Melissa both wobbled unsteadily on their legs. She had to have felt as cold and exhausted as he did.

At gunpoint, they were handcuffed and forced into the back of an army transport truck. As the truck jerked into motion, the leader, the one everyone else referred to as captain, sat on the bench seat across from them and leaned forward.

"Why did your comrades destroy the airport and then leave you behind?"

Alex laughed. "Obviously I'm not very good at picking friends."

The soldier on his right slammed a rifle butt into his gut, leaving him doubled over and gasping for air.

Melissa spoke up. "They destroyed the airport trying to kill us."

The captain cocked his head and looked her up and down. "What's so important about the two of you?"

She met his stare. "Whatever it is they're planning, they know we can stop them."

"Just what is it you're trying to stop?"

"I'm not really sure." She nodded her head at Alex. "He might know."

The captain looked at him, raising an eyebrow to indicate he was asking him the same question. It was likely, no matter what he said, the soldier would not believe him. So he led with the truth.

"They are planning to assassinate the President of Russia."

The captain of the small military force did not laugh. Instead, his eyes grew darker. "I am sick of your jokes."

"It's not a joke. And when my friends find out I'm still alive, they'll be back to destroy everything else. They will kill everyone in this town just to get to me."

"And who are these people, who want you dead so much?"

"Chechen terrorists."

The captain barked out a laugh. "Ha. Now I know you're lying. Chechens don't have access to Russian MiGs. And they certainly wouldn't be out here on the East Coast blowing everything up. They have nothing to gain by attacking Provideniya Bay."

"It doesn't matter what you believe, it's the truth."

"And where is your proof?"

Proof. Of course he would want proof. "Give me a moment. Skyler? Are you there?"

Skyler didn't respond.

"Skyler? Can you hear me?"

The captain glanced at Melissa, a look of confusion on his face. She shrugged her shoulders and shook her head.

He looked back at Alex. "Who are you talking to?"

Still silence from the comm unit on his tooth. "Skyler. Now is not the time to be ignoring me."

Skyler's voice came through, but it was hard to hear him over the captain's insistent demands to know who he was talking to. He gave the captain a stern look.

"Be quiet, I can't hear both of you once. Go ahead Skyler."

Skyler's voice came in loud and clear. "Sorry for the

delay. I've been listening to your conversation and realized he would want proof. I picked up some chatter on a rarely used military channel. Two of the jet fighters that shot at you requested refueling, and rearmament, at a nearby military base. It was approved, but only after a private citizen agreed to pay for it."

"Do you know who agreed to pay?"

"It was Umarov."

"He must have some connections high up in the military to pull that off so quickly."

"He's a billionaire. I'm sure he has connections everywhere."

"Then why is he funding terrorists?"

The captain interrupted him. "Who are you talking to?!"

He ignored the grizzled soldier. "What's the name of the base where they landed?"

He could hear Skyler typing furiously. "Ugolny Airport. They will be ready for takeoff in ten minutes. They're just waiting for confirmation of your deaths from the earlier attack to see if they need to return."

The captain grabbed him with both hands and shook him, his face mere inches from his own. "Who are you talking to?!"

A thought suddenly occurred to Alex. "Why were you on the runway?"

The captain pushed him against the side of the truck and leaned away, ignoring his question.

This nagging thought tickled on the edge of reason and he couldn't let it go. "You came out with armed men looking for us. How did you know we would be out there?"

The captain looked uncomfortable with this line of questioning. Alex pressed further.

"How did you know we were out there?"

The captain looked off to one side, as if formulating his response, and then looked back at Alex. "What makes you think we were looking for you?"

"Because as soon as you found us, you left the airport. If you were looking for survivors, or bodies, you would've left some of your men behind to continue the search. I didn't see any other search teams picking through the rubble. As soon as you saw us come out of the lake, you knew your search was over. How come?"

"I was ordered to confirm that the two of you were dead."

"With all the destruction, how come you were only looking for two bodies?"

"Before the MiGs landed, we were instructed to clear the airport of all personnel. There would be nobody else."

"Who told you to clear the airport?"

Surprisingly, the captain was forthcoming with his answers, as if forgetting who was the captor, and who was the captive.

"The orders came through the proper channels."

"And you didn't question removing everyone from the airport?"

The captain shrugged. "Happens more often than you think. Being the closest airport to the United States, we have a lot of high-profile traffic pass through our little town. But this is the first time someone blew it all up."

"And if you don't act correctly, they'll be back to finish the job."

"That is where you are wrong. I will report to my superiors that I found you both alive, that I have you in custody, and they will come to pick you up."

"That is where you are wrong. If you tell them we're alive, they will come back, not to collect us, but to kill us. And they will kill everyone else around us."

"Why would they do that?"

"Because they can't risk that I've already told you about their plans."

"What plans? You mean the assassination of the President?"

"Yes. Exactly that."

"That is ridiculous. You have no proof."

"You want proof? Call somebody you know at Ugolny Airport. Someone you can trust outside the chain of command. Ask them about the MiGs that are being refueled right now."

"I don't know anyone at Ugolny."

The army truck jerked to a stop. The captain looked out the back and stood up. "You two, out of the truck."

Alex stood, hunching slightly to keep from banging his head on the roof of the army truck. "Where are we?"

"The only prison cells we have are in the town jail."

As they stepped down out of the truck, Alex continued to plead his case. "You can't tell them you found us alive."

The captain ignored him as he led them into the tiny building on the end of the block and locked them up.

The captain borrowed the phone on the small wooden desk and dialed a number from memory.

Alex pressed his face against the bars. "Don't do this Captain."

Somebody must've answered on the other side of the line because he stopped looking at Alex and turned away.

"Yes, this is Captain Oleg. I have the two prisoners. Yes, they are alive."

He looked back at Alex. "They are locked up in the police station in town. Yes. Yes. Of course. They are not going anywhere sir."

Captain Oleg hung up the phone without taking his eyes off of Alex.

"They are sending someone to pick the two of you up."

Alex pressed his face farther into the bars. "Did they ask if I told you about the assassination of the president?"

Captain Oleg's brows knitted. "Yes."

Alex slumped against the bars.

"Then you are as dead as we are."

Chapter 75

Two minutes after being cleared for takeoff from Ugolny Airport, the MiG pilot's new orders were filtering down the chain of command to him. What he heard, was not what he had expected.

He thumbed the button on his comm panel.

"Say that again Control."

The soft female voice crackled through the speakers in his helmet. "Your primary target is the Provideniya police station. Secondary targets are anyone attempting to flee the primary target. Do you copy?"

In a world where it was his sole responsibility to receive orders, and to follow them, there was only one thing he could say.

"Copy that."

He switched off the comm and glanced over at the other MiG flying alongside him. The pilot gave him a thumbs-up, indicating he had received the same orders and was ready to proceed with their preselected attack vectors.

He banked hard to the left, while the other MiG banked hard to the right.

Thirty seconds later, with the target in his sights, he armed the missiles. With the press of a switch, he released them at precisely the right time. He flew low over the center of town at the same moment the building that housed the only police station in Provideniya erupted in a massive fireball.

The other MiG screamed overhead and confirmed that nobody had survived to present themselves as secondary targets.

After two more flyovers to confirm the total destruction of the primary target, the MiGs broke off their attack and disappeared into the deep blue sky.

Chapter 76

As black smoke billowed into the sky from the rubble of the police station, a small group of people stood looking out the window of a building on the other side of town. They watched as the MiGs danced back and forth across the sky, searching for additional targets.

Searching for them.

Alex turned his head to look at the captain. "Do you believe me now?"

Captain Oleg turned to Melissa. "You've been quiet this whole time."

She shrugged. "This is his show. I'm just along for the ride."

"Do you believe him?"

"I wouldn't put it past the people he's going up against to go after the president."

"What ties do you have with him?"

She shook her head. "None. We only just met."

"Then why are you here?"

"I have a bad habit of sticking my nose in where it doesn't belong. This is just another one of those times."

"Can you corroborate what he's telling me?"

"No."

He regarded both of them for a long time, and then his face set as he decided on a course of action. He turned to his second-in-command, who had been carefully watching the prisoners.

"Un-cuff them, and get me a cell phone."

The soldier could not keep the look of surprise from his face. "Sir?"

"Release them. That's an order."

"Yes sir!"

He unlocked Alex and Melissa's handcuffs and then took a step back. Alex massaged his wrists, happy to be free from the shackles.

Another soldier handed Captain Oleg a cell phone.

Alex held up a finger. "Be careful who you call. Your chain of command thinks you're dead."

He paused, halfway through tapping in a phone number. "When you and your friend get to Moscow and save the president, be sure to tell him it was I who helped you."

Alex smiled. "You looking for a medal?"

"No. I want the president to know that the people of the Chukotka Autonomous Okrug believe in the Russian Federation, and will do whatever it takes to keep the president safe, even if we are on the other side of the continent."

"Even if that means going against your superior's orders?"

Captain Oleg smiled. "How can I be expected to follow orders if I am already dead? Now if you'll excuse me, I have some calls to make."

He started to dial again on the cell phone when a thought occurred to him. "So just who is it I am helping? You both sound American. Are you CIA?"

Alex and Samantha looked at each other, and then Alex looked back at the captain. "Honestly, I'm not sure who I'm working for, but I'd lay ten to one odds that you've never heard of them."

The captain abruptly stopped punching numbers on the phone. "You don't even know who you're working for?"

Alex shook his head. "I only know who I'm working

with. And right now, she's in a jet fighter headed to Moscow without us."

The captain continued dialing. "Don't worry, I can get you there in a little less than five hours. Maybe not as fast as a fighter jet, but a lot quicker than hitchhiking across Siberia. I have a cousin in the FSO. I will call him and tell him to meet with you."

"Do you think he can help?"

"I can at least make him listen to what you have to say. After that, it's up to him how much he is willing to believe an American."

"So, you're letting us go?"

Captain Oleg put the phone to his ear, waiting for someone to answer.

"No. You will stay in my protective custody until the truth is uncovered."

Chapter 77

Samantha had almost forgotten she was traveling at Mach 2 until the MiG rolled to one side and executed a tight turn, the weight of seven gravities pressing her into her seat. Flying at this new angle, she could finally see the ground. She could make out the concentric rings of freeways that carved through the city below and made it look somewhat like a massive target from the air. She could just make out the group of buildings at the center of the city-sized target.

It was the Kremlin.

That could only mean one thing, she thought, as the jet fighter leveled out and began its descent. She was about to visit Moscow for the first time in her life. And she was certain she was not coming as a welcomed guest.

The pilot circled the city once and then set down at the Chkalovsky military air base. As soon the jet fighter was rolling slowly down the runway, she removed her helmet and mumbled quietly.

"Skyler, are you there?"

She waited a few moments of silence and mumbled again.

"Skyler? Can you hear me?"

Her request was met with more silence. She hoped he was trying really hard to regain contact with her.

The jet fighter came to an abrupt stop and the canopy lifted. With a clear view of the sky, she didn't bother to look for the other jet fighters she knew wouldn't be coming. Not knowing she understood Russian, the pilot had not bothered to disconnect her comm unit and she had been able to eavesdrop on the pilot's conversation regarding the failed attempt to kill Alex and his unknown associate, and the subsequent destruction of the Provideniya police station; with no signs of survivors.

She was on her own until Skyler could regain contact.

Even if he did reappear inside her head, she didn't know what she could do about her current situation, which at the moment, was her being led at gun point across the tarmac to a waiting military jeep.

As soon as she climbed into the jeep, a hood was placed over her head. They drove for what seemed like hours, but couldn't have been more than forty-five minutes. She had no idea if she had been taken deep into the center of Moscow, or if they had driven around in circles to keep her disoriented and she was less than a kilometer from where they started.

The jeep braked to a stop and rough hands pulled her out of the vehicle. She wished her hands were not tied behind her back so that she could cover her ears as she was taken through a noisy construction area.

As she was led blindly down twisting corridors and through hollow sounding rooms, each door that closed behind her muffled the construction noises in succession until there was nothing but a faint rumble in the background. She was jerked to a stop by her arms and forced down into a chair.

The hood was yanked off her head, and as her eyes adjusted to the sudden brightness, they focused on the smiling face of the Thin Man.

"Hello again, Ms. Fox."

It wasn't as much a surprise to her that he knew her name, as it was that she couldn't bring his up from the depths of her memory. She always prided herself on matching names to faces, even after only a single introduction. "Have we met before?"

His smile widened. "We have. But you wouldn't remember. The patches I used to make you little more forthcoming with the truth, the last time we spoke, have the bonus effect of short term memory loss. It was rather convenient all around when I decided not to kill you."

That would explain the gap in her and Alex's memory between leaving the old lady's house, the one with the cookies, and waking up in her car hours later. But that didn't answer the most burning question in her mind.

"Why did you let us go?"

"You said something that piqued my curiosity."

"Yeah? And what was that?"

"It had been my understanding that a certain military organization had been unfunded and disbanded. All of my sources confirmed this until you came along claiming to be part of said organization; with the disgraced leader still in charge."

"I don't know what you're talking about."

He clicked his tongue at her and frowned. "Tsk, tsk, Ms. Fox. It won't do you any good to lie to me now. I took the liberty of installing a second transmitter over the first one in your mouth. I've been listening to everything you and this Skyler have been saying to each other. From what I gather, he is your support team. Of course, I use the term support team loosely as it seems he is alone and in quite the pickle himself. Robert has made the mistake of rebuilding the Peacekeepers with a disorganized bunch of buffoons. He even let you recruit someone straight out of prison. Not one of your better decisions I might add. Unfortunately, it will also be one of your last. Within the next couple of days, everyone, including your esteemed leader, will be dead."

"Why are you telling me this?"

"Oh, I'm just blathering on until Skyler locates you with his stolen satellite."

The Thin Man had her at more than just a disadvantage. He knew everything they had planned, albeit it wasn't much, and they were working off of limited information with fast dwindling resources. Obviously, he did not see the Peacekeepers as any kind of threat to his plan.

"Since we're wasting time, why not tell me who you are."

"How rude of me. I keep forgetting you don't remember. My name is Umarov."

"Okay, Umarov, why did you let me live?"

"Because, I knew you could help me."

"Torture me all you want. I won't help you."

"There will be no need for that. You will help me, and you will do it willingly."

"Just what is it you think I'm going to help you do? Destroy the Peacekeepers?"

He dismissed her comment with a wave of his hand. "The thought had crossed my mind, but you seem to be doing a much better job at dismantling your own little group than I ever could. No, I have a much bigger, more important, job for you."

"Like what?"

His smile returned.

"You are going to kill the President of Russia for me."

Chapter 78

Deep in the underground Dungeon of MI6, Skyler placed a hand against the titanium door. It was warm. Warmer than it should have been.

It didn't look like he was going to get the full thirty-six hours before they cut through it. At this rate, they would be storming his little castle sooner than anticipated.

Much sooner.

He returned to the monitor and called up his hacked version of Google Earth that displayed the location of his satellite currently, with a visual trail showing where it had been recently. The dull green trail crisscrossed in a search pattern over the massive city of Moscow, while the satellite listened for the return signal from Samantha's tooth transmitter. A signal it would receive once she was in range.

He had also assigned a blinking red dot to represent the approximate location of the commercial flight Alex, Melissa, and the Russian captain had boarded in Anadyr, from the very same airport that had refueled the MiGs. They were only two hours away from Moscow, and he still hadn't located Samantha. His biggest fear was that she hadn't been taken to Moscow, and he was looking in the wrong place. But there was no other place he thought she could be, so he set the satellite to begin along the outer edges of the city, and work its way in to the center. He started his search outside the city since, if he were going to hide someone who didn't want to stay hidden, he would take her to one of the deserted farmhouses that were separated by acres of untilled fields. Even if she tried to escape, there would be nowhere for her to go without getting caught. It would also keep her close by, but not too close, while they went after the Russian president.

He sat in the chair and watched the clock in the corner of the monitor ticking away the milliseconds in a blur. It wasn't doing him any good to stare at the monitor. He needed to be ready to devote his full attention when he found Samantha and shouldn't be expending his concentrative energies now.

Besides, it was time for another round of bathroom breaks with his hostages.

He leaned forward to turn up the speaker volume, so he could hear the alert tone when the satellite finally found Samantha, at the precise moment something collided with the back of his chair, right where his head had been the moment before he moved.

He threw himself sideways out of the chair just as the steel rod smashed down on his keyboard, scattering little plastic keys in every direction.

He crab walked swiftly across the floor, trying to regain his feet as Basil charged at him, raising the steel rod he had dislodged from a server rack over his head.

Skyler rolled to one side as Basil brought the steel rod down hard, chipping the cement floor. He continued rolling until he somersaulted to his feet, slipped the gun out of his belt, and thumbed off the safety. As he swung it around toward his attacker, the steel rod connected with his hand. While the painkillers coursing through his body suppressed the pain that had to be shooting up his arm, he still involuntarily let go of the gun. It skidded across the floor, stopping within a few feet of the second hostage, who was still frantically trying to work free the steel rod he was tied to on his server rack. If he got loose, it would be two against one. He couldn't let that happen.

Basil swung again.

Skyler ducked under the swing, charged forward, and tackled Basil at the waist, lifting him off his feet. He twisted in the air and slammed Basil down hard on the cement floor, using his full weight to knock the wind out of his surprised victim.

He slammed his elbow into Basil's chin, knocking him out cold.

A rubber bullet grazed his shoulder. He spun around to see that the other agent had worked himself loose and was pointing his own gun at him.

He charged, letting out a primal scream as he ran. The agent panicked, firing off two rounds that slammed into his chest as he drove forward, letting the momentum carry him into a full tackle. A head butt sent blood gushing again from the agent's already swollen nose, and drained all the fight out of him in an instant.

Skyler wrestled the gun from the agent's grip and sliced it across the man's temple, rendering him unconscious.

When the assault team finally broke through the door, and took one look at his hostages, they would not think twice about killing him.

He got unsteadily to his feet and tucked the pistol back into his belt. He dragged Basil over next to the other agent and, using more plastic zip ties, bound their hands and feet together behind their backs and secured them to each other, before securing them to another server rack using zip ties around their necks. If they tried to break the support bars off of these racks, they would only end up strangling themselves. He didn't care how uncomfortable they felt when they woke back up. It was only going to get worse for them. They had just lost their bathroom privileges.

A beeping tone sounded from the computer monitor.

The satellite had found Samantha!

He dashed over to the computer terminal, and stared at the shattered keyboard. The satellite was not too smart, and if he didn't transmit a stop order, it would continue on its programmed trajectory and move out of range of Samantha's transmitter in a few minutes.

He scooped up a few of the keys that were scattered on the table, ready to place them back on the keyboard in any order. He knew how to type by touch, so it didn't matter which keys he put where. He never needed to look anyway.

He picked up the keyboard to reposition it, and only part of it lifted off the table.

"Bloody hell!"

The keyboard base itself was in pieces and the satellite would be moving out of position any minute. He had to find another keyboard. And he had to do it quickly.

A quick glance at his hostages confirmed they were still out cold. At least they wouldn't be causing any more trouble, any time soon.

His first stop was the supply closet he'd seen earlier. If this place was like any other place he'd worked, there be a stack of old keyboards somewhere on the upper shelves. As soon as he switched on the light, he saw the cords trailing down from a couple of keyboards that sat next to a pile of old mice on the second shelf from the top.

Jackpot!

He grabbed both keyboards, in case one of them was truly broken and deserved to be relegated to the junk pile because, God forbid, an IT person ever threw anything away, and dashed back to the computer terminal.

He swept away the pieces of the old keyboard and tossed the cable over the edge of the desk closest to the wall.

He dropped on his back and slid under the desk, fumbling around behind the desk until he found the loose keyboard cable. He yanked out the old cord from the terminal switch, and plugged in the new one.

He was back in the chair in a flash and hammered on the keyboard to redirect the satellite back into position.

A loud pop from behind nearly gave him a heart attack.

Whatever that was, it had come from the direction of the main door. He finished entering the commands to bring the satellite back over the area where the signal was strongest before going to investigate.

He peeked around the server rack at the titanium door.

He didn't see anything unusual. He walked forward, and the fluorescent lights reflecting off the curved door showed a dark spot that wasn't there before. As he got closer, he noticed it was a tiny hole in the door.

I faint hiss emanated from the hole.

Oh crap! They were gassing him.

Not content to let him have free rein of the systems in this room for the thirty-six hours it would take to get through the door, they were pumping some form of gas in the room that would render him unconscious when he breathed enough of it.

He tucked the collar of his undershirt over his nose and mouth and drew his pistol. Aiming for the small hole, he fired.

At this close range, he didn't miss. The rubber bullet lodged into the hole, shutting off the flow of gas into the Dungeon. With nowhere else to go, the gas would spill back through the hole and out into the main server room. He wondered how many people would collapse before they realized their attempt to slow him down had backfired.

In any event, he had to stay alert for whatever else they might try.

A loud tone emanated from the terminal workstation, indicating the satellite was back in position. Within seconds, he would be able to contact Samantha.

The fact that her transmitter was still active meant it was still clinging to her back molar. He hoped she was in a better position than he was.

Chapter 79

Inside the small room, Samantha watched Umarov closely as she struggled to understand his ultimate goal. The constant buzz and hammering of construction taking place in other parts of the building echoed softly through the closed door.

He seem to be watching her just as intently, waiting for any indication that her team had made contact again through her tooth transmitter. She vowed not to give him the satisfaction.

"What can you gain from killing the president? What are the Chechen terrorists offering you that you couldn't afford on your own?"

He smiled at her. "So, you do recognize me?"

"Anytime there's a big financial partnership deal between Russia and some other nation, you're right there, practically with your arm around the president. Your net worth must measure in the millions."

His steely gaze locked under hers. "It's billions."

"Then what did the Chechens do to make you turn against your own country?"

"Since we will be working so closely together, I guess it's safe to tell you."

He stood up, crossed over to the window, and pulled aside the curtain, letting the view through the window shine into the room. Through the brown colored mesh covering that spread across the outside of the window, she could see the capital of the Russian Federation on the other side of the river. He pointed to the tall spires of one of the world's most recognizable buildings.

"All my wealth is tied up inside that building. My money is the blood that flows through the beating heart of the Russian Federation. And the three regimes before it. That money has been in my family for generations, and I can't touch any of it. I am a man dying of thirst in the middle of the ocean. What good is it to be the richest man in Russia, if I don't have access to my own money, anytime I want?"

"How is killing the president going to get you your money?"

Umarov chuckled. "I asked the president if I could be given free access to my money to do with as I please. Do you know what he told me? Over my dead body. If that is what he wants, then by the gods that is how it shall be.

"The Chechens agreed to help me. I would fund the assassination of the president, and they would claim responsibility. In the ensuing chaos, I could grab the money that is rightfully mine. And then, if I choose to stay in Russia, it will be on my own terms."

"You were going to start a war, for money?"

"No. I am going to start a war, for a lot of money. And it's my money anyway."

"How was this war going to free up your money? It's not like it's just sitting in a room in the Kremlin for you to walk in and grab it."

"Actually, it kind of is." He produced a small USB thumb drive from his pocket. "All I have to do is plug this into the correct computer, and then I can move my money anywhere in the world in a matter of seconds. But to get to that computer, I needed a way to gain access to a part of the Kremlin I normally cannot go. Helping to carry a bleeding president back to his private quarters, and the location of a very specific computer, is my way in."

"So you don't care about the Chechens desire for independence from Russia?"

"Of course not. They were a means to an end. But now I have something better. I have you."

"Well you can forget it. I will not help you."

"It cost me nearly three times the original price to have the code rewritten, just for you, in such a short time. But it will be worth it."

She was about to respond again when Skyler's voice echoed in her head. "Sam? Can you hear me?"

She tried to keep the look of surprise off her face, but Umarov noticed it in an instant. Before she could respond, Umarov was at her side. He gripped her face in his hands and applied pressure on the back of her jaw, forcing her mouth open. He spoke into her gaping mouth as if it were microphone, which it was.

"Hello Skyler. If you can hear me, tell her and then she will tell me."

Skyler's voice echoed in her head. "Is that Umarov?"

"Yes." Her answer was for both of them.

Umarov gripped her head even tighter and moved in close. "Good, because I'm only going to say this once. Your girlfriend here is going to kill the President of Russia. But before she does that, she's going to record a video saying that she did it under direct orders from MI6. If you think I am bluffing, think about Moscow, Idaho. After the president is dead, and the whole world logs on to YouTube to find out that the British government was behind it, I will be free to do as I please."

Before she could react, he reached into her mouth and twisted the transmitting cap off her tooth.

He dropped it on the floor and crushed it under his heel,

severing the last connection with her team.

He took a step back and smiled down at her. "There. That ought to keep everyone busy for a while."

Chapter 80

Skyler stared at the monitor as the transmission went dead. His first instinct was to call upstairs to the head of MI6 and let him know what was happening. But then, that would create a flurry of activity throughout the agency that would look, to the outside world after-the-fact, like they had been gearing up for the assassination.

It didn't matter what the truth was. The YouTube video would be enough to bring Russia and England to the brink of war, with every nation the world over picking sides.

No. He couldn't contact MI6 and warn them. It was better to stick with the original plan. He glanced over at the Google maps graphical display and saw the plane Alex was on would be landing within half an hour. Just enough time to move the satellite into position and regain contact with him.

As he entered satellite movement commands into the terminal, his mind thought about Uncle Robert's goal to rebuild the Peacekeepers X-Alpha unit. Despite the failures of the past, Robert had convinced his superiors to let him form an autonomous organization that operated outside the boundaries of committees, subcommittees, and oversight that plagued the other agencies under UN control. They would be allowed to operate without the red tape associated with organizations as large as the United Nations. But if the Peacekeepers X-Alpha couldn't save the world, while operating independently, maybe Robert had been too quick to send them out on their first mission, without first ensuring that they could work together as a cohesive group. Of course, this mission was supposed to be a simple snatch and run. Get a cell phone from a tiny police station in the Midwestern United States. What could be easier? But it had quickly blown up into a much larger operation than any of them were prepared to handle.

No, maybe prepared wasn't the right word. They had spent most of this mission reacting to the situation. If they had any hope of stopping the assassination, they had to get out in front and start forcing the bad guys to react to them.

He glanced over to a side monitor that showed the view of a security camera he had hacked into. From the angle of this camera, he was able to watch the group of MI6 agents outside his room. When they had realized that their attempt to gas him had failed, they had proceeded with the task of cutting through the titanium door. He looked at the progress they had made, crunched the numbers in his head, and realized they were cutting much faster than he originally thought possible. They would be through the door in less than twelve hours, when he should have still had more than twenty-four.

The ticking clock had just taken a giant leap forward.

Whatever Umarov had planned, if he didn't do it soon, the Peacekeepers might not be in a position to stop him.

Chapter 81

The wheels of the commercial airliner touched down with a screech, accompanied by puffs of white smoke, at the Vnukovo International Airport, twenty-eight kilometers southwest from the center of Moscow, Russia.

Before the fasten seatbelt sign was even turned off, Captain Oleg stood up from his seat and flashed his badge at the flight attendants. He, Alex, and Melissa would be getting off first.

The plane taxied to the gate; the accordion-like jet bridge extending out to connect the plane with the terminal. As soon as the flight crew opened the main door, Alex stood and followed Melissa into the aisle, with Oleg leading the way.

Someone from inside the plane behind him called out his name.

"Alex?"

Nobody on this flight, filled mostly with Russian nationals, would have any idea of who he was, let alone call out his name as if they knew him. He turned around to see who was trying to get his attention when the voice echoed from behind him again, even though he was facing a different direction.

"Alex? Can you hear me?"

The voice wasn't coming from inside the plane. It was coming from inside his head.

He didn't know if he would ever get used to this.

He mumbled quietly, trying not to draw attention to himself by speaking too loudly.

"Loud and clear Skyler."

"We have a big problem, Alex."

"What do you mean?" he whispered back.

"Sam told you about the technology to reprogram people?"

"Yes?" he said, drawing the word out longer than he needed to.

"Umarov is using it on her."

"What?" he said, still talking quietly.

"He is going to make her kill the president."

"What?!" he yelled, not caring who heard him.

Skyler continued. "Umarov said he was going to have Sam assassinate the President of Russia, and claim she did it under orders from MI6. She's going to record a video and post it on YouTube, telling the world that Britain was behind the assassination of the Russian president."

"Can't she resist?"

"The programming happens at the subconscious level. She might be able to fight someone off if they tried to put headphones on her. But if they pumped the sounds in through speakers... as long as the audio waves are heard by the ears, there's nothing anyone can do."

Alex stopped at the threshold of the aircraft before stepping out into the tunnel of the jet bridge. "What does this mean?"

Skyler paused for a moment, the pain of what he had to say evident in his voice. "Once programmed, she will work toward her goal with unwavering determination. You may have to kill her to keep her from killing the president."

Someone touched his shoulder and he jumped. The flight attendant spoke in perfect English, with only the slightest hint of an accent.

"Is everything alright?"

He looked deeply in her eyes, searching for an answer that was not there.

"No. Everything is not alright."

Chapter 82

Alex crossed the threshold of the aircraft into a new world. A world where the one person he knew he could trust had just become the enemy.

A new line had been drawn in the sand placing him, and the person who'd hired him, on opposite sides. He didn't like it one bit. If he wasn't able to help save the President of Russia, his chances of staying in the organization that had recruited him were slim, at best. They were even less if he killed the very person who recruited him.

Melissa walked back onto the jet bridge toward him. "What's the matter Alex?"

He looked at her. "Whatever happens, promise me you will do your best to not harm Samantha."

She squinted at him. "Well, when you put it that way, I can't promise anything. What's going on?"

He turned to Captain Oleg. "When do we meet your cousin?"

Oleg glanced at his watch. "He should be waiting for us in the VIP hall now."

"Take us to him."

The captain led the way through the crowded airport. He flashed his badge at a security checkpoint and got the three of them through without needing to provide any documents for Alex or Melissa, other than his verbal assurance they were prisoners in his custody, despite neither of them wearing handcuffs.

They entered a less crowded section of the airport. No, not less crowded. Practically deserted.

Captain Oleg led them into one of the private suites in

the VIP hall.

As soon as he was in the room, he held his arms wide and walked briskly to a uniformed soldier. "Cousin!"

They gave each other a big hug and a kiss on each cheek. Oleg spun around and pointed toward Alex and Melissa.

"These are the ones I told you about."

His cousin's eyes shifted back and forth between them. "Good. Separate them."

Strong hands grabbed Alex from behind and ushered him to a small room off to one side. He didn't struggle, or resist. It was important he showed a high level of cooperation if they had any hope of working together to stop Samantha.

He was forced into a chair at the only table in the tiny room. One of the two soldiers spoke to him with a thick accent, "Wait here."

Chapter 83

According to the clock on the wall above the door, Alex had been seated at the table of this tiny room for nearly an hour, with only one guard. The Russian's shoulders stretched the entire breadth of the doorway, so it was obvious only one guard was needed.

Fortunately, the time spent alone, well almost alone, in this room had given him and Skyler a chance to formulate a plan to prevent the assassination. After the first few times of him talking out loud in the tiny room, and assuring the muscular soldier he was only talking to himself, the guard had gone back to ignoring him.

The best plan they could come up with hinged on the most unlikely of scenarios. It was a simple plan, all the best plans were, but it still required the cooperation of the Kremlin Regiment, the bodyguards for the Russian president.

They were still arguing with each other about how to convince Oleg's cousin of what was coming when the door opened and the guard sidestepped out of the way. Captain Oleg's cousin walked in and sat down in the chair opposite Alex.

He leaned forward and placed his elbows on the table.

"My name is Viktor. And you are?"

"Alexander Chase."

"And you work for?"

"I'm not really sure."

"Your friend, Melissa Stone, has not been very helpful either. She insists she does not know anything about the attempt on our president, which is a ridiculous notion to begin with. The Kremlin Regiment provides the best security in the world. No one can get to our president."

Skyler's voice echoed in his head. "Ask him about the state dinner tonight."

Alex cleared his throat and looked the soldier squarely in the eyes. "I'm not here to tell you that there's a flaw in your system, but there is."

Skyler pushed again. "Ask him about the state dinner."

"I'm getting to that," he mumbled.

Viktor was about to respond to his earlier comment, but then suddenly looked at him strangely. "Who are you talking to?"

Alex gave him a disarming smile. "The little voice in my head?"

Viktor snapped his fingers and the soldier by the door pulled a Zippo lighter from his pocket. He flipped open the cover, just like you always did on the world's most famous lighter, and flipped the rocker switch that sat where the flame should have been. He snapped the lighter closed and set it on the table in front of Alex.

Viktor frowned back at him. "Did that take care of the little voices in your head?"

"Skyler?" he mumbled quietly. There was no reply.

Viktor sat back in his chair and crossed his arms. "Now where were we?"

"Before you silenced the voice in my head with that box, it told me about the state dinner tonight."

A look of shock flashed across Viktor's face, and then it was gone, replaced again with his standard neutral expression. "I don't know what you're talking about."

"Is Umarov going to be there?"

Viktor leaned forward. "Supposing there was a formal

dinner tonight with the president, of which I'm not admitting to, and that the richest man in the Russian Federation was invited, what do you know?"

"I know that Umarov will bring someone not on the guest list. And because he is who he is, he will get her in. That is the flaw in your security."

Chapter 84

"Alex! Can you hear me?!"

It was the tenth time Skyler had said that, and there was still no response. He slammed his fists on the table.

"Bollocks!"

A voice from behind shattered the silence. "Having a bit of a problem?"

He spun around in his chair and looked it Basil, tied awkwardly to his coworker, and then to the server rack, craning his neck to look up at him. With no one else to talk to, Basil was as good as anyone to unload his troubles to. Even if he was an MI6 agent, and working against him, it still helped to talk through a problem out loud.

"Yeah, I guess you could say that."

Basil shifted uncomfortably; bring up a muffled complaint from his companion, who was still half asleep.

"In fact, I would go is far as to say you could use some help."

Skyler laughed and waved his arms around the room. "If you haven't noticed, my options are very limited."

"But you still have options."

"What options?"

"Me."

"You?"

"I was listening to you talk to that guy, Alex, on the terminal. Are you really trying to stop an assassination attempt on the President of Russia?"

"Yes."

"If it's such a credible threat, why aren't you warning the FSO?"

"The source of our information was not obtained through standard channels. We're unable to provide the proof most government agencies would require, and a warning would be summarily dismissed along with all the other false claims that happen on a daily basis."

"What makes you think this one isn't another false claim?"

"It isn't."

"But how do you know?"

"I can't tell you how we know. But the source of our intel is infallible."

Basil laughed. "If it's so infallible, what are you doing trapped down here, helpless to your operatives in the field?"

"The intel is infallible. Once we move on an operation anything can happen, and then we have to improvise."

"How's that working for you?"

Alex glanced over at the monitor showing the progress of the team outside cutting through the titanium door. He looked back at Basil, his shoulders drooping. "Not so well."

"I've been watching you, kid. You're smart, but you don't have street smarts. I would wager that improvisation is not your strong suit."

"I do much better with logic."

"Then here's some logic for you. Untie me, and I will help you."

Skyler sat up in his chair. "Help me with what?"

"Help you stop the assassination of the President of Russia, if you still believe that is going to happen."

"Why do you want to help me?"

"I heard what that other voice said earlier, the one with the Russian accent. I'm not about to let him drag Britain into a war. As long as he wants to blame MI6 for the death of the President of Russia, and you want to stop him, you and I are on the same side."

"Can I trust you?"

Basil nodded toward the monitor showing the progress of the team outside the titanium door. "They'll be through that door in the next hour. If you don't switch over whatever program you're trying to decode to the Newton algorithms, you'll never crack it in time. You need to trust me. And you need to start right now."

Chapter 85

A couple hours after telling everything he knew to Viktor, or rather more like spilling his guts in the midst of an interrogation, Alex found himself sitting in the main security room of the Kremlin with his hands cuffed behind his back. Security room was a rather loose term for something that looked more like ground control for NASA. Monitors lined the walls, while dozens of personnel watched their private screens without blinking, and even more people flittered back and forth picking up completed activity logs and dropping off new blank ones.

Alex had been seated at one of the end stations with the monitor switched over to show the main entrance to the dining hall. Viktor stood next to him while they both watched the monitor waiting for Umarov to arrive for the private state dinner. If he arrived alone, it would be the last thing Alex would ever see.

Anytime someone knew something bad was about to happen, they usually hoped they were wrong. In this case, Alex hoped he was right so that Viktor wouldn't take him out back and execute him by firing squad, or whatever method was the current favorite in the new Russia.

On the monitor, guests arrived in a steady stream. By his count, Alex had already tallied thirty people in attendance for the small, intimate, private dinner. And the limousines were still lining up outside.

Alex didn't know how the technicians could sit there for so long without blinking. He had only been staring at this monitor for less than an hour, and his eyes were already starting to dry up. He was about ready to concede defeat and accept his punishment, just to relieve the burning sensation in his eyes, when the soldier sitting next to him pointed at the screen. "There he is."

Alex blinked several times, trying to re-wet his eyes, and watched from the bird's eye vantage point of the security camera as Umarov walked away from his limousine and ascended the steps to the front door.

Alone.

Alex blink a few more times and tried to focus on the screen. The limo sped away without anyone else climbing out. Clearly he was missing something.

He watched as Umarov approached the checkpoint, held up his arms up for a cursory weapons check, and gave his name to be verified against the roster. A security guard waved a wand up one side and down the other of his body while a second verified he was an invited guest. Umarov dropped his arms, thanked the two security guards, and walked into the private residence of the President of Russia.

Still alone.

Something was very wrong. Skyler had said that Umarov told him point blank that he was going to use Samantha to assassinate the president.

Tonight.

But where was she?

Why wasn't she with him?

Viktor grabbed him by the shoulders and lifted him out of the seat. "You've wasted enough of my time."

Viktor shoved him down the aisle, past rows of technicians all staring at their own screens. He had to think of something, anything, to get Viktor to believe him. And he had to do it fast.

"Viktor wait! She must be coming in with somebody else.

Or maybe Umarov snuck her in as part of the serving staff."

Viktor was not buying any of it. "For all I know, you and the woman were sent here to assassinate the president. I gave you the benefit of the doubt for my cousin's sake. I'm afraid I've been too lenient with you. Tomorrow, I will decide what to do with the two of you. And since nobody knows you're even here, my options will not be limited to the constraints of the Geneva Convention."

He had to get Viktor to believe him before the President of Russia was assassinated, Britain and the Russian Federation went to war, and took the rest of the world with them. "Viktor, you have to…"

He was interrupted by a technician who turned in his chair just as they passed him. "Excuse me sir, Governor Yezhov of the Ryazan Oblast is requesting an exemption from the guest list."

Viktor stopped, still gripping Alex's shoulder tightly.

"Show me."

The technician tapped a few keys and the screen showed an older gentleman in a tuxedo with a beautiful blonde-haired woman, many years his junior, hanging on his arm. It was apparent they had both been drinking.

Viktor squinted at the screen. "That's not his wife."

The technician smiled knowingly. "Wouldn't be the first time."

"Go ahead. The Ryazan Oblast's support is very important to the president."

The woman flipped her hair back and Alex's eyes nearly popped out of his head.

"That's her! That's Samantha!"

Viktor pinched a nerve in his shoulder, causing him to wince in pain.

"Nice try, do you think me the fool?"

"You have to believe me! That's her! She's getting in!"

Viktor shoved him into the arms of two security guards waiting at the end of the aisle. "Take him down below and lock him up with the woman."

Chapter 86

After being politely told to shut up, or he would be shut up, Alex let the two guards walk him out of the security control room. He thought about trying to overpower them, but he was in the middle of the Kremlin, with his hands cuffed behind him. Even if he overpowered his two guards, he wouldn't get far before being swarmed by dozens more.

The elevator ride, down several floors, occurred in silence.

What more could he say? They had failed.

He chuckled to himself taking in the irony of it all. They had more than just failed. They had become instrumental in helping the enemy achieve his goals.

It was Samantha's job to stop something like this from happening. And now, she was smack dab in the middle of it, playing for the wrong side. She had become the enemy's biggest ally, by being in the wrong place at the wrong time. It could just as well have been him. It would've been a harder sell to claim he was acting under orders of the United States military, but from what he'd seen watching the television mounted in the corner of the rec room while in prison, the news rarely cared about the facts. Given the chance, they would sell the sizzle on a steak still sitting in the freezer.

The elevator slowed to a stop and the doors opened, accompanied by the faint ding of a bell. Down at the end of the hall, a guard stood with his face pressed against an open slot in the metal door, rubbing at his crotch.

One of Alex's guard called down to the man. "What do you think you are doing?"

The guard never took his face away from the slot, but waved at them to come closer and join him.

The two guards looked each other, and then both broke into a smile. Alex knew what they were thinking. The door guard must've confiscated the women's clothing. And everyone loved a peep show.

The two guards rushed Alex down the hallway. As they got closer, the door guard stepped sideways, readjusted his hat while looking ashamedly away from them, and pointed to the open slot in the door.

Ignoring Alex, the two guards pushed at each other, trying to be the first one to peek through the slot.

Alex was the first to notice that the door guard's uniform was several sizes too large for him.

As the door guard looked up at him, and his face became visible below the brim of the hat, Alex gasped in surprise.

Melissa, dressed in the baggy guard's uniform, gave Alex a wink and a smile before cracking her baton across the heads of the two guards in a single sweeping motion.

Their heads ricocheted off the metal door, and they both went down, piled one on top of the other.

Alex couldn't believe Melissa had gotten the drop on her guard.

"How did you…"

She shrugged. "Soldiers and guards both lead very lonely lives. I took advantage of his overwhelming desire to get it on with a willing woman."

Alex spun half around, showing her the handcuffs. "Tell me you've got a key for these."

She did, and he rubbed at his wrists once he was free. It seemed he had been in handcuffs more often in the past few days than in his entire two years of imprisonment.

"Samantha's already in the building."

Melissa couldn't hide the look of surprise on her face. "She's here?"

"Yes."

"Good."

"Not good. She's going to kill the president."

"What?! I thought you guys were trying to stop it?"

He quickly explained what little he knew about the technology that could turn anyone, even Samantha, into an assassin. "That's why she's the one we have to stop."

Melissa looked up and down the hallway. "I don't know if you've noticed, but we're both fugitive Americans who just escaped from a prison cell in the middle of the Kremlin. I don't think we're in a position to stop anybody from doing anything. We'll be lucky if we can get out of here alive."

Alex shook his head. "I won't accept just getting out. I have to save Samantha, and by saving her, I can save the president."

"I understand why you'd want to prevent war by saving the president, but why Samantha?"

"She recruited me. If I have any hope of staying in the organization she works for, I have to save her."

Melissa crouched, retrieved a gun and a radio from one of the unconscious guards, and held them out to Alex. "Well, if we plan to save the world, we're going to need these."

Chapter 87

Samantha stumbled, laughing loudly as she leaned heavily on the governor to keep from falling down. All it had taken was a few drinks in a nearby bar, and a make out session in the limousine on the way over, to get into one of the most exclusive parties in all of Eastern Europe.

She had done many things for Queen and Country, but tonight would be the pinnacle of her career in MI6. It was not the place of a British agent to question her orders, but she had to admit to herself at having second thoughts about the assassination order she had received a month before.

She had requested a secured call to the director of the SIS himself, and verified the authenticity of the order. She apologized to him for having any doubts about the mission and resolved herself to carrying out her sworn duty to the best of her ability.

So here she was, in the private residence of the President of Russia in the very heart of the Kremlin, dressed in a slinky cocktail dress, and looking much drunker than the governor.

She opened her clutch purse and extracted a stick of gum. Unwrapping it, she waved it in the governor's face while partially slurring her words. She spoke in English, accentuating her lilting British accent. "I don't want anyone to smell alcohol on my breath, or they'll know I've been drinking. You want one?"

He teetered on the balls of his feet, clearly finding that standing still was much more difficult than moving forward. "No one cares we've been drinking."

She gave him a wry smile, shoved the gum in her mouth,

and slurred her words while smacking the gum loudly. "But I'm a lady."

As they stumbled down the hallway to the main dining room, she spotted the ladies restroom.

"If you'll excuse me guvnor," she layered on a thick cockney accent to that last word, which, for some reason, he loved more than anything. "I need to freshen up. You go on ahead, I'll find our table."

He wobbled slightly as he looped his arms around the small of her back. "Don't be too long my turtledove."

She brushed her lips across his, and then whispered into his ear, "How could I stay away from you any longer than necessary?"

His hands slid lower, and he gave both buns a tight squeeze. She laughed and pushed away from him.

"Save that for later, love."

He grabbed her hand and pulled her close. "How about you and I get out of here after the second course?"

She tilted her head and smiled up at him. "I would like that very much."

As she pulled away, their hands extended all the way out until only the fingertips were touching. She let their touch linger for a moment before stumbling away out of reach. As she wobbled unsteadily toward the bathroom, she kept spinning back around to make eye contact and giggle. He was clearly enjoying every moment of it right up until the point she stepped into the bathroom and closed the door behind her.

Once inside, she stood up straight. Any indication that she had had even a single drink melted away in an instant.

She had a job to do, and not much time to do it.

Bending down, she checked the stalls and made sure she

was the only one in the restroom.

She was.

She snapped open her tiny purse, ripped at the lining, and slid out a bright neon pink piece of paper. Unfolding it revealed the words "OUT OF ORDER" written in big block Russian letters on the brightly colored paper.

She's spit out her gum, wadded it up, and stuck it to the back of her handmade sign. She opened the door to the bathroom, stuck the sign to the outside of the bathroom door, and closed it again.

She was alone, and would not be disturbed.

Now to make sure of it.

She kicked off her shoes and wedge the heels under the restroom door. That would keep anybody from walking in and surprising her before she was done.

Now for the weapon.

Unfortunately, a skimpy cocktail dress, along with the constantly groping hands of the governor, meant there was no way she could sneak anything bigger than a piece of paper into the Kremlin.

Fortunately, everything she needed, was hidden in this restroom.

Dropping to her knees, she felt around under the marble sink until her hands found the Walter PPK, Hollywood's favorite British secret agent gun, taped to the underside. While not packing quite the punch of its larger sibling's in the handgun world, it easily fit into a cocktail purse, and would give her a fighting chance to escape the Kremlin in the chaos that was sure to accompany the death of the president.

She slipped the gun into her purse, and left that on the edge of the marble sink where she could grab it on her way out.

She made her way to the first stall and pulled open the paper seat-cover dispenser and began removing various black polymer and metal components.

She did the same with the other two seat-cover dispensers until she had all the parts to a Dragunov sniper rifle, complete with two ten-round magazines and flash suppressor, laid out on the tiled floor, ready for assembly.

Chapter 88

Alex couldn't remember the last time he took his pants off in a closet, with a woman doing the same thing less than a foot and a half away from him. This time, however, sex was the last thing on his mind. He glanced over at Melissa. She was already stripped down to her underwear and bent over the laundry pile of waiter uniforms. Okay, maybe not the last thing on his mind.

She selected two sets of uniforms and tossed a white shirt, bow tie, cummerbund, and black slacks to him. He caught them with one hand, while still holding his pants halfway up with the other.

She gave him a quizzical look. "Really?"

He realized he had been staring, snapped out of it, and cleared his throat.

She ignored his gawking and got right to business as she buttoned up her white waiter's shirt. "How long do you think we have before they notice were missing?"

He was glad she chose to ignore his impropriety. "I've been thinking about that. Fortunately, we were relegated to an empty part of the basement, so nobody should hear the guards when they wake up. And with the state dinner going on, I doubt anyone will be checking on them too often. Still, our time crunch is not how quickly will they find us, but how quickly can we find Samantha. We have to find her before she does anything we'll all regret."

They finished dressing and slipped out of the closet, following their noses to the kitchen. Right before they walked through the double doors into the kitchen, Melissa grabbed his arm and held him back.

"How's your Russian?"

"Serviceable. Yours?"

She grimaced. "A little rusty, but I think I'll manage."

He gave her a reassuring smile. "Let's just get in there, find Samantha, and get out of here."

She smiled back. "You make it sound so easy."

He placed a hand on her shoulder and squeezed, adopting a mocked serious look on his face. "Don't worry, it won't be."

Chapter 89

With the sniper rifle assembled, Samantha made her way over to the wall and began tapping lightly on each tile, starting with the row closest to the floor, until she found the one that sounded hollow.

Digging her fingers around the edge of it, the plaster crumbled away easily until the tile felt loose. She gripped the corners and popped the tile off the wall, exposing a hole in the drywall behind it.

She worked off several more tiles around the first one, until she exposed a much larger hole in the wall. She could now see the back of the electrical outlet in the wall that faced the dining area.

She spent the next few minutes slowly dismantling the back of the electrical outlet, being careful not to electrocute herself as she pulled out the wiring.

As she worked, she heard the scuffling sounds of someone ignoring the out-of-order sign on the bathroom. She held her breath as she watched the door.

Her heart skipped a beat when she saw one of her shoes shift slightly from the pressure exerted by someone on the other side.

She rose silently to her feet and crept across the floor until she was at the door. She slowly pressed her shoulder against the door, easing it back into the doorframe.

Whoever was on the other side was insistent about getting in. Using all her weight, she held the door fully closed until the person on the other side gave up and left.

She let out the breath she had been holding and wedged the heels of her shoes tighter under the door before returning to her work on the outlet.

Chapter 90

Alex was in the kitchen, loading plates of salad onto a serving tray. While cruising through the dining room empty-handed, he had been threatened with immediate termination if he didn't get back to work. He didn't like the inconvenience of having to do actual server duties, but it was better than being ejected from the Kremlin altogether before finding Samantha.

Melissa pushed through the double doors leading out to the dining room, spotted him, and hurried to his side.

"I just checked all the bathrooms. She's not in any of them, and the one by the entrance is out of order. Are you sure he said she went to the bathroom?"

"Yes. I asked him when he was expecting his companion to join him. He said she was freshening up and that she would want a glass of champagne waiting for her. Where else do women go to freshen up?"

"Well, she's no longer in the bathrooms. Maybe she was coming in to the dining room while I was going out."

Alex hefted the tray full of salad plates onto his shoulder. "I'll keep an eye out for her as I do a round."

She gave him a disapproving look. "You're serving food?"

He spun back around to face her. "The supervisor's already yelled at me. I suggest you grab something to carry when you go back out there. It won't do us any good to attract unwanted attention for being lazy on the job."

He pushed backward through the double doors and headed out into the dining room.

He continued to scan the room as various dignitaries,

politicians, and celebrities got his attention to demand a plate of salad. As he dropped salads, he took the empty soup bowls and added them to his tray. The last thing he needed was for the supervisor to see an empty tray and make good on his threat. That would force Alex's hand too soon and he didn't want to draw his pistol, currently shoved down the back of his pants, until he absolutely needed to.

He made another complete turn of the dining room, smiling and nodding at people courteously as he loaded more dirty dishes onto his tray until it threatened to topple over from being overloaded.

He was headed back to the kitchen, to unload his tray, when he passed by two other servers complaining in Russian.

"I've had the chafing dish plugged in for over an hour, and it's still cold."

"Maybe it's broken, just like everything else in Russia."

"No. I verified it worked before I left it."

"You know the wiring in this old palace. It works even less than our leaders."

"Shush. Not so loud. You don't want anyone to hear you."

"Look at them, they're all drunk. Nobody cares anymore."

As he walk past, he glanced down at the outlet on the wall, between the two skirted tables, where the chafing dish was plugged in. The dishes nearly slid off his tray, and clattered to the floor, as he came to an abrupt stop.

He stared down at the outlet and saw something you should never see through the holes of an electrical plug.

Light.

That couldn't be right.

He looked more closely.

Light was showing from the other side of the outlet.

Realization dawned on him in that split second. There was a hole going all the way through the wall to the other side of that outlet. The light he was seeing was coming from the adjacent room. But what room was that? And what would somebody see if they were looking through the wall from the other side?

He spun around slowly and, in his mind's eye he saw a bright red line, indicating line-of-sight from somebody on the floor on the other side of that outlet, draw itself straight through the room, tracing an unobstructed path to the very same podium that the President of Russia was just stepping up to, to give his welcome speech.

He glanced back just as the tiny circle of the three-pronged outlet popped out and silently landed on the carpet. If he had been six inches in either direction, the two skirted banquet tables on either side of the outlet would've blocked his view, and he would've missed it completely. In that instant, he realized the other side of the wall was the bathroom Melissa had said was out of order.

His tray canted wildly as he let go of it and reached behind him.

Unfortunately the noise of every dish on his overloaded tray shattering on the floor drew all eyes to him at the same moment he drew his pistol out into the open.

The world slowed to a snail's pace as Alex swung his pistol around and sighted down the barrel on the outlet.

Someone yelled "gun" in Russian, causing an immediate reaction from everyone in the room. As expected, the reaction was not a calm and orderly response to the stimulus of a maniac with a gun in the same room as the Russian president. And it only got worse when he began firing into the wall.

He managed to fire off seven rounds before being tackled by security and pinned to the floor by several heavy men in expensive suits. It seemed everybody wanted to get in on the act of being able to say they saved the president's life.

Chapter 91

Before chaos had erupted in the dining hall of the Kremlin, Umarov was seated at a table closest to the stage. His heart raced in anticipation as he watched the president ascend the steps and approach the podium to give his welcome speech.

In moments, he would be one of several brave souls who risked their own safety to help carry a dying president back to his private chambers.

The micro USB device burned a hole in his pocket and he reached in to fiddle with it. During the confusion, he would plug it in to any of the computers in the president's private office. By the time the civilians, like himself, were asked to leave the presidential care to professionals, and ushered safely out of the Kremlin, he would have access to all of his money.

He had been lost in thought, deciding which private island in the Caymans to buy, that it almost didn't register when someone yelled "gun" right before several loud pops echoed in the massive dining hall.

The gunshots were loud.

Louder than he would've expected.

He had provided a flash suppressor for the sniper rifle that would also serve to dampen the sound of each shot fired.

Why hadn't she used the flash suppressor?

He had paid extra to program her with the skills of a master sniper. If something went wrong, because the programming was faulty, he would demand a full refund. It didn't matter that his supplier had the reputation of always delivering at one hundred percent, without fail. He did not like the thought of being her first mistake. And if she had made a mistake, the woman who called herself Hannah had just made a dangerous one. And if she couldn't correct it, she would make a dangerous enemy.

Commotion on the stage brought him back to the present.

He jumped from his chair and vaulted up on to the stage. "I can help carry the president."

One of the president's bodyguards stopped him with a stiff arm to the chest. "I'm going to have to ask you to leave, sir."

Umarov tried to look past the six-foot-five behemoth for the president's body lying on the floor. "If the president is hurt, I want to help. He's a close personal friend of mine."

The bodyguard pushed him back. "The President's fine. I'm going to have to ask you to exit through the main doors with the rest of the guests."

He gave the bodyguard a panicked look. "The president's been shot."

The bodyguard looked at him strangely. "The president was not hit. Please leave with the others. I will not ask you again."

Umarov backed away. The bodyguard instantly turned to stop another guest who wanted to help. With the bodyguard no longer blocking his visibility, he was able to see the president, surrounded by a wall of bodyguards, rush out through the side doors, unharmed.

The president was alive.

He had failed.

No. It wasn't him who had failed. It was his assassin who had failed.

No. Neither of them had failed.

It was Hannah who had failed.

With the recent attempt on his life, the president's security services would be on high alert. It would take months, if not years, to be able to get this close to him again.

Hannah had failed him completely.

He glanced around him, trying to regain his bearings.

The dining hall was nearly empty now, with half of the guests all crammed on one side, still trying to funnel through the main doors.

Directly ahead, security guards were lifting one of the servers off the floor by his bound hands. While not quite mistreating him, the guards weren't treating him in a friendly manner.

As the server got to his feet, he glanced over at the podium and made direct eye contact with Umarov.

A hint of recognition flashed across his face, and a smile formed on his lips. He was letting Umarov know who had beaten him.

Umarov's list of new enemies was growing longer.

Chapter 92

Before the formal dinner had shifted instantly into pandemonium, Melissa had been refilling someone's water glass at a nearby table and was the first to notice Alex's tray tipping wildly as he reached for his gun.

That could mean only one thing. He had spotted Samantha. And if he was drawing his gun out now, in front of everyone, the president was in immediate danger. So she did the only thing she knew to save his life at that moment in time.

She yelled "gun" as loud as she could in Russian, knowing the president's private bodyguards on the stage would spring into action immediately.

When Alex fired, he didn't shoot at Samantha, or at anyone, but at the wall.

Why had he done that?

The other side of that wall was the out-of-order restroom.

She cursed herself. It'd been too long since she'd had to operate at a hundred percent capacity. She'd gotten lazy since the last time she was tasked with saving a world leader's life.

She forced her way through the panicked crowds that surged for the main doors. All she had to do was get carried along with the flow of bodies, and she would be led right past the restroom door. As she pushed through the crowd toward Alex, she called out his name over the noise. He craned is neck and they made eye contact. She nodded, indicating she was hot on Samantha's trail. Relief washed over his face and he let his head drop back down to the floor.

Bodies pressed on her from all sides as everyone forced their way through the door, like grains of sand all fighting to be the next one through the thinnest point of the hourglass. Once in the hallway, she pushed her way over to the wall and ran to the bathroom door with the out-of-order sign on it.

She slipped the pistol out from the back of her slacks and chambered the first round. She kept the gun down at her side, out of sight from everyone running past in their hurry to get out of the building.

She pushed on the door. This time, there was no resistance, and it swung open easily.

She glanced inside. A Dragunov sniper rifle sat perched on a bipod on the bathroom floor, pointed at a large hole in the wall.

The bathroom looked deserted. If Samantha had been here, as evidenced by the sniper rifle, she probably left when Alex started firing through the wall.

But she had to be sure.

She slipped into the bathroom, letting the door swing closed behind her.

With her pistol raised, she ducked down and scanned under the bathroom stalls.

Nobody was standing on the floor in any of them. But if somebody was standing on the toilet in one of them, she wouldn't be able to tell from this angle.

Slowly she walked sideways, her arms holding the pistol rigid in front of her. One by one, she verified every stall was empty.

Samantha was no longer in the bathroom.

Whatever head start she had, was lengthened because

Melissa had to stop and check.

If Samantha had gotten out of the building, and into the city, there was no way Melissa could find her on her own.

It was time to include the Russians in their plan.

She unclipped the radio from her belt and pressed the talk button.

"Is the president safe?"

She recognized Viktor's voice as he replied quickly over the radio, "Who is this?"

"Hello Viktor, it's Melissa. Don't do anything to Alex until we have a chance to explain."

"Why should I listen to you?"

"Because the president is still in danger."

Chapter 93

It took nearly half an hour for Umarov to get out of the Kremlin, walk across the river, and enter the house at Sofiiskaya Embankment 18. This house had been the perfect rally point for his assassination plan. It was directly across the Moskva River from the Kremlin, and rather than being an active residence, the outside was completely covered with a photo printed canvas that showed the façade of a generic red brick building with windows to hide the fact that it was an abandoned property in disrepair, and suffering from rampant vandalism.

He entered the front room to find Samantha sitting in a chair in the semi-darkness. She sat with her back to him and stared at the Kremlin across the river through a square hole she had cut in the canvas just outside the broken window.

Without turning around, she spoke to him.

"Leave the lights off."

"I wasn't going to turn them on."

"Who did you tell?"

"What?"

She spun around in the chair to face him, the gun in her hand partially lit by an outside streetlamp.

"Someone yelled gun as soon as I was ready to take the shot. The only way that could've happened was if they already knew I was there. Didn't the British government pay you enough?"

"What?"

"You were hired to make sure the rifle was delivered to the bathroom. That was all you had to do. Nobody else knew there would be a gun in there but you."

Suddenly he realized what was happening. She was still living with the fantasy programmed into her that MI6 had ordered her to assassinate the Russian president.

"Nobody paid me. That was my plan. I'm the one that wanted you to assassinate the president."

"I received my orders from the director of the SIS himself; otherwise, I wouldn't be here. Do you want more money? Is that it?"

He shook his head, becoming a victim of his own plan.

"You did not get your orders from the SIS. Your orders came from me."

"That is ridiculous. You're nothing but a tool to get me what I needed to accomplish my mission."

"Go ahead, call the director. He will deny any knowledge of giving you the order to assassinate the Russian president."

"Of course he will deny it. Besides, my orders are to stay dark until the job is done, however long that takes."

"No, he will deny it because your orders came from me, not him."

"Funny, I don't remember discussing anything with you. But I do remember my call with the director."

"Listen to me…"

She stood up abruptly. "No! You listen to me! How are you going to get me access to the president?"

"I can't. And who knows how long it will be before anybody can."

"Then I have no more use for you."

She lifted the pistol and pointed it at him.

He held his hands up in front of him. "Wait!"

He heard her fire three shots, but his brain only registered the first bullet as it shattered the bones in his hand, kept traveling along its trajectory, and punctured a lung, right before his body went into shock.

He collapsed backward to the floor. His chest burned, and it was impossible to catch his breath. It felt like he was drowning.

As he lay there on the floor, staring at the ceiling and gasping for air, Samantha's face came into view.

"The Crown thanks you for your assistance. But I can handle the rest from here."

He tried to say something, but found it impossible to speak.

She stood and pointed the pistol at his face.

The last thing he saw was the flash from the muzzle, and then nothing.

Chapter 94

Basil sat alone, on his side of the conference room table, on the third floor of SIS Headquarters at Vauxhall Cross. His face was still swollen, but the painkillers they had given him deadened the pain.

Agent Baird of SIS Internal Affairs had been grilling him for several hours, on and off, about the events that had taken place in the Dungeon.

Baird reviewed his notes and looked at Basil over the rims of his glasses.

"If I can go back to the point when you first discovered that there was an unauthorized individual in the Dungeon. What did you do?"

"Per protocol, I locked down the terminal right away."

"And were you successful in locking down the terminal?"

"Yes."

"At any point, did the individual gain access to the terminal?"

"No."

"Did he ask you for the code to unlock it?"

"Look at my face. What do you think?"

"And did you give it to him?"

"Of course not. I would die before letting anyone have access to the Dungeon terminal. And if the strike team had not breached the door when they did, I was afraid it was going to come to that."

The internal affairs investigator flipped through the pages of his report.

"So the only crimes our perpetrator had committed were breaking into a secure government facility, assaulting British

Intelligence agents, and getting locked in the Dungeon for a few hours."

The painkillers were starting to wear off, and he was starting to feel how his face must've looked. "Sounds about right to me."

"While these crimes are pretty severe, they wouldn't result in the death penalty. Why do you think he open fired on the assault team as soon as they entered?"

"You would have to ask him."

"Rather unfortunate, wouldn't you think, since the assault team was forced to terminate him."

"That is most unfortunate."

The investigator opened a bright red folder, flipped through a couple of the loose pages inside, and closed it again.

"The autopsy report showed there was an abundance of narcotics in his system. Why do you think that was?"

"I don't know."

The investigator removed his glasses. "Do you think he went in to that room expecting to die?"

"I wouldn't know."

"Did he say anything that would lead you to believe he was suicidal, or off balance in anyway?"

"Like I said before, our conversations were limited to 'give me the password' and 'no'. We never talked about anything else."

The investigator stared at him silently for a long time before jotting down a quick note, closing the folders, slipping them into his briefcase, and snapping it shut.

He stood abruptly, grabbing the handle of his briefcase as he did so. "This concludes my investigation. You are free to go."

With that, he spun around and exited the conference room.

It had happened so suddenly, Basil couldn't believe it was actually over. He watched the conference room door, expecting the investigator to return at any moment and give the "don't leave town" line. But that didn't happen, and the door remained closed.

He had been sitting there for a full five minutes when the door finally did open and in walked the custodian dragging a vacuum behind him.

He spotted Basil and his bushy eyebrows shut up in surprise. "I'm sorry. I thought this room was empty."

Basil stood up. "I was just leaving."

Once out of the conference room, he walked briskly down the hall to his office, trying his best not to walk with a limp. The painkillers were really wearing off now, and he felt every bump and every bruise. Maybe if someone did notice the limp, they would attribute it to how he looked, and think nothing more of it.

As he entered his private office, he shut, and locked, the door behind him. This was the first time he had been alone since the assault team burst through the door into the Dungeon.

He sat down, more like fell actually, into his chair and kicked off his left shoe. Picking it up, he pulled out the Dr. Scholl's sole insert and retrieved the USB thumb drive that had been digging into the arch of his foot.

He held it up between his thumb and forefinger and inspected closely, as if the significance of the data locked inside was inscribed on the tiny aluminum shell.

The information they had unlocked, when he and Skyler had decoded the message, was important enough, and time sensitive enough, that Skyler willingly gave up his life to protect it.

It was important enough that Basil felt compelled to lie to his superiors about everything that had taken place in the Dungeon.

He glanced at his watch. He had less than eight hours to get this information to the people Skyler was working with before the message they had decoded would become old news, and then the world would never be safe again.

He switched on his desktop computer and plugged in the thumb drive. The programs, embedded on the thumb drive and hand coded by Skyler himself, took over his system. His screen filled with multiple windows of running programs, picking right back up where they had left off.

He moved his mouse and expanded one of the windows to fill the screen. Right now, it showed a flat line cutting horizontally across the screen. If the field operatives Skyler was working with tried to contact him, that one thin line would suddenly expand and contract, responding to the quality of the transmission. It would give Basil a visual cue that somebody was on the other side of the open comm link.

Somebody he needed to talk to, desperately.

Somebody that needed to know what only he could tell them.

Chapter 95

Alex had been sitting in the small interrogation room for hours, his hands fastened together in front of him with several plastic zip ties. He didn't like the fact that the table and chair were both bolted to the floor, or that the bare cement walls terminated at drains that formed the entire base of all four walls. It was obvious, bad things happened in this room.

The door opened and Viktor entered, not smiling.

Of course, in the few hours he had known him, he'd never seen Viktor smile once. So it was conceivable he could still be in a good mood.

Viktor snapped his fingers at the guard standing in the corner behind Alex. "Cut him free."

The guard stepped forward, slipped the combat knife out of the sheath on his side, stuck the knife quickly between Alex's hands, and sliced through the zip ties in a single fluid motion.

Viktor sat down in the chair across the table from him.

"I have reviewed the security footage, and it is exactly as you say."

Alex leaned over the table, the guard behind him shuffling forward, ready to stab him in the back with that same knife if he made a move against his boss.

"Did you catch her? Is she alive?"

Viktor raised a hand, waving the guard back, without taking his eyes off of Alex.

"Using security cameras around the city, we tracked her to a house across the river. The camera showed two people entering shortly after the attempt on the president's life, and only one person leaving a short while later."

"Who left?"

"The woman."

"So you got Umarov?"

"When the police arrived, they found his body. He had been shot several times in the chest, and once in the head while he lay dying."

Whatever personality Umarov had programmed her with, was now loose out in the world. Had Samantha overcome her programming and eliminated Umarov? Would she be making her way back to the organization that had recruited her, before she recruited him? Or was she still living out her programmed reality and changing her plan to fit the new situation?

Could she still be considered an ally?

Or had she become a new enemy?

The answer terrified him all the way down to his core. He looked at Viktor.

"Where is she now?"

"We tracked her to an Aeroexpress station. We are reviewing the security tapes for every station along that line to see if she got off before reaching the airport. Nothing yet."

"I would like to offer my help, in catching her."

Viktor shook his head.

"That will not be necessary. We will find her before she gets out of the city. She is in unfamiliar territory, with no access to resources. She killed the only one who could help her, so it is only a matter of time."

He looked down at his hands, newly freed from the bindings.

"What about Melissa and I?"

"We're securing transportation to take the two of you out of Russia. Where you go from there, is up to you. Before you leave, there is someone who would like to speak with you."

"Who?"

"The president."

His heart leapt into his throat, and he swallowed it back down.

"I don't want to sound insulting, but would it be possible to talk to my people before I meet with your president?"

Viktor furrowed his eyebrows. "I'm sorry, I cannot allow you access to a phone in the Kremlin."

"You don't need to give me access to a phone." He motioned to the Zippo lighter on the edge of the desk. "You just need to turn that off for a moment."

Chapter 96

Basil was exhausted, and his body needed the sleep to heal, so he leaned back into his ergonomic office chair, and let himself doze off. He had turned the volume up on his computer, so if anyone on Skyler's team tried to make contact, it would alert him immediately and wake him up.

For the first time, in several hours, he fell asleep rather than getting knocked unconscious.

His brain, trying to process all that had happened in the past day, started to dream.

Basil found himself back in the Dungeon, sitting next to Skyler as they worked to decode the message. Fortunately, in his dream, he was not as battered and bruised as he had been in real life.

With the message finally decoded, and the time sensitive nature of its contents weighing down on them, Skyler glanced over at the monitor showing the progress of the assault team. He shut down the terminal and crawled under the table to unplug the USB drive.

As he crawled back out, he looked up at Basil.

"I need you to do something for me."

Basil didn't respond verbally, and Skyler took that as an affirmation of his desire to help. He held the USB thumb drive out to him.

"As soon as you get the chance, plug this into a computer and wait for Alex or Melissa to contact you. Give them the information we decoded. Once you've done that, you can destroy the thumb drive and be done with it."

Basil took the thumb drive. "What about you?"

Skyler looked at him, sadness written all over his face.

"You need to lock this terminal down, and then I'm going to tie you back up. No one can know I accessed the Dungeon systems."

"What are you going to do Skyler?"

Instead of answering, Skyler gave him more instructions. "I need you to hide that thumb drive where no one will look for it."

Basil removed his shoe, and tucked it under his arch support.

Skyler nodded. "Good. Lock down the terminal."

As soon as he had entered his private code, and locked the terminal, Skyler followed him back to the server racks. The other MI6 agent was still unconscious, and had no idea his partner was helping the man who had broken into the Dungeon and attacked them.

As he let Skyler zip-tie him to the server racks, he looked him in the eye. "You don't have to die. You'll spend time in jail, admittedly a long time, but this doesn't have to be the end for you."

Skyler averted his eyes as he finished securing him to the rack. "You make sure Alex gets that information as soon as possible."

An explosion reverberated throughout the room as the assault team finally broke through. Skyler raced back to the terminal, scooped up his pistol, and spun around to point it at the open entrance. He ignored the shouted commands from the approaching assault team and fired three shots.

The shots sounded strange.

They didn't sound like gunfire, silenced or otherwise.

They sounded more like someone knocking lightly on a wooden door.

The assault team responded with three shots of their

own.

That's not how he remembered it. The assault team had let loose a hailstorm of bullets that tore Skyler to shreds before his eyes.

They hadn't responded with only three shots.

And they certainly hadn't sounded like three more knocks on a door.

Instead of going down under a barrage of gunfire, like he had only hours before, Skyler responded with three more shots. This time, the strange sounding shots brought Basil out of his dream, and partially awake.

He looked around the semi-darkness of his office, disoriented for a moment, his breath coming in shallow gulps while perspiration seeped from every pore in his forehead. Another light rapping at his office door brought him fully awake.

A muffled, female voice, came through the door.

"Basil? Are you in there?"

He leaned forward, shut off the monitor, cleared his throat, and stood up.

Which he did far too quickly, forcing him to grip the edge of the desk for balance as the room spun around him.

Another faint knock was followed by the same, melodic voice. "Basil? It's me, Elise. Are you okay?"

The room finally righted itself, and he called out to her. "I'm fine."

"I got the alert that the situation in the Dungeon had been resolved. I've been waiting for you to finish your interview to see if you're okay."

"I'm fine."

There was a moment of silence, and he could sense her leaning against the door to his office. "Can you open the door?"

"I'm okay, really. But I'm not up for visitors right now."

"You should go home. I can take you home."

"I just need to rest for a little bit."

"Will you open the door?"

"I'm not a pretty sight right now. I don't think you should see me like this."

"I don't care what you look like. Just open the door."

He closed his eyes, taking a deep breath.

"If I ignore you, will you go away?"

"I just ate a whole bag of crisps from the snack machine. I'm not going anywhere."

He knew she was being more than honest with him. She would sit in front of his office until he opened the door to let her in. He glanced at his monitor, double checking that it was off, and then went and unlocked the door.

She'd heard him disengage the lock and responded by pushing the door open. She slipped in and shut the door quickly behind her, re-engaging the lock.

She glanced around. "You're keeping it dark in here. I like it."

"Elise, I…"

She held up a finger, silencing him. "Don't worry Basil. We don't have to do anything until you feel better."

"I let you in so you can see I'm okay. But you have to go."

"I'm not going anywhere dear. I'm going to stay by your side and nurse you back to health." She tilted her head, and let a playful smile tease the corners of her lips. "And when you're feeling better, I can leave the nurses uniform on."

That comment elicited a tiny response from his pants. He had to get her out of here.

"Yes, yes. That sounds great. Right now, I have to finish filing my report…"

She interrupted him. "They're making you file your report now?"

"They're not making me do anything. It might be several days, maybe even a week, before I come back to work. I want to get it all down while it's still fresh in my mind."

Her eyes searched his desk in the darkened office. "The computers off. And I can't see you writing in the dark."

"I was sitting in my chair…"

"In the dark?"

"Yes. In the dark. I was sitting in my chair gathering my thoughts when you knocked."

"I wanted to make sure you were okay."

"And as you can see, I'm fine."

"You don't look fine."

"I'm not comatose in some hospital somewhere. I'm standing here talking to you, in immense pain, but still generally okay."

"Can I at least take you home?"

"Of course. But right now, I need to be alone."

"I'll just sit over here and be real quiet."

"No. You have to go."

"Why?"

"I can't explain right now."

"Can't? Or won't?"

"Don't start this again."

"I have higher clearance than you. There is no secret you can know that must be kept from me. Unless, I'm not the only girl in your life?"

"Of course you are."

She crossed her arms in defiance. "Then why are you

trying to kick me out of your office?"

He was about to say something when a noise echoed from the speakers of his computer. Unfortunately, it wasn't a noise he could easily dismiss, or explain, as it was a man's voice coming through the speakers of his computer, loud and clear.

"Skyler, this is Alex. Do you read?"

They looked at each other, both stunned to silence as the speakers crackled again.

"Skyler? Now's not the time to be silent, I need you."

She looked from the computer speakers back to him, shock registering on her face. "Oh my God! I am the only woman in your life. The only one. And I let you... do... things... to me!"

"What? No! It's not like that at all."

The voice interrupted again. "Skyler! Come in!"

She glanced at the computer speakers, and then back to him. "Skyler? Isn't that the name of the bloke who broke into the Dungeon?"

He gripped her shoulders. "Okay, you want to stay? You get to stay."

He guided her to the chair in the corner. "Just sit here, and don't say anything."

He rushed back to the computer, switched on the monitor, and pressed a key on his keyboard.

"I'm afraid Skyler can't come to the phone right now. Is this Alex?"

The voice replied with a question of his own. "Who is this?"

"My name is Basil, and I have an urgent message for you."

Chapter 97

Alex sat silently in the interrogation room and listened to the strange voice in his head.

"Right before the assault team breached the Dungeon, Skyler and I decoded a message that discussed a shipping container that was being loaded on a cargo ship in Lewiston, Idaho."

"Who are you again?"

"My name is Basil. I was one of the of MI6 agents in the Dungeon when Skyler broke in."

"And why are you telling me this?"

"After I heard Skyler talking to you earlier, I could tell he was trying to stop the assassination of the President of Russia... Oh my God! Did you do it? Were you able to save the president?"

"Yes. He's safe."

He could hear the relief in Basil's voice. "Good. I helped Skyler decode the message because I wasn't about to let anyone kill the President of Russia and blame it on Britain."

"Okay, so the message said they were loading a shipping container onto a cargo ship. So what?"

"Skyler believed that a shipping container is the only thing big enough to hold and transport the computer used to program people into assassins. If we lose that shipping container, we lose the computer that could be used again to program another assassin."

"So why don't we just intercept the ship before it gets to the delivery port?"

"Because there's not enough time."

"Those ships are slow. We should have plenty of time."

"The message wasn't just about the shipping container. It detailed plans to hijack the cargo ship and load the container onto a submarine as soon as it was out to sea."

"Then why don't we inform the United States Coast Guard? They can stop that from happening."

"Skyler insisted that it had to be you and your associate, Melissa, who got to the container first."

"Why us?"

"You are the only ones willing to destroy the computer built into the cargo container. Anybody else would keep it for themselves. As long as that computer exists, even if there is only one of them in the world, nobody is safe from anybody. The ship is scheduled to depart in four hours. You have to destroy that container before the ship makes it to the open ocean."

The plan sounded ludicrous.

Sounded ludicrous?

It was ludicrous.

All Alex had to do was get he and Melissa back to Idaho, find the shipping container that housed a supercomputer capable of programming people into master assassins on a ship bound for the Pacific Ocean, and destroy it.

Simple.

Despite the many things that could go wrong with such a plan, he saw one big major flaw, and he told as much to the voice inside his head.

"There's no way I can get from Russia to the United States in less than four hours."

The voice was not swayed. "Yes there is. But you need to convince the Russians to help you. And I'm sure the only one who could do that would be the Russian president himself. If you could somehow talk to him, you could get access to their scramjet. It travels a hundred kilometers above the earth and can get you to Idaho in less than an hour of flight time. Do you think there's any way you can ask to speak with their president?"

"I actually delayed a meeting with him to talk to you."

"Perfect. We don't have much time. Meet with the president, get on that scramjet, and destroy that computer. I'll stay here and try to help you any way I can."

Alex viewed the overhead map of Idaho in his head. He was glad he had studied it earlier, because now he was going back. The airport he had followed Umarov to, what felt like years ago even though it had been less than a couple of days, was the closest one he could think of to the port in Lewiston.

"The Pullman airport is only a half hour away. Are you able to find us a ride from that airport to Lewiston if we can make it in time?"

"I can help you in many ways, but I'm not sure how I could do that."

"I'm going to give you a phone number. Call it and ask for Nate. Tell him where to pick us up, and when."

He rattled off the number from memory and there was a pause as Basil was either writing it down or committing it to his own memory. "Who is this Nate fellow?"

"He's a friend. He'll drop everything and go wherever you tell him to go as long as you say it's for me."

He looked up at Viktor. "I'm ready to see the president now."

Viktor leaned forward and flipped the switch on the Zippo lighter. "You understand, your conversation with the president must remain private."

Alex nodded. "Of course."

And then another thought occurred to him.
He pointed to the lighter.
"Do you think I can keep that?"

Chapter 98

The audio signal strength, displayed on the monitor of Basil's computer, flatlined. Whatever had been interrupting the signal before, was doing so again.

Behind him, Elise approached silently. "Basil?"

He replied without turning around. "Yes?"

"Who was that?"

He spun around to face her. "I need you to keep an open mind about what I just did."

"And what, pray tell, did you do?"

"What did it look like?"

"It looked like you used MI6 resources to contact a third party, a third party I might add, who is connected with the man who broke in to the Dungeon and nearly killed you. But you didn't just make contact, you instructed him to conduct illegal activities, and assured him you will use MI6 resources to assist him."

"I told you to keep an open mind."

"An open mind?! You're committing treason."

"No I'm not. I didn't ask him to do anything against the British government."

"You shouldn't have asked him to do anything. We're analysts, Basil. We don't conduct clandestine operations. And we certainly don't initiate them!"

"I had no choice."

"What are you talking about?"

"Once we decoded the message, Skyler and I knew there wasn't enough time to involve anyone else in this. It would take too long to explain to someone that such a thing even existed. And any delay would result in losing the only chance we had at destroying that computer."

"Are you listening to yourself? You've got Stockholm syndrome. That's the only explanation for your current behavior."

"He did not turn me because he treated me well. I mean, look at me. He did not treat me well at all."

"Then why have you violated every oath we gave to this country to help him?"

"I listened in on what he was doing, and knew he was doing the right thing."

"Breaking into the SIS headquarters is never the right thing to do."

"In this case, it was."

"Never."

"Skyler told me who he worked for."

"Who?"

"I... I can't tell you that."

"How do you know he wasn't lying?"

"He died to protect his organization."

"An organization that asked him break into a secure British facility."

"I know it looks bad..."

She laughed nervously. "Looks bad? Someone, who could very well be an enemy of the Crown, broke in to where we work... where you work! And now you're helping them?"

"I can't explain it right now."

"Just try."

He closed his eyes. "I can't. There are less than five people in the world who know about this organization. And now I'm one of them."

"I thought what you and I had was beyond keeping

secrets."

"This is bigger than the both of us. This is bigger than everyone in MI6. This is bigger than all the intelligence agencies in the world, combined."

She stuck her hands on her hips. "And now you're part of it?"

"This wasn't something I asked for."

She shook her head and took a step back. "Why are you going along with this? Why didn't you turn over everything to Watson?" Her face suddenly shifted as a thought popped into her head. "You lied to Watson. Why would you do that?"

"Because I'm convinced that this organization needs to stay a secret. We operate in an environment that succeeds, no thrives, on secrets. And this is the biggest one of all."

"And when they ask you to turn your back on your own government to help them, what will you do then?"

"I would never do that. They are not the enemy, Elise. But right now, they are the only ones who can stop the enemy."

"And you are making this judgment call, all by yourself?"

"No. I'm asking you to make it with me."

Chapter 99

Viktor led Alex out to the plaza that surrounded the Tomb of the Unknown Soldier in the Alexander Garden, just outside the Kremlin wall. At this time of night, the plaza was deserted, save for the increased presence of the Kremlin Regiment.

The bodyguards were interspersed at twenty meter intervals throughout the plaza, most likely because the president had chosen to meet with a stranger outside the Kremlin walls, fully exposed mere hours after the failed attempt on his life.

Viktor stopped at the bottom of the steps and motioned for Alex to keep going.

As he walked up the steps leading to the Tomb of the Unknown Soldier, and the eternal flame that burned brightly in front of it, the guards kept a wary eye on him. He was an outsider, an American no less, and he was approaching the most powerful man in the Russian Federation. A man they had sworn to protect with their very lives.

He stopped next to the president and watched the flame lick hungrily at the air from the center of the bronze star embedded in the ground.

They stood together; quietly watching the flickering orange flame for several minutes, before the president finally broke the silence, speaking in English. "Your name is unknown, your deed is immortal."

It was not often that Alex met with powerful men. In fact, he couldn't remember the last time he found himself standing face-to-face with a world leader. It was just not a situation he was prepared for. He didn't know what to say, so he said nothing.

The president turned to him, indicating the bronze lettering, illuminated by the eternal flame, with a wave of his hand.

"It is the English translation of the brass inscription. This tomb is dedicated to everyone who shall forever remain unknown to us, but sacrificed all that they had to keep Russia strong. Viktor tells me it was you who thwarted the assassination attempt."

"I had some assistance from your security team."

"Come now, Mr. Chase. Russians are a proud and honest people. We own our mistakes rather than cover them up and point fingers, like some other countries that shall remain nameless. If it were not for the risks you took, putting yourself between me and a bullet, I would not be standing here tonight."

"I only did what needed to be done."

"I asked to see you because I wanted to thank you personally for what you did for me, and for Russia."

"It was my pleasure sir."

"I do not know many people who would have the balls to draw a weapon in my own house. Did I say that right?"

Alex smiled. "Yes sir. You said that right."

The president smiled back. "Good. American vulgarities are just not as colorful as good old-fashioned Russian swearing."

"We'll, you're very good at it sir."

"You know what else I'm good at? I'm good at driving my bodyguards crazy. When I told them I wanted to meet you, they urged me to do it with a big plate of bulletproof glass between us. I'm pretty sure Viktor had to change his underwear when I told him I wanted to meet you out here.

Did I say that right too?"

"You doing fine, sir."

"Excellent. Even though I am wearing Kevlar body armor under my suit, I'm sure they're all jumping at every little night sound around us."

"That explains why Viktor tried to convince me to request to meet with you in the library. I told him I was fine with whatever place you wanted to meet."

"Thank you, because I had a very specific reason to meet with you at this particular spot. This place signifies the need to maintain secrecy about what really took place here tonight. While the events of what happened have been immortalized by every news station around the world, it is still important that your part in all of this remain unknown."

"That works very well for me, sir. The organization that sent me to save your life seems to prefer to stay hidden in the shadows."

"Out of curiosity, does this organization have a name?"

"I guess you can consider us just another of your unknown soldiers."

"Well, whoever you are, I am forever in your debt."

"And if I'm not being too forward, Mr. President, I know how you can repay that debt."

Chapter 100

Alex and Melissa, both encased in aviator g-suits over their flight suits, looked like a pair of cosmonauts ready to go into space, which was not too far from the truth.

They both stared up at Russia's entrance in the race to turn space into a destination for the ultra-rich. The Cosmopolis XXI Aerospace System was a two part system that consisted of a carrier aircraft, the M-55X Geofyzika high altitude aircraft, and a manned rocket module, the C-21. The C-21 itself was built around a 3-seat passenger capsule, with integrated life support systems, and an engine unit that could be best described as a giant rocket strapped to the back of it. The C-21 rocket module was mounted on top of the M-55X and would be carried partway on its journey through the sky until it was released to continue the rest of the way under its own power.

The original design set the C-21's top speed at over four hundred miles per hour on its journey to the edge of space. The scramjet modifications pushed that speed to over four thousand miles per hour. He and Melissa were about to join an elite club of the fastest people on earth, or above it. A club reserved for space pioneers and the astronauts circling the planet in the International Space Station.

Melissa tugged on his sleeve, and he knew why without turning around to ask her. The square boxy design of the spaceplane did not look at all like what he would have expected a state-of-the-art jet-propelled plane, that could take them a hundred kilometers above the earth's surface and then glide back down through the atmosphere to land safely at their destination over five thousand miles away, would look like.

It didn't help that the spaceplane had been painted in primary red, white, and blue colors, making it appear more like something that should be standing in front of a grocery store to place a toddler in, deposit a quarter in the base, and watch it rock back and forth, brightening the child's day.

The C-21 pilot walked up and slapped his hand on Alex's back.

"Are you ready to travel to the other side of the world at Mach 6?"

Alex took a deep breath and let it out slowly. "As ready as I'll ever be."

The pilot laughed. "It's not as bad as you think. As long as you plug your g-suit into the control panel, the computer on the plane will make sure all the blood in your body doesn't pool in your legs."

He laughed again as he walked toward the piggybacked planes.

Melissa watched the pilot ascend the ladder to the top plane before turning to Alex.

"Are you sure this is the only way?"

He barely nodded his head. "We have three hours to get to Idaho, find the computer, and destroy it. We should just count ourselves lucky that Skyler knew about this. Nothing else in the world could get us there in time."

Melissa watched the pilot disappear into the spaceplane. "I must admit, I was skeptical the first time you told me about it. From what little I know about the scramjet, it sounds more like science-fiction than science."

"It still sounds like science-fiction to me, even after the briefing we just had. The rocket engine on the back of the spaceplane has to push us up to near-hypersonic speeds before the supersonic ramjet engine can even kick in. And once that happens, then we'll really be moving."

"How did the president react when you asked if we could use it?"

"To be honest, he had to make a couple of calls to verify they were even working on something like I described. That's why it took so long to get here. He wasn't sure 'here' even existed."

The pilot for the M-55X approach them. "Are you ready to go?"

Alex looked at Melissa. She nodded slightly and he understood her hesitation. He felt it too. He looked back to the pilot and tried to give him a confident smile. "Let's do this."

They followed the pilot to the stacked planes. Melissa climbed the ladder first to the spaceplane mounted on the back of the carrier aircraft. As soon as she had settled into one of the two passenger seats, Alex climbed the ladder and joined her inside the world's most heart-stopping carnival ride.

He connected his g-suit to the computer control panel and clamped his helmet to the O-ring on the neck of his suit. The flow of oxygen from the spaceplane's internal supply started up immediately. Rather than fill the cabin with air, the pilot and his two passengers would each have their own air supply delivered directly through their helmets.

One of the things needed to get up to scramjet speeds was as light a payload as possible. And, believe it or not, filling the entire cabin with enough air pressure to match breathing at sea level, actually made the plane heavier. It was a grueling process of shaving off every ounce of mass to get the maximum potential out of the spaceplane.

Less than a minute after he had settled in, Alex felt the seat rumble under him as the pilot of the M-55X taxied out onto the runway. His stomach somersaulted as the carrier plane lifted off the ground. There was no relief for pressure on his inner ear as the plane continued on its steep trajectory and climbed higher into the sky as quickly as possible.

The brain's concept of time was one of the most flexible constants in the universe. It felt like they had been leaning back in their seats forever, even though it couldn't have been more than a few minutes, when they finally leveled out. Despite knowing that the worst was still ahead of him, it felt good to have this momentary relief from the constant acceleration.

Only the acceleration didn't let up, and the pilot pushed the engines harder, gaining speed for the next climb that would bring the carrier plane high enough to finally release the spaceplane.

These were the moments Alex hated the most.

He was not in control, and just along for the ride. Any error made by the pilots of either plane, could result in his death.

And there was nothing he could do about it.

The carrier pilot's voice came through the comm system of his helmet.

"How's everybody doing up there?"

The C-21 pilot responded. "Not trying to breaking any speed records today, eh Yuri?"

"I'm just trying to give our passengers a comfortable flight."

Alex toggled the comm switch to join in on the conversation.

"Don't take it easy on our account. We are on a very tight schedule."

The carrier pilot laughed. "Okay then. But just remember, you asked for it."

Melissa's voice echoed through the speakers of his helmet. "Don't encourage them."

But it was too late. He heard the engines on the M-55X build to a high-pitched whine right before the plane tilted up at a sharp angle. It felt as if a giant invisible hand pressed his whole body into his seat, everything inside of him threatening to squeeze out through any opening they could find.

A sudden jolt rocked the spaceplane, followed by the sensation of weightlessness that lasted for half a second before the C-21's rocket engaged and smashed him even deeper into his seat under the massive force of acceleration.

But the pressure was nothing compared to the force the g-suit exerted on his legs, doing its job to keep the blood circulating throughout his entire body.

Just when it felt like it was never going to end, they hit the ceiling of their journey and, if he hadn't been strapped into his seat, he would've floated right out of it.

The C-21 pilot's voice crackled through the speakers in his helmet.

"What did you think of the ride?"

Melissa was the first to respond. "I don't think I've ever been as terrified before in my life as I was just now. And I've cut the cords on my own parachute while still thousands of feet in the air."

The pilot chuckled. "Well if you believe in a god, now is the time to pray. Because you haven't seen anything yet."

Chapter 101

Five thousand miles away from where Alex and Melissa were preparing themselves for something that nobody could ever really prepare themselves for, a dark-haired woman sat on the sofa in the Governor's Suite of the Red Lion Hotel in Lewiston, Idaho.

Despite having the best view of the Lewiston skyline through the windows of her room, the woman was more interested in the open Skype window on her laptop, because it currently showed the person she was most upset with.

She was doing her best to rein in her anger as she spoke with Vakha, who had been Umarov's second-in-command until his untimely death.

"I'm sorry to hear about your boss, Vakha, but it's not because of..."

It was evident he was doing his best to hold in his anger as well, since he interrupted her again; the fifth time in less than two minutes.

"It was your program, Hannah, which resulted in Umarov's death."

"That had nothing to do with my program. That was not my fault."

"You created the assassin who killed Umarov. Of course it's your fault. What are you going to do about it?"

Hannah did not usually handle things personally, but with the recent threat of a mole in her own organization, she'd had to cut back to dealing with only a select few people whom she trusted without question. Based on his current actions, it appeared Vakha would need to be scratched off of that list.

"I'm not going to do anything."

Vakha was no longer able to hold back his anger. As his face filled the screen of her laptop, she could see the vein pulsating on his forehead. "What do you mean nothing?! You need to clean up the mess you made."

Once she'd made the decision to no longer deal directly with Vakha, her own anger dissipated. She was in control. She leaned back on the couch and felt better about her decision.

"I have reviewed the security tapes from inside the Kremlin. The person who stopped your assassination attempt knew exactly where she was hidden. I suggest you look at those closest to you for why your plan failed."

She wasn't about to tell him that, after reviewing the footage, it was evident that the latest recruit into Robert's Peacekeepers had figured it out based on the information presented to him only moments before. She would have to keep an eye on that one if she planned to maintain her position of always one step ahead.

Vakha was not swayed. "There was no leak on my end."

She smiled, glad to still be one step ahead of someone, and leaned forward to look directly into the tiny camera along the bezel of her laptop. "Frozen assets or not, I expect full payment, or else you will personally discover that my program works flawlessly."

She closed the Skype window on her computer before Vakha could respond. Let him stew over that for a while.

She didn't need the money, but if she made it look like she was ignoring a lack of payment, rumors would quickly spread among the underworld that Hannah was growing soft. And she couldn't have that. Fear was her most precious commodity, and she was good at cultivating it.

She glanced at the digital clock on the display of the DVD player, nestled in the cubby below the 32-inch flat screen TV. She still had a little over an hour before she had to make her way to the docks and supervise the loading of the semi-trailer-sized computer.

It would not take her long to destabilize the organization that directed the actions of leaders, for nations and extremist cells alike, as if they were mere chess pieces on a board game. She had worked hard to increase her worth to that organization, beyond the lowly pawn, only to hit a glass ceiling and be disallowed from the higher ranks; because she was a woman.

Soon, she would no longer need to use fear to control those below her. And those above her? They would quickly learn that she could not be so easily dismissed.

No longer would she be forced to follow the orders of the Phantom Council. She would discard them, as easily as they had discarded her, and become the Phantom herself. And as long as she controlled the minds of all who could hear, nobody would ever say no to her.

But before she could wield that kind of power, she had to get the computer to a place where nobody else could reach it. And that place had cost her a considerable amount of money to build. It was not an easy task, nor a cheap one, to build a facility on the bottom of the ocean and tap into the intercontinental phone cables that stretched across the sea floor.

She had wanted to wait until it was in place, and unreachable by those wanting to stop her, before using the brain reprogramming technology at her disposal. But once Umarov found out about it, during a night of heated passion that she was feeling less and less proud of, he hastily developed his assassination plot and insisted she run a test proving it could be used on anyone.

Since she needed to get her house-sized computer out to sea, and ironically, there was a city only twenty-eight minutes away from the easternmost west-port city in the United States also named Moscow, it seemed the perfect scenario.

Umarov had come to Idaho personally to observe the program in action. He had even gotten himself invited to the judge's fundraiser and was able to witness, firsthand, the young woman kill him in front of everyone before turning the gun on herself. The program worked.

The program worked too well, as Umarov had discovered.

When the first assassination attempt failed, the woman programmed to kill the Russian president would continue to pursue her goal until she succeeded. She must have determined Umarov was no longer useful to her, and eliminated him. It's what the assassin Hannah had modeled the program after would've done.

It would be interesting to see how this newly created assassin dealt with forming her own plan to accomplish her task. How adaptable was the program beyond the initial mission, were that mission to fail? And how long would the human brain function with a second identity suddenly forced upon it?

Only time would tell.

Hannah started to close the laptop when she saw the active window in the taskbar on the bottom.

Oh yeah.

Her.

She clicked on the task bar, and the program expanded

to fill the screen.

It was a frozen video image from the Kremlin security tapes. It showed a woman with blond hair, and wearing a waiter's uniform, pushing her way through the crowd of panicked dignitaries and politicians. Hannah tapped the space bar on the keyboard, and the video resumed playing. She watched closely as the woman made eye contact with Robert's new Peacekeeper, and nodded to him.

Hannah tapped the space bar, and the video froze again.

She looked closely at the image of the woman.

There was no mistake.

It was definitely Melissa.

And it was clear by her actions that she was working with the Peacekeepers, made more significant by her presence in the Kremlin at that particular moment.

Things had become a little more complicated for Hannah.

Chapter 102

It wasn't so bad, screaming along the edge of space at over five thousand miles per hour.

Scratch that.

It was the worst thing Alex had ever experienced.

Despite the cramp forming in the back of his jaw, he kept his mouth clamped tightly shut. He wasn't so much worried about losing his lunch as he was losing his stomach, lungs, spleen, and everything else that was supposed to stay inside his skin.

But that wasn't the worst part. The worst part was when the pilot sent the C–21 occasionally into a barrel roll. He claimed he did that so he could look out the window to see where they were on their journey.

Alex saw it for exactly what it was. The pilot might never get a chance to do anything like this again, so he was hot-dogging it.

On the last barrel roll, Alex ventured a glance out the window and saw the eastern seaboard of the United States rolling by under them. In less time than it had taken him to walk from his home to the nearby high school as a kid, they had traversed nearly halfway around the world.

The pilot rolled the spaceplane away from the ground, his voice crackling through the speakers in the helmet.

"Ladies and gentlemen, this is your captain speaking. Please return your trays to their upright position, extinguish all smoking materials, and observe the fasten seatbelts sign. We are now beginning our descent back to planet earth."

Apparently, the earth had other plans. The entire passenger compartment vibrated violently as the plane resisted diving back through the atmosphere. The only reason Alex didn't scream out in terror was because, if he opened his mouth, he might turn inside out.

He knew it was only his imagination, but he could feel the heat as they burned through the atmosphere. He could feel it through the ceramic heat shielding of the spaceplane, through his seat, and through the multiple insulated layers of his flight suit.

The mind was an amazing thing. Under hypnosis, people could be told that scalding hot water was about to be poured on their hand. When ice cold water was splashed on them, their skin reacted by turning red and blistering, as if the water had actually been hot enough to burn skin.

He knew his mind was compiling his worst fears together and telling his body to react to stimulus that wasn't even there.

The speaker in his helmet crackled, Melissa's voice came through barely above a whisper. "Does it feel warm in here to you?"

Chapter 103

Basil's heart raced when he heard the faint knock on his door. Elise had rushed out of the room half an hour earlier, claiming to need to use the facilities. He knew what she was really planning to do, but rather than try to stop her or escape, he decided it was best to sit in his office and wait for them to come and take him away.

The army on the other side of that door was very polite as they knocked quietly again.

He opened the door slowly, half expecting it to be shoved open by armed security, knocking him to the ground while they pounced on him ferociously.

His heart rate slowed when he saw Elise standing in the hallway, alone; a sandwich in each hand. She had not bolted from his office to turn him over to the authorities. She was putting her loyalty to him above her loyalty to Queen and Country.

But he was helping an unknown secret organization in direct violation of the oath he gave when he took this job. It was a dangerous place for either of them to be. A road fraught with peril. But they had already averted one major disaster, and they were not finished.

Behind him, a melodic tone emanated from the computer speakers.

He reached out and pulled Elise into his office, closing the door after her.

He rushed over to his desk and, using the mouse, clicked the green phone icon in the newly opened window.

"Hello?" was all Basil said.

A man's voice came through the speakers. "Who is this?"

Not wanting to give away too much information early in the game, he parroted back the caller's question. "Who is this?"

After a brief moment of silence, the voice spoke again, a little more hesitantly this time. "Is... is Skyler there?"

Okay, the caller knew Skyler. He had to be the one Skyler told him about. "Is this Robert?"

The voice did not reply.

Even though this was an audio only call, he leaned in close to the webcam stuck to the top of his monitor.

"Wait. Don't hang up. I have a message for you from Skyler."

There was no response from the other side of the line, but at least whoever it was had not hung up.

He told whoever was listening all about the events that had unfolded in the Dungeon, and how he just received confirmation from Alex that the President of Russia was still alive and the assassination attempt thwarted. He then described how he and Skyler decoded the message detailing the planned theft of the supercomputer that could program people into assassins, and how he sent Alex and Melissa back to the United States to destroy it.

Only then, did the voice respond.

"Well then, I am forever in your debt, whoever you are."

"My name is Basil, and I am here to help."

"Where are you now, Basil?"

"In my office."

"Is it secure?"

"Nobody can listen in on our conversation, if that's what you're worried about. I have a high clearance and I'm beyond reproach as far as my superiors are concerned. Nobody's checking on what I do."

"Then I thank you for your help, and instruct you to destroy whatever you used to intercept my call."

"Destroy it? But you need my help."

"My people can take it from here."

"Then let me ask you this. Are you out of the hospital yet?"

There was no reply.

"That's what I thought. Maybe you don't fully understand your situation. Your tech guy sacrificed himself for this operation, your primary agent has been reprogrammed into an international assassin, you are in the hospital recovering from a stroke, and right now I am the only one capable of helping your new recruit intercept that computer. This is the only chance we will get, before it's gone. If that thing is allowed to continue to exist, the world will never be safe. You need me to finish this operation."

There was a momentary pause before Robert spoke. "Does anyone else know you're doing this?"

He hesitated before answering, but finally decided the truth was the best course of action. "There is another MI6 agent with me."

"Then I must respectfully decline your offer."

"She can be trusted as much as I can. I want... We want to help you."

"I'm sorry, but the risk is too great to the both of you."

"Then let me say this to you, Robert. Try to stop me."

He closed the window on his computer screen, disconnecting the call before Robert could reply.

Elise was at his side. "Why did you do that?"

"Because he wants our help, he needs our help, but for some reason he can't say it."

"He's trying to protect us. What we're doing will be seen

as treason."

"Only if we get caught."

"And how do we keep from getting caught?"

"It's easy. We don't get caught."

Chapter 104

Alex's seat bucked wildly under him, like the mechanical bull at a western-themed night club. At the speed they were traveling, the slightest shift in air pressure buffeted the spaceplane like turbulence on steroids. He envisioned them skipping off the atmosphere like a rock skipping off the top of a lake. But unlike the rock on the lake, every time they skipped, it created friction that heated the thermal ceramic tiles built into the underside of the spaceplane.

Melissa's question had confirmed that it wasn't his imagination getting the best of him. It was definitely getting warmer. And if he could feel the heat through his insulated suit, it must be a sauna in the passenger compartment.

He found the comm button on his suit.

"Excuse me, pilot? Does the cabin normally heat up this much?"

There was no reply. He pressed the comm switch again.

"Excuse me, pilot? Can you hear me?"

There was still no reply.

He and Melissa looked at each other. Even though they could not see each other's faces through the tinted helmets, he guessed her face matched the same worried expression as his.

He pressed the comm switch again.

"Pilot?"

Still no reply.

He reached to unbuckle the five point harness that held him in his seat when the pilot's voice echoed in his helmet.

"I wouldn't do that. You might bounce around the cabin and damage some of my equipment."

"We thought something happened to you. Why didn't you reply?"

"I'm a little busy right now."

As if making the pilot's point, the cabin bucked wildly to one side. If he had managed to unhook the harness, he would have been tossed about the cabin. The pilot grunted as he fought to maintain control of the spaceplane. The plane righted itself and continued along its agitated path.

Alex still wanted to know how much danger they were in. "Should we be worried about the heat?"

The pilot replied with a single word. "Yes."

Chapter 105

Basil was impressed with the software program Skyler had built. He had successfully created software that could access any secured system in the world, and built that into a device that plugged straight into the USB port of any computer. The more powerful the computer it was connected to, the greater the capabilities of Skyler's USB thumb drive.

Right now, it was connected to the central computer network of MI6, so he was able to monitor the North American Aerospace Defense Command's internal communications system. There was a sudden flurry of activity as they began to react to the spaceplane that had unexpectedly entered US airspace. Skyler's system also allowed him to insert new data into the stream, and not just passively observe.

He began furiously typing out a string of emails that looked like a conversation between two technicians who were working diligently to reset the warning systems after loading a simulation test program, and forgetting to switch the system to test mode. It didn't take long before someone picked up on the emails, and began to spread the misinformation he had planted into the network. Part of his deception relied on the fact that people were more willing to except that somebody had majorly screwed up, rather than believe an enemy nuclear missile was dropping into the heart of America.

By the time NORAD figured out that the emails were faked, the spaceplane would have already touched down in Idaho, and hopefully, Alex and Melissa would be free to complete their mission.

Before they had even taken off from the Zhukovskiy Air Base in Moscow, the Russian president was already preparing his statement to apologize to the world for the emergency landing of a Russian aircraft on American soil during a failed scramjet test.

The official word from NORAD would be that they were aware of the test, and had monitored the spaceplane on its flight over, and ultimately into, the United States. They would keep the secret that somebody had infiltrated their communications network and implanted false information. That was something they would look in to internally, and it didn't need to become public knowledge.

A melodic chime alerted him to answer another phone call from Robert. The two angels on his shoulders battled with the decision as to whether he should answer the call or not as the mouse cursor hovered over the green telephone icon.

The good angel won and he clicked the button.

Robert did not wait, but began speaking as soon as he knew his call had been answered.

"Since you have decided to help, I'm going to give you additional information you don't know. I just received a call from a friend at NORAD where they have been tracking the spaceplane Alex and Melissa are on."

"I've already taken care of that."

"Right. The phony emails from the technicians. I'm glad to report that they are believing that for the moment. But it's why he called me. He wanted to know what I knew about it."

"What did you tell him?"

"I told him I was in the hospital, and not in direct

contact with my team."

"Did you tell him that it was your team on the spaceplane?"

"He asked me that point blank, and I didn't deny it. That's as good as admitting it at the level we operate."

"So what you going to do about it?"

"My guy works on the switchboard for radio intercepts, and the reason he called me was because he got an alert about a call going out from NORAD on an unauthorized channel. He wasn't able to listen in on the conversation, but he said the call terminated in Lewiston, Idaho."

"That's where Alex and Melissa are headed."

"How soon before they get there?"

"They should be touching down in fifteen minutes."

"How quickly will you be able to regain contact with them?"

"As soon as they are on the ground. I already have the satellite in position."

"Good. Be sure let them know that somebody, I'm guessing it's the owner of that computer, has been warned that they're coming."

"Do you know who owns the computer?"

"I have a pretty good idea."

"Who?"

Without warning, the call terminated abruptly from Robert's end.

Basil sat back in his chair and looked over at Elise.

She shrugged her shoulders. "I guess he wants to keep that a secret from you."

Chapter 106

Robert sat up in the hospital bed when his cell phone suddenly cut off, reset itself, and then started ringing again.

He answered it quickly, not wanting the nurses in the hallway to hear he had managed to smuggle a cell phone into his room.

"Sorry about that Basil, my phone cut off."

The voice on the other end was not Basil's. "I find it so tiring to keep up with the names of all your new little friends."

"What do you want Hannah? I'm busy."

"Busy trying to take what's mine away from me."

"What you created cannot continue to exist. It's not like a nuclear bomb, where all sides can continue to stockpile them as a deterrent."

"Are you saying I don't know how to handle my own toys?"

"I think that was made evident when you programmed my agent to assassinate the Russian president, and now she's loose out in the world doing God knows what."

He could hear the slightest hint of regret in her voice. "I am truly sorry about that. I had no idea Umarov had taken one of your people when he asked for a change in the program. But I didn't call you to talk about that."

"But that is what we're dealing with right now."

"Not entirely. Melissa is working for you and I want to know why."

"In case you haven't heard, I've been in the hospital, in surgery, and haven't spoken with her. She joined on her own."

"Then contact her, and tell her to leave this alone."

"And why would I do that?"

"You know why."

"Since you already know she's coming right to you, why don't you tell her yourself?"

"I don't want to force a confrontation with her."

"You mean you don't want to drive her away even farther."

"If you think, by using her, I will just give up and let you have the computer, you are wrong."

"I don't think any such thing. I already told you, she's there on her own."

"We used to be so close, Robert. I can't believe you would stoop so low as to use her against me. That is not something friends do to each other. Even old friends."

"You have the power to stop all of this, right now. Destroy the computer yourself, and then Melissa will be out of harm's way."

"I can't do that, Robert. I have to answer for my actions just like you do. I wish we were in charge, but we're not. You and I are the same."

The heart monitor attached to Robert's chest started beeping rapidly. "We are not the same."

"Yes, we are. We are the doers. The people who make things happen for those in charge. We don't decide what we do; we just make sure it gets done."

"We used to be on the same side, Hannah."

"Yes we did. We were going to change the world, Robert. All of us. But instead of changing the world, you changed."

"I realized peace was the change we were after. Not chaos."

"Do your superiors know about your colorful past?"

"They know all they need to know."

"And if I were to tell them of your exploits before joining with them?"

"It wouldn't make any difference, Hannah. They know who I am now. It doesn't matter who I used to be."

"Are you sure about that?"

"The only thing they care about is that I keep the world safe. And right now, that computer you created is the most dangerous weapon ever made."

"Only in the wrong hands."

"For a weapon like that, there are no right hands."

"That is not for you to decide."

He looked out the window of his hospital room, at the peaceful city of London as it stretched out before him. His reply was nearly whisper.

"Yes. Yes it is."

Before Hannah could reply, he hung up the phone, pulled out the battery, and dropped it into the trash receptacle next his hospital bed.

Alex and Melissa would be landing in Idaho any minute now.

It was up to them to destroy that computer.

Chapter 107

Alex sweated profusely as the heat became nearly unbearable in his suit. Fortunately, the ship had not broken apart or exploded yet. The pilot had been rotating the ship back and forth, spreading out the friction caused by reentering the atmosphere to different sides of the ship. As one side began to heat up to critical levels, the ship would spin to present another side to the unending friction. The pilot was spinning the ship faster as each side barely had time to cool before being called back into service to keep them from becoming a fireball streaking across the sky.

Right before he was certain he was going to die from dehydration, having already sweated out every ounce of water from his body, the pilot's voice came through on the comm.

"We're slowing down and the heat is starting to dissipate."

"How soon before it cools off in here?"

"That won't happen until after we have landed."

"And when is that?"

"In about a minute."

The spaceplane was now an unpowered glider, dropping through the air at high-speed. They were going too slow for the scramjet engine to function, and they'd already expended all their fuel pushing them to scramjet speeds. It was now all about the skill of the pilot in a box that was barely meant to fly.

The pilot tilted the spaceplane forward into a steep angle, and Alex could see the approaching runway through the front window. At this speed, they would disintegrate at the same moment they created a massive crater, when they hit the ground.

"You're coming in too fast!" screamed Alex.

The pilot replied with a chuckle. "Smoke'em if you got'em."

Just before they impacted with the earth, the pilot yanked up hard on the flight stick and the wheels hit the ground hard with a squelch.

At the speed they were traveling, he estimated it would take them close to a minute to slow down. But he also remembered how small this airport was from when he had chased Umarov's plane down the runway with his car, and he figured they had less than fifteen seconds of runway left.

Without warning, his whole body was thrown forward, straining against the harness, as they slowed quickly, rolled right up to the edge of the runway, and stopped when the front wheel dropped softly off the edge of the tarmac.

Before the spaceplane had even stopped rocking back and forth in the divot along the edge of the runway, the pilot removed his helmet and stood to open the canopy. He looked at them with a massive grin on his face. Clearly, he had enjoyed the ride.

He finished pushing open the canopy with his hand and addressed Alex and Melissa together.

"Thank you for choosing Kremlin Air for your nonstop flight to Idaho. Be sure to have the world famous potatoes while you are here."

Alex pulled off his helmet and started to remove his gloves.

The pilot waggled a finger at him. "Keep the gloves on. The outside of the plane is very hot."

Alex looked over to Melissa, who was just pulling off her

own helmet. Her hair was matted to her head in sticky wet clumps. She looked over at him and frowned. "Next time, I think I'll walk."

He laughed. "I'll be right next to you."

Outside, a car screeched to a halt on the runway.

The pilot pointed out of the spaceplane. "Friend of yours?"

Alex unhooked his harness and peered over the edge of the canopy.

Nate was standing next to his car gawking at them. He saw Alex and waved.

Alex and Melissa climbed out of the spaceplane and sloughed off their insulated flight suits. Their clothes underneath were damp from sweat, but there was nothing they could do about that. Besides, the clock was ticking if they hoped to get to the docks before the computer was gone forever.

Nate ran up to them. "That was awesome! You guys were coming in so fast, I thought you were going to hit the ground and... BOOM!"

Alex grimaced from the memory. "So did I."

Nate looked at Melissa and frowned. "This a different girl?"

Melissa reacted. "Girl?!"

Alex pointed to him. "Melissa, meet Nate. Nate, this is Melissa. The one you met earlier is... On another assignment."

Nate stuck his hand out. "Pleased to meet you Melissa. You a spy too?"

Melissa didn't shake his hand, but snapped her head toward Alex. "How much does he know?"

Before Alex could reply, Nate spoke up. "It's okay Mel.

I'm cool."

Her head snapped back to him. "Mel?"

"I'm sorry. Didn't mean to offend. You prefer Lisa?"

"I prefer Melissa."

Nate looked at Alex with a wink. "She's a lot more uptight than the last one. And that's saying something."

He could see Melissa starting to get hot under the collar, and he had to change the subject before it got any worse. "Hey Nate, why don't you get us out of here before the cops show up."

It was as if Nate suddenly remembered why he was even there. "Oh, right. Right. Let's go."

As Nate ran toward the car, Melissa looked over at Alex. "I don't think he's firing on all cylinders."

"Just do your best to ignore him. He'll drive us to the docks and be on his way."

"How well do you know this kid?"

"Samantha and I met him when we hijacked his car a couple days ago."

"Hijacked his car?"

"It's okay. He wants to help."

"Why?"

"He's got a thing for spies. And he won't tell anyone."

"How can you be so sure?"

"As near as I can tell, he's a small-time pot dealer. I don't think he's interested in talking to the police about anything."

"And based on this, we should trust him?"

"No. We should trust him because he showed up."

Nate honked the horn and leaned out the window. "You guys coming?"

Alex held his hands out, pleading with her. "We just need a ride to the docks."

"I can't believe you're bringing a civilian into a combat situation."

"What combat situation? He'll drop us off at the docks in less than half an hour and be on his way. If anything's going to happen, it will happen at the docks, not between here and there."

Melissa let out a big sigh. "Fine. But I don't think you should tell him anything more about you or me. Especially me."

Chapter 108

Hannah shut down her laptop and loaded it into the small rolling suitcase. It didn't matter that Robert thought he could stop her. She would head for the docks, supervise the loading of the cargo container, and then steal it back again as soon as it was in open waters. It would safely be tucked away at the bottom of the ocean before the Coast Guard even responded to the SOS from the cargo ship.

She was one step ahead of everyone, and that's how it would stay.

She took one last glance around the hotel room and, confident she hadn't forgotten anything, opened the door.

All she saw was the flash of bright red right before the fire extinguisher slammed into her face. Stunned, she stumbled back into the hotel room, tripped over her suitcase, and landed on her back.

Through the blurry haze of disorientation she saw a single person enter the hotel room, close the door, and swing the deadbolt to the locked position.

The figure leaned in close, coming into focus. It was a slight woman with auburn hair, hard angular features, and smooth movements.

She moved with the practiced grace of a highly trained assassin.

But Hannah did not recognize her.

The woman snapped her fingers in front of Hannah's face until she focused on her. "Can you hear me?"

Hannah nodded, the movement sending shooting pain up and down her spine.

"Good, because I need to talk to you."

The woman grabbed Hannah by the wrists and pulled her over to the bed, sitting her up against the edge of it. She hunched down in front of her, snapping her fingers again a couple more times in front of her face, drawing her attention back to her.

"Do you know who I am?"

Hannah shook her head. She really had no idea who this woman was.

"My name is Madina. Now do you know who I am?"

Hannah's senses were returning back to her, and her brain spun through the names in her head like an old-fashioned Rolodex until it settled on everything she knew about someone named Madina.

"You're one of Umarov's hired guns."

"I was his lover. That is until you killed him."

"I didn't kill him."

"The MI6 agent you programmed did. And since you programmed her with your machine, you're responsible."

"Is there anything I can do to convince you otherwise?"

"No."

"What do you want from me? Revenge? Money? What?"

"I want your machine."

Hannah laughed. "It's not mine to give, and it's certainly not yours to take."

Madina smiled. "It's good that you find this funny, because I've already taken it. I just stopped by to let you know that it was me who did it when you discovered it missing."

"No you haven't."

Madina looked at her watch. "It was supposed to be loaded onto the cargo ship fifteen minutes ago."

She looked at the packed suitcase on the floor. "And you

were just headed out to verify that. Well, you don't need to bother. Instead of being loaded on the cargo ship, it was placed on my semi-trailer and is already on the highway headed away from here. But I'm not going to tell you where it's going. That's for me to know, and you to never find out."

"You underestimate my abilities."

"No, you overestimate what you can do when you are dead."

Hannah smiled at her. "You'd be surprised at what I can accomplish when I'm dead."

Madina took a step back, drawing a pistol out from behind her back. "I don't believe in ghosts."

Hannah moved quickly, jumping up and grabbing the pistol just as it went off. The bullet's shockwave pounded at her eardrum, deafening it for the time being.

Hannah slipped her thumb into the trigger guard, on top of Madina's finger, and repeatedly squeezed the trigger until the gun was empty. There was no doubt that several people were already dialing 911 from the sudden outbreak of gunfire in the hotel. In such a small town, it wouldn't take long for the police to respond.

Hannah pinned Madina against the wall with one hand against her throat and twisted the gun out of her grip with the other. As she squeezed the life out of her, she leaned in to whisper into the assassin's ear.

"I have been a ghost since before you were a twinkle in your father's eye."

As she held her iron grip on the assassin's throat, Madina grasped at her hands, trying to pry them off her neck. But it was no use. Hannah kept her pressed against the wall with all her weight until Madina's eyes rolled back into her head and she collapsed to the floor.

In less than a minute, the hotel would be surrounded by police. She had to get out of there, without drawing suspicion to herself. She couldn't afford to wait around while the police filed their reports.

She wiped off the pistol, smearing any trace of her fingerprints on the gun, and placed it back in the hand of her unconscious assassin. She yanked open the mini-fridge door, removed several miniature bottles of alcohol, and carried them over to the sink. She unscrewed the caps on the tiny bottles and poured the alcohol down the drain, emptying out all but one of them. After rinsing the sink with water, she carried the bottles over to the woman lying on the floor and haphazardly scattered them around her. She picked up a couple of the bottles and shook the last of the alcohol on the woman, making her smell like she had been drinking.

She slipped the hotel key from her pocket and placed it on the nightstand by the side of the bed. Standing back, she surveyed the scene. When the cops arrived, they would see someone who had broken into a hotel room, got drunk, and fired off several rounds before passing out. The only thing left to do was create an alibi that placed her well away from the hotel when the gunshots occurred.

Reading the number off the stationary on the desk, she dialed the main number to the hotel on her cell phone.

After two rings, it was answered by a too cheery, but hurried, voice. "Thank you for calling the Red Lion Lewiston, how may I direct your call?"

"Hi, I checked out earlier this morning, and just remembered I left my key in the room without informing you I had already left."

"No problem. What room was that?"

"Room 402."

"Okay. Ms. Smith?"

"Yes."

"I can check you out over the phone."

"Thank you."

"Did you have anything from the mini-bar?"

She stared at all the tiny bottles strewn around the unconscious assassin. "No."

"Can I place the charges to your credit card on file?"

"Oh, they're calling my flight. Yes, just use the credit card I gave you at check-in."

"No problem. Would you like me to mail you the receipt?"

"That's okay, my accountant will take care of it."

"Very well. Thank you for choosing to stay at the Red Lion Lewiston, Ms. Smith."

"Thank you. If I ever come back to Lewiston, I will definitely stay there again."

"I'm very glad to hear that Ms. Smith."

She hung up the phone, grabbed her suitcase, and walked out into the hallway, closing the door behind her. As she exited the hotel through the back stairwell, she could hear the faint wail of sirens in the distance.

She was in her car, and on the road, before three police cruisers shot past her in the opposite lane at high-speed.

As always, she had made a clean getaway. Unfortunately, her unique room-sized computer was not so lucky. And every minute that passed meant that the truck pulling her cargo container was getting farther away.

Unfortunately, she'd only been here to supervise the loading of the container on the ship, and did not have a team on the ground under her command.

That left only one person she could contact, who was not only nearby, but was more than capable of stopping the semi-trailer.

All she needed was internet access for her laptop. As she cruised through of the small downtown area of Lewiston Idaho, she scanned the windows of various retail buildings looking for a sign offering free Wi-Fi access to patrons.

Chapter 109

Nate kept his foot pressed down on the accelerator, acting as if the signs indicating that they were traveling south on Route 95 meant that they should also be traveling at ninety-five miles per hour. This close to Moscow, Idaho the road was still a single two-lane highway. It had not yet expanded out to the larger four-lane highway with the grassy median separating the opposing lanes. Nate expertly maneuvered the corners as the road twisted past isolated farms.

He had also been incessantly chatty ever since they had left the Pullman-Moscow Airport.

Alex was about to interrupt him, to ask how much longer till they made it to the docks, when a female voice interrupted his thoughts.

"Testing. Testing. 1. 2. 3."

He glanced back at Melissa, the only female in the car. She looked at him expectantly with a raise of her eyebrows. It hadn't been her that he'd heard in his head. So who was it?

The voice intruded again. "Can you hear me Alex?"

"Hello?"

"Good, you can hear me."

"Who is this?"

"I'm a friend of Robert's."

"Who?"

"He's the guy in charge of the Peacekeepers."

"The Peacekeepers?"

"The organization you are currently working for."

"Okay. What do you want?"

"I have new intel for you regarding the cargo container you are after. It's no longer onboard a ship. It's been loaded onto a semi-trailer and is traveling overland."

"Who is this again?"

"If you plan to recover the computer that can program the human brain to kill, I suggest you listen instead of asking questions that don't matter."

"Okay, I'm listening."

Melissa leaned forward from the back seat and spoke at the same time as the voice in his head. "Who are you talking to?"

He waved her back with a hand.

"I'm sorry, I missed what you just said. Can you repeat that?"

"The trailer you are looking for is blue with white letters painted on the side. VHA13857."

"VHA13857. Got it. Do you know which way the truck is headed?"

"Not yet, but I'm working on it. I will contact you again when I have more information."

"Wait."

But it was no use, he could tell the voice was already gone.

The car drifted across the center line and into oncoming traffic. Neither Alex nor Melissa had noticed Nate's inattention to the only task he been given. They had both been too busy for either of them to realize Nate, too, had been more interested in what Alex was doing rather than paying attention to the road.

The massive blare of a horn brought Nate's focus back to what he should've been doing the whole time, driving. He yanked on the wheel and pulled back into the proper lane.

Instinctively, Alex and Melissa both looked out the back window at the truck that nearly claimed their lives. Alex did a double-take as he noticed the letters on the trailer matched the ones he had just been given by the new voice in his head. By sheer luck, the truck he was looking for had selected the same highway they were on.

"Turn around!"

Nate did not take his eyes off the road as he replied. "What?"

Alex twisted in his seat, pointing out the back window. "We have to catch up with that truck."

"No. That was entirely my fault."

"That's the truck!"

Nate looked at him. "Right. That's the truck that almost killed us, but I crossed over the lane. We shouldn't take it out on the driver."

"No. No. No. I just received new information. That truck has the cargo container we're looking for."

Melissa, and unfortunately Nate too, craned their necks to look out the rear window at the truck as it sped away from them.

Since they were alone on the road, Alex felt confident in what he was about to do. He stuck his foot over the drive train hump on the floor and smashed his foot on top of the brake pedal. The car skidded to a halt, careening wildly to one side.

He leaned over Nate, opened his door, and pushed him out of the car. "It's my turn to drive."

As he settled into the driver's seat, Nate ran around the front of the car and hopped into the passenger seat. "Are we really about to have a high-speed chase?"

Alex jammed the car into reverse and looked over at

him. "Yep."

Nate's smile was almost too wide for his mouth as he strapped himself in with the seatbelt. "Cool."

He smashed the pedal to the floor and the rear tires squealed in delight as the car rocketed backward. With a twist of the steering wheel, he spun the car in a quick one-eighty before shifting back into drive to pursue the truck. He would've much preferred to have a muscle car with a five-speed manual transmission, giving him better control, but he would just have to deal with the subcompact and its automatic drive.

As they raced up behind the semi-trailer, Melissa leaned forward again. "I hope you're not thinking about trying to ram him off the road? He outweighs us by several tons. He'd drive over us like were nothing but a bump in the road, and keep going."

She wasn't saying anything he hadn't already considered. Nate's tiny two-door subcompact was no match for the massive semi. He would need something with a little more kick if he planned to stop that truck.

"Nate, you got anything volatile in the trunk?"

"What, you mean like explosives or something?"

"Sure. Anything like that?"

"Sorry man, I just deal in weed. I stay away from all that dangerous stuff. I know what can happen if you're not careful."

"You got anything at all that can be used as a weapon?"

"Just a crowbar and spare tire I think."

"Okay," said Alex, "we're going to have to do this the hard way."

He darted out from behind the truck to pass it, when lights flashed at him from an oncoming car. He slammed on the brakes and swerved back behind the semi as the other car shot by, blaring its horn.

Swerving back out into the opposing lane, he saw that this time the path was clear, and he was able to speed past the semi and get in front of it.

The truck driver blared his horn as Alex swerved in front of him and slowed. He wondered how easy it would be to keep slowing down until the truck stopped. He got his answer soon enough.

He was pushed back in his seat as the truck slammed into the trunk of the car, pushing them off the highway and onto the shoulder. They spun out in a plume of dust, the little gray sedan stalling after being forced off the road.

Nate clutched at his seatbelt. "What the hell?!"

Alex twisted the ignition key, firing the engine back up again. He looked over at Nate. "You want to get out?"

Nate smiled. "No way man, this is freakin' awesome!" His smile faded as a thought seemed to occur to him. "But you're going to pay me back for the car, right?"

Without saying a word, Alex focused his attention back on the truck as he shifted the car into gear. The subcompact bounced wildly back onto the highway as he pushed the weak four-cylinder engine to catch up with the truck.

This time, as he tried to get around the truck, the driver swerved back and forth on the road, preventing him from passing.

He crossed the center line into the opposing lane, the truck swerving over the same line to hold him back. Without warning, he jerked the wheel, bounded off the road onto the shoulder, dust kicking up behind him, and pushed the poorly maintained engine to overtake the truck before the driver had a chance to notice he was coming up on the other side.

Once in front of the truck, he floored it. Glancing at the rearview mirror, the grill of the semi filled the entire view of his back window. His little four-cylinder subcompact was no match for the twelve-cylinder behemoth bearing down on him.

The truck slammed into the back of the car, throwing Alex forward against his seat belt as he fought with the steering wheel to maintain control. The truck backed off, gained speed, and slammed into them harder. The subcompact fishtailed and spun off the road again as the truck roared by, blasting its horn in triumph.

Nate clawed at his seatbelt. "Okay, I want to get out now."

He unhooked it, and had just opened his door, when Alex got the engine started again.

He paused, white knuckle still clutching his seatbelt as he stared at Alex with wild eyes. "You're not seriously going after him are you?"

Alex had no choice. If the computer inside the cargo carrier was not destroyed, more people would become like Samantha. "I have to stop that truck."

Melissa finished his sentence behind him. "Or die trying."

Alex twisted back to look at her. "You don't have to come along."

"Oh I'm coming. You'll need somebody to steer while you jump onto the back of the truck."

"Jump on the back?"

"Well, you can't stop him with brute force. He'll just swat you off the road again. You going to have to get on board and handle the driver personally."

He hated to admit it, but she had a point. "You're right."

She looked at Nate as she climbed between the seats to the front and settled in. "Just sit tight. We'll come back for you."

She shut the door, buckled up, and nodded to him that she was ready for whatever insanity he had planned.

He smashed the accelerator to the floor, kicking dust up as they sped back onto the highway.

He caught up quickly to the semi. As they rounded another bend on the road, he tried his best to stay in the blind spot of the driver as he brought the subcompact to within inches of the rear trailer.

He glanced over at Melissa. "I guess this is where I get out."

She reached over and grabbed the steering wheel while simultaneously stepping a foot over the drive train hump to take over the accelerator from him.

He rolled down the driver's side window, climbed out of the car, and stood on the hood. Fortunately, they were close enough to the trailer that they were drafting behind it. There were no gale force winds trying to knock him off the hood of the car. Instead, it was the twisty road trying to throw him to his death with each curve of the pavement.

He kept his stance wide as he crouched and leaned forward to reach for a handhold on the back of the trailer.

Just before he grabbed hold of something, Melissa slowed unexpectedly, throwing off his balance and almost toppling him forward over the front of the hood. He collapsed to all fours and glared back at her. She ignored him as she guided the car back up to nearly touch the back of the semi-trailer.

He reached forward, grabbed onto the trailer, and hauled

himself up onto the back of the truck. Melissa slowed, and backed away.

He climbed up the back and, as he clambered over the top edge, he was hit full force by sixty mile per hour winds trying to knock him off the trailer.

He leaned into the wind and crawled across the top all the way to the front. Peering over the edge, he saw just enough room for him to slide down between the trailer and the cab of the tractor.

The truck suddenly swerved, and if he hadn't been holding on, he would have been thrown off the side. The truck swerved again, crossing the center line.

Melissa was trying to pass him. Only, he knew she wasn't trying to pass him as much as she was creating a distraction. With the truck driver focused on his left-hand mirror, paying attention to the car racing up on his side, Alex would be able to clamber around to the right, open the side passenger door, and hop into the cab.

At least that was the plan.

As he angled around the cabin, the wind threatened to tear him from the side of the truck and discard him along the side of the road like a piece of trash.

He clung to the different impromptu handholds he found on the side of the truck as he made his way to the door. Alex gripped the side mirror with one hand, and the door handle with the other, as he lifted himself up and ventured a peek into the cab of the truck.

The motion of his head appearing at the window must've attracted the driver's attention, because all of a sudden, he was facing down the barrel of a shotgun.

He released the door handle and swung forward, hanging on to the side mirror to keep from falling off the truck, as shotgun pellets shattered the side window.

Now would've been a good time to have a weapon of his own. But he had nothing, save his wits.

They would have to do.

The driver veered off the edge of the road, the truck vibrating in Alex's hands as he held on for dear life. Looking ahead, he saw what the driver had planned.

He was steering them straight toward a stand of trees along the edge of the road. The driver was going to brush him off the side of the truck like someone brushing a bug off their sleeve.

He pulled himself in tight against the side of the truck as they crashed through the edge of the trees. Branches tore at his jacket as they desperately tried to pull him off the truck.

The semi bounced back onto the road and barely made the next corner.

Alex edged back along the side of the truck, grabbed the handle, and flung open the passenger door. Just as he was about to step up into the cab, the driver twisted the steering wheel sharply to the left, throwing the door open even farther. Alex quickly looped an arm through the shattered window and hung onto the door frame as it swung outward.

The driver twisted the steering wheel sharply to the right, swinging the door back toward the truck. If he had not been clinging to the door, this action would've slammed the door shut again. But his arm was in the way, and pain shot up through his shoulder as the swinging door caught his arm in a crushing vise.

Inside, the driver was reloading the shotgun with one hand.

Just as the driver raised the shotgun and pulled the trigger, Alex kicked at the side of the truck with his legs, swinging the door open again.

The buckshot narrowly missed him. Instead, it peppered a yellow sign on the side of the road, that warned of an impending sharp curve up ahead, as they roared past it.

The driver, more focused on his unexpected passenger, and reloading his shotgun, failed to notice the sharp turn until his truck crossed over the line and headed straight for the cement barriers lined up along the side of the highway.

He dropped the shotgun and gripped the steering wheel in a panic, twisting it sharply a little too late. He caught the cement barriers with his front tires at an oblique angle. With the center of gravity already set pretty high on semi-trailers, the cement barriers acted like a tripping hazard as they flipped the truck onto its side, and off the road.

Chapter 110

Melissa slammed on the brakes and skidded to a stop, nearly colliding with the cement barrier herself. All along the edge of the road, and into the field beyond, were the shattered and twisted remains of the semi-tractor and trailer. It had rolled several times, disintegrating in large chunks as it trampled the grass beneath it on its final journey. She could see smoke coming from the dry grass that had been ignited by the heat of the exposed engine. It wouldn't be long before this whole area was ablaze, and once the gas tanks heated up, the resulting explosion would permanently render the computer inside the cargo container useless, if the crash hadn't already accomplished that.

A sudden flash erupted from inside the wreckage of the truck. The flames reached higher as they hungrily devoured the dry grass.

She jumped from the car and vaulted the cracked cement barrier, screaming at the top of her lungs.

"Alex! Alex!"

A moan emanated from the tall dry grass to her right and she followed the sound to Alex who was just sitting up. She reached out a hand and helped him to his feet. He didn't look too much the worse for wear, but she ducked under his outstretched arm to support him as she guided him back to the car.

He squinted at her and winced as he favored his left ankle. "What happened?"

"The truck hit the barrier and rolled."

He glanced over her shoulder at the burning wreckage and then picked up his pace, hobbling quickly alongside her.

She helped them over the barrier and to the idling car. She eased him into the passenger seat and ran over to her side.

Before she shifted the car into gear, the first of the hundred and forty gallon tanks of gasoline exploded.

Every window in the subcompact car shattered from the concussive wave. She slammed the car into reverse and smashed down on the accelerator.

The little car shot backward, the gears whining in protest.

She twisted the steering wheel, performing a one-eighty maneuver, while simultaneously shifting the car into drive. She stomped on the accelerator just as the second gas tank exploded, disintegrating what was left of the semi, and igniting even more bone dry grass in an ever expanding radius.

As she rocketed down the highway, she remembered that this was not the first time she was forced to outrun a raging fire. But this time, she had a smooth, paved highway, and was able to get away quickly.

Chapter 111

Hannah sat in the air-conditioned comfort of her rental car as she crawled along Route 95 at less than five miles an hour. She guessed that, out of the long line of cars that stretched for miles in either direction around the accident, she was the only one who actually wanted to be there. She had to see for herself if her computer was salvageable, or if the news reports she'd been hearing on the radio regarding the crashed semi were accurate.

Despite the initial incident taking place the day before, the local fire brigades were still dealing with isolated pockets of burning grass that still threatened the livelihood of dozens of farmers.

The state police had only recently opened up the highway again, so here she sat, waiting to see if it was gone.

While she had promised the supercomputer to the organization she worked for, she had no intention of ever giving it to them. But they didn't know that. All they would see was that, for the first time in a long time, she had failed to deliver on a promise.

If the computer really was destroyed, it would set her back immeasurably. She had already eliminated every scientist and programmer who had been involved with it. She wanted to ensure no one could build a second one.

If the news reports were true, her one-of-a-kind weapon was lost forever.

She finally reached the cordoned off area where the semi had crashed. She could tell at first glance that the news reports were more than accurate. There was nothing left of the cargo container but twisted and charred metal.

As soon as she passed the accident, the traffic miraculously disappeared and she was exceeding the posted speed limit in no time, heading toward the city of Moscow, Idaho, where it all began.

She didn't stop in Moscow this time. Instead, she kept going, heading northward with no specific destination in mind. It was time to make herself scarce for a while until her bosses came to terms with the loss, even though they didn't know they would never have gotten their hands on it in the first place. She would wait until they needed her expertise again before making contact.

Chapter 112

Basil stood in front of one of the myriad of patient rooms in the long hallway of the London hospital. He checked his suit again, satisfied that he looked presentable, and knocked lightly on the door.

The voice that echoed from inside the room was muted by the closed door. "Come in."

He cleared his throat and entered the room.

Sitting in the hospital bed, with wires poking out of the hospital gown and connected to various beeping and flashing equipment, a frail old man stared back at him. Despite how thin and pale he looked, when he spoke, it was a voice of strength.

"You must be Basil."

Basil nodded his head. "Yes sir."

"You were with Skyler, until the end?"

"Yes sir."

"What did he say to you to convince you to betray your oath to England and help me?"

"It wasn't so much what he said, sir. It was what he did."

"So what did he do?"

"He averted an international crisis that just might have pulled Britain into a war."

"And that inspired you?"

"That, amongst other things."

"What things?"

Basil paused, unsure of how to proceed.

The old man's face warmed and he smiled. "It's okay Basil. You can tell me."

I might as well come clean, he thought.

"My thesis at Academy was on your organization. I found nothing beyond whispers and rumors. The only thing I could nail down was your name; The Peacekeepers. The people in my own organization at MI6, who should have known about you, claimed ignorance. Others recommended I do my thesis on something that wasn't fiction. I knew you existed, but I had no proof. And then Skyler broke into the Dungeon. And suddenly, I had proof.

"At first, I thought I'd finally get vindication. But when I saw what he was doing with his access in the Dungeon, I knew the conclusion of my thesis had been entirely wrong. I was only just now seeing who you really were."

"And what was your conclusion?"

"You're the last hope for an equitable peace. You work in the shadows, content to remain hidden. You ensure that everyone is given a chance at peace, and you don't do it for glory. You do it for peace."

The old man nodded his head. "Can I rely on you to keep my secret?"

Basil kept his hands behind his back, hoping that their nervous shaking would not tremor upward to his shoulders and give away how he felt at this moment.

"I would like to do more than that sir. I want to help."

"What makes you think I need your help?"

"Begging your pardon sir, but, you're in the hospital and your team has been decimated to the point of nonexistence."

"Rather harsh criticism from someone asking to join my little outfit."

"I understand that sir, but I can be very valuable to you in my current position with the SIS."

The old man regarded him thoughtfully. "Something has

come to my attention that is time sensitive. I am open to the possibility of a trial period to see how much you can help me without committing yourself to something you don't fully understand."

"Let me rebuild your team again, starting with myself, Alex, and Melissa."

The old man visibly grimaced. "I'm afraid Melissa is gone."

"Gone? Where did she go?"

"So, per your proposal, it looks like it will just be you and Alex for now. Will that be enough to do what needs to be done?"

"What is that you need done?"

"I need someone transported out of South Africa."

"Legally? Or illegally?"

The old man winked. "I still have resources. People who owe me favors. You go in and rescue the target, and we can discuss a more... permanent relationship. Will that be acceptable?"

Basil thought long and hard before replying, "It's a start sir."

"Good. Contact Alex and let him know his probationary period is nearly over. Let him know he is now the lead agent in the field, with you as his primary contact. You will also use your access to the Dungeon to provide operational support during this mission."

Basil snapped to attention. "Yes sir."

The old man stared at him, hard. "The only reason I'm using the two of you to rebuild my team is because you both showed initiative, and courage, in the face of danger. I am breaking every rule and protocol I personally put in place."

"Thank you for your confidence sir."

"Now that you are one of us, you can never again admit you know anything about us."

"Understood sir."

"And one more thing."

"What is it sir?"

"Don't call me sir."

Basil smiled. "Yes sir."

Chapter 113

Alex stayed an additional day at the hospital in Moscow, Idaho after Melissa had left. He asked if he would ever see her again, and she replied in her normal witty style, "never say never".

He sat up in the hospital bed, doing the opposite of enjoying a meal of dry chicken and bland potatoes with what seemed to be gravy. Alex dipped the tines of a fork into the sticky substance ladled on top of the mound of mashed potatoes and took a taste. He decided it was not gravy after all but couldn't describe it beyond the word brown.

He purposely kept himself in the hospital longer then needed. The doctors had told him he could be released the previous day, but he convinced them he should have a few more days of monitoring by feigning headaches. He normally detested hospitals, but it was the easiest way to ensure he was found.

The voice he had been waiting for echoed in his head.

"Alex, can you hear me?"

"Loud and clear, Basil. What did he say?"

"Congratulations. You are currently the lead agent of the newly reformed Peacekeepers X-Alpha initiative."

"Good. When do I meet with Robert?"

"You won't be meeting with him personally. I will remain your contact through the comm unit in your tooth. I know you're still at the hospital, how do you feel?"

"I'm only here so you can find me. I'm ready to leave any time."

"Good. I booked a flight for you out of the country

under a false identity. Are you ready to go?"

"I'm ready to go wherever you send me, but at some point, I would like to meet with Robert."

"I work on that. I'll be back in a little while with the details on your new mission."

"Alright then. Over and out."

Basil's voice left his head and he was finally alone with his thoughts.

He climbed out of bed, and walked over to the freestanding closet in the corner of the room. He reached into the pocket of his jacket and removed a newly purchased prepaid cell phone and the specially modified Zippo lighter; a gift from Viktor.

He flipped open the lighter and activated the radio jamming frequency before dialing a number from memory on the cell phone. His call would not be overheard through the transmitter on his tooth.

The other side rang twice before answering.

"Was it worth it?" the female voice on the other side asked.

Alex had almost forgotten how she affected him. He could feel his heart speed up at the sound of her voice. His body reacting from rote memory. He could now say for certain that the last two years he had spent behind bars, and the four years of training and planning with her before that, were definitely not wasted. They would soon have everything they worked so hard to get.

"It was worth it. I'm in."

Other Books by the Author

A is for Apprentice (Fantasy)

Oliver Twist: Victorian Vampire (Fantasy Horror)

A Tale of Two Cities with Dragons (Fantasy)

Shade Infinity (Science Fiction Thriller)

Peacekeepers X-Alpha Series (Thriller)
    Inherit the Throne
    The Warrior's Code

Steampunk OZ Series (Science Fiction Novellas)
    Forgotten Girl
    The Legacy's World
    Emerald Shadow
    The Future's Destiny
    The Dangerous Captive
    Missing Legacy
    Shadow of History
    The Edge of the Hunter

Fugue: The Cure (Science Fiction Short Story)

Jason and the Chrononauts (Kid's Adventure)

Be the first to know about Steve DeWinter's next book. Follow the URL below to subscribe for free today!

http://bit.ly/BookReleaseBulletin

www.ingramcontent.com/pod-product-compliance
Lightning Source LLC
Chambersburg PA
CBHW021132260626
47169CB00005B/1571